Robyn Cadwallader has published numerous prize-winning short stories, poems and reviews, as well as a book of poetry and a non-fiction book based on her PhD thesis, which explored attitudes to virginity and female agency in the Middle Ages. When she isn't travelling to England for research, visiting ancient archaeological sites along the way, she lives among vineyards outside Canberra.

Further praise for *The Anchoress*:

'Elegant and eloquent.' *Mail on Sunday*

'A perceptive and arresting debut.' *Bookseller*

'Absorbing and finely structured . . . The contemplative tone of this beautiful novel leaves behind a feeling of calm and restoration, and a deeper sense of the power of the written word.' *Australian Book Review*

'The small scale of Sarah's world allows an exact literary appreciation of detail, often through sound and smell because Sarah can hardly see out: the sounds of a thatched roof, the smell of rain, the importance assumed by a visiting cat and a nest of birds under the eaves.' *Guardian*

'Cadwallader has chosen a rich subject, for while a story located in a single small room might sound claustrophobic, this is in fact what heightens Sarah's observations. It is precisely this limitation that drives the narrative – in the same way it does in Emma Donoghue's *Room* . . . *The Anchoress* achieves what every historical novel attempts: reimagining the past while opening a new window – like a squint, perhaps – to our present lives.' *Sydney Morning Herald*

'A detailed, sensuous and richly imagined shard of the past. [Cadwallader] has successfully placed her narrator, the anchoress, in that tantalizing, precarious, delicate realm: convincingly of her

D0173769

own distant era, yet emotionally engaging and vividly present to us in our own.' Geraldine Brooks, author of *People of the Book*

'A gripping tale of faith, temptation, grief, defiance and self-acceptance.' *Daily Telegraph* (Australia)

'An intense, atmospheric and very assured debut.' *Booktopia*

'Cadwallader is a poet of loneliness ... Few writers have captured so completely the essential madness that accompanies hermitage.' *Kirkus*

'A fantastic exploration of what it is to be human in any era, and ... a wonderful work of literary historical fiction.' *Bookworld*

'Cadwallader's vivid period descriptions set a stunning backdrop for this beautiful first novel.' *Booklist*

'*The Anchoress* addresses issues of contemporary interest within a historical framework, and does so with more ease and accuracy than many a historical novel ... It deals with its heavy themes gracefully.' *shinynewbooks.co.uk*

THE
ANCHORESS

Robyn Cadwallader

FABER & FABER

First published in Australia in 2015
by Fourth Estate, an imprint of
HarperCollins*Publishers* Australia Pty Limited
Level 13, 201 Elizabeth Street, Sydney NSW 2000, Australia

First published in 2015
by Faber & Faber Ltd
Bloomsbury House
74–77 Great Russell Street
London WC1B 3DA

This paperback edition published in 2016

Printed and bound in England by CPI Group (UK) Ltd, Croydon CR0 4YY

All rights reserved
© Robyn Cadwallader, 2015

All renditions of *Ancrene Wisse* are based on translations from the original by Dr Judy King.

The right of Robyn Cadwallader to be identified as author of this
work has been asserted in accordance with Section 77 of
the Copyright, Designs and Patents Act 1988

*This book is sold subject to the condition that it shall not, by way of trade or otherwise, be lent, resold,
hired out or otherwise circulated without the publisher's prior consent in any form of binding or cover other
than that in which it is published and without a similar condition including this condition being imposed on
the subsequent purchaser*

A CIP record for this book
is available from the British Library

ISBN 978-0-571-31334-1

FSC
www.fsc.org
MIX
Paper from
responsible sources
FSC® C101712

2 4 6 8 10 9 7 5 3 1

For Anneliese

'Tis not that Dying hurts us so —
'Tis Living — hurts us more —
But Dying — is a different way —
A Kind behind the Door —

The Southern Custom — of the Bird —
That ere the Frosts are due —
Accepts a better Latitude —
We — are the Birds — that stay.

Emily Dickinson

I HAD ALWAYS WANTED to be a jongleur, to leap from the shoulders of another, to fly and tumble, to dare myself in thin air with nothing but my arms and legs to land me safely on the ground. An acrobat is not a bird, but it is the closest a person can come to being free in the air. The nearest to an angel's gift of flying.

But that was as a child, when my body was secure, like that of a boy, and I felt myself whole and able to try anything. That was before my arms and legs grew soft and awkward and my woman's body took away those strong, pliant surfaces of skin, before I knew I could bleed and not die or, worse still, carry a life inside me and die because of it.

In spite of my body, the dream remained. It was the idea that I loved; I understood enough of the world to know that I could never be a jongleur.

I remember Roland especially, though in my child's fancy I called him Swallow. He was part of a travelling troupe that visited our town one market day and began to perform in the middle of the crowd, the music and the colours of the costumes nudging us to stop and watch. A circle formed, with Swallow as its centre. His costume was grey striped with red, his face painted with blue on his cheeks and forehead and red on his nose. He balanced the hilt of a sword in each hand, the blades standing tall above him, and danced, lifting his knees, pointing and scooping his feet in front and behind. When he stopped, his confrère gently placed an apple on the tip of each blade. Making sure they were still, the balance certain, Swallow stepped right then left, forwards and backwards, a slow and graceful single carole, smiling at us all. Finally he threw the swords up and caught them in one hand — though someone shouted, 'Blunt, you fraud' — and gathered the apples with the other. He bowed deeply and ran to join his companions who were building a tower, three on the bottom then two on their shoulders. With dancing feet, Roland climbed from leg to arm to leg to arm and onto the shoulders of the men on top. He stood still for a moment, arms in the air, stretching out to the heavens, face tilted up, then leaped and tumbled. I gasped to see him swoop like a swallow in the grey sky beyond. He landed surefooted and still on two slippered feet and the six men formed a line, bowed deeply, then turned around, pulled down their breeches and farted at us, one at a time. The crowd laughed and cheered but I was still leaping in the air with Swallow.

When I saw him later that day with his face cleaned of colour, I saw his nose was not at all like a swallow's beak, but sat to one side of his face as if it had been dough flattened by a rough hand. He told me he had fallen when learning to tumble; his own knee had broken his nose as he landed.

The day after I was enclosed I thought of Swallow. I'd thrown away everything in this world and leaped into the air, lighter than I'd ever been, flying to God, who would catch me in his arms. Here, like Swallow, I was a body without a body. Even inside the thick walls of my cell I felt I could see the sky all around me, blue and clear, and I thought I had what I wanted.

I didn't know then that I had landed on hard ground and broken my bones with my own body.

The Church of St Juliana
Hartham, English Midlands
St Faith's Day, 6 October 1255

⊰ SARAH ⊱

I WAS NEAR THE door, where women should stay. The floor
was hard, refusing me, though I lay face-down, my arms
outstretched, embracing it, wanting this life, this death. I knew
there were people nearby, those from the village who had come
to look or pray, but I saw none of them. Voices in the sanctuary
that seemed so far away sang a dirge, a celebration of loss,
prayers for me. I knew the words: I had read and reread them,
memorised them, prayed on them, but now they were nothing
but sound. The dank cold of stone crept into my bones; I did
not feel the drops of water on my back, their chill blessing. I had
become stone.

The bishop lifted me to my feet, my legs leaden, and guided
me toward the altar. I took the candles they gave me; now a
flame glowed in each hand and I could see nothing beyond them.
From somewhere outside my ring of light, the bishop's words
implored me: 'Be fervent in love of God and your neighbour.' I
knelt and prayed.

Then words, paper and more words: I signed to all I had asked
for. The clinking of the thurible's chain and the bitter-sweet

smell of incense drifted close, quietly wrapped around me like a shroud, like arms that loved me.

They led me through the front door, away from the gathered light of candles and people, and out into the night, black and chill. We walked through the graveyard, wet grass under my feet, the dead all around me. Singing came from the darkness, 'May angels lead you to paradise'; this was the hymn we'd sung for Ma when she died, and later for Emma, too. At the cell we stopped and the warm hands that held my arms let go. I shivered. The bishop's voice commanded, 'If she wants to go in, let her go in.'

The dark mouth stood open. I took a breath and stepped inside. Blackness yawned around me, damp on my face. But voices were nearby, sweet ones, singing, 'Be of good courage, thy desire from God is at hand.' They laid me down on the floor, scatterings of dirt and words falling on me, into my mouth and eyes. Death desired me and I accepted: 'Here I will stay forever; this is the home I have chosen.' I could feel my bones, white and still in the black soil; worms wove among my ribs like wool on a loom. Deep in this darkness I am dead. My body dissolves, crumbles, turns to earth. They turned and walked away, left me alone.

I startled, fright hot and sharp in my chest. Blows shuddered the door. I stood and pressed my hands against it, felt nails splintering wood, the sound sharp in my ears, then echoing inside my head. These hammer blows that sealed my door were the nailing of my hands and feet to the cross with Christ, the tearing of his skin and sinew. The jolt of each blow pushed me away but I strained to feel it, the shiver of resistance humming in my body.

When she was dying, Emma had opened her hand for mine, held on to me, held on to life. Another nail, and another, the judder running through my arms and into my chest, through my jaw and into my teeth. The taste of blood sharp on my tongue. Christ made no noise, his face tight with pain; Emma didn't speak, just looked at me, her eyes fading. Blood dripped, then ran.

The hammering ceased but still my arms throbbed and silence rang in my ears. Then scuffling, tools clinking, the church door banging shut, the dull click of its latch, low and serious voices fading. I stepped away from the door, the smell of incense floating up from my robe to touch my cheek.

Two candles burned on my altar; they must be the ones I had carried in the church. I took two or three steps toward the bed and sat down delicately, as if not to disturb someone else's sleeping place; the straw rustled. I stood up again and peered into the gloom. Of a sudden my body came back to me: my heart was beating hard, my legs were shaking, and my belly ached. I needed to piss, now. I looked around for the bucket, found it at the end of the bed, pulled up my robe, and squatted. The ache in my belly lessened and I felt calmer. I reached out, touched the cold stone wall, rough and gritty on my hand. The clotted smell of dampness, the earthy smell of moss. This was to be my home — no, my grave — for the rest of my life.

I knelt at my altar and began Compline: 'The Lord Almighty grant us a quiet night and a perfect end ...' but my words ran out. I'd prayed these words each night since I was a child; they were part of me, like breathing, and now they had deserted me. But this was my life, to pray. I began again, my breath fast and shallow, hoping that the thread would catch and the words be pulled along. Nothing; they would not return however much I concentrated. It was as if I'd never learned them. My first night alone and I had no prayer. I snatched at some lines: *Iesu*

Criste, Fili Dei uiui, miserere nobis ... Domine, labia mea aperies ... I sang *Veni creator spiritus* over and over until my heart settled and slowed. My head drooped. I blew out the candles and crawled over to my bed, crossed myself and closed my eyes. It was done.

THE CLANG OF A bell, loud and close by. I started awake, opened my eyes but everything was black. Fright pounded in my head. The bed was hard, the blanket rough, and as I sat up, stone grazed across my hand. My cell. Letting out a long breath, I crossed myself and began my day as always: *Veni creator spiritus, mentes tuorum visita* ... To my relief the familiar rhythm of the prayer settled into me, and I let myself move beyond its forms and words to the memory of candles and darkness, to the vows I had made the night before, giving all to God.

This life meant that I was to pray all day, as I woke, as I dressed, as I ate, as I read. I wanted to light my oil lamp, but I had no idea where my maid had left my flint and tinderbox, so I fumbled for my shoes, pulled on my robe and buckled my belt, reciting my *Pater Noster*, saying the *Credo*.

I stood in the darkness. The things of my old life made no sense now. I touched my lips; there they were, but when I moved my hand away, my mouth was gone. A flicker of light nearby. It must have come from my squint, my way of seeing into the church. I took a step or two toward it, felt along the stone until I found a ledge and the niche cut into the wall above it. Someone was moving around in the sanctuary on the other side of my wall, lighting candles, beginning prayers. It was

Martin, the priest's assistant; I could tell his eager voice from the day before when he had rushed in and out, carrying messages, straightening the altar cloth, lighting the thurible. Even though he was only an assistant, it was a relief to hear him and I knelt once more and whispered my prayers in time with his. I was alone, as I wanted, but it was a comfort to know that my cell hugged the church.

The church door banged as Martin left, but I stayed on my knees, listening to my breath going in and out. The familiar ache was still there in my chest: Emma gone and in the ground, my little sister's life dragged from her body. Her wails of pain, then her whimpers that terrified me even more, the desperate grip of her hand that weakened and finally let go. I took a deep breath, let it out slowly. Here, inside these walls, Christ would heal me of my grief, help me let go of my woman's body, its frailty and desire. I would learn to love him above all others, to share his suffering.

Patches of dull light glimmered through gaps in the thatch and a soft golden glow came from somewhere above me. I looked up. Over my altar, and just below the roofline, was a window covered with strips of horn that kept out the wind but were thin enough to let through some light. I could see only dimly, but found my flint and lit the oil lamp on my desk.

Next to it was a book, simply bound and without a clasp, my Rule of Life. I picked it up and held it between my hands, felt the smooth leather of the cover. Inside were page after page, row after row of letters, here and there a simple red capital. Plain words, no illuminations such as I had seen in Books of Hours, not even a flourish around a capital, or a curl of leaves. I had thought there would be something. Even the bishop said that mine was a calling few could undertake. If I was to read this book each day, look to it for guidance about how to live this hardest of lives, surely I deserved better.

I moved nearer the lamp to read the first page.

You, my dear sisters, have begged me for a Rule for many a day and so I have written down these words for you, that you may be encouraged in your love for Christ as you hang with him.

My dear sisters. I was one of these dear sisters. The bishop told me the Rule had been written by a godly man for some anchoresses who had lived not far from here. God had blessed the diocese with more women like them, he said, and there were now many copies of the Rule. The one used by the women in this cell had been given elsewhere, so a scribe had made one more, just for me. I wondered about the man who had written out all these words, one by one, and drawn the plain red capitals. Just for me. Perhaps the other copies had been plain as well. This was my life now; I should not expect more.

The parchment whispered as I turned the pages, word after word.

A quiet knock, then a little louder, and a muffled voice.

'Sister Sarah? 'Scuse me, Sister, for disturbing you. It's Louise, your maid.'

I looked toward the rattling shutters. Louise would be standing at the maids' window cut into the back wall of her room, the one adjoining my cell on its narrower side. I walked across to it, pulled back the bolt, and swung open the wooden shutters. They banged as they hit the stone wall and I winced.

The window was low, just above waist height, and we both had to bend to speak.

'Pardon again, Sister, but I'm Louise, as you'd remember from yesterday. It's me as will be caring for all your needs till the second maid comes.'

'Yes, Louise. I remember.' I sat down on the end of my bed and looked through the window. In the light of her room, I could just see Louise's face when she straightened, the shadows emphasising its cobweb of wrinkles. Her hands were folded across her belly in a stance that I would ever after connect with her voice, patient and longsuffering. 'Your room is enough for your needs, I hope?'

'Yes, Sister. There be enough room to cook and for two women to sleep, though if I may say, it be—'

'Yes, Louise. I trust you understand your duties.' I suddenly felt awkward; Louise was a maid, and I had dealt with servants, but most likely she knew more than me about this place, this cell, how I would survive. And now I was to teach and guide her path with God. 'Can you read, Louise?'

'No, course not, Sister. Where would I have learned to read? Me as was born here, in that house just over—'

'Then I will read to you from my Rule and from my books. And you must pray and be quiet when you're indoors, and modest when you go out.'

'Yes, I will, Sister.' I heard her make a clucking sound with her tongue. 'And if I do say, Sister, that's always been my way; that's why Father Simon, he's the priest here, he said to Bishop Michael as I would be most suitable to be maid to the new anchoress. "A pious widow of good life", they were the very words Father Simon said of me.'

'He said that to me as well. But you're under my care and instruction now.' I began to feel easier.

'Yes, ma'am ... Sister. I wonder, Sister, if you'll be wanting some food after your long fasting, and after walking here all that way.'

Her words made my belly growl; I thought of roast venison and baked quince. 'A little pottage and some water, I think.'

As Louise opened her door, early morning light hazed through the maids' window and softened the darkness in my cell. I left open the shutters, stood and looked around.

You might think there would be nothing to tell about those four walls, two windows, a squint, and darkness, but the stones carried so many stories. And they would carry my story, every moment of my time here. My only witness.

A few steps to my left, in the same wall as the maids' window behind me, was the parlour window with shutters like those to the maids' room, though still closed. Two narrow eyes: one open, one shut. Nearby, along the outer wall, the few books I carried from home had been set neatly on my desk: my Breviary, my Psalter, and a collection of devotions, and now my Rule of Life as well. Tucked in close to the desk was a small chest where I could keep my clothing, and next to it was the fireplace with its rough chimney. In the far wall, opposite the two shuttered inner windows, was the door through which I had entered, the only way in or out, nailed shut. I shivered. It could be opened only by my confessor or by Father Simon, and only if I was in need. To its right was a simple altar with a wooden crucifix hanging above it, and a mere step or two past that, but in the church wall, were my squint and ledge. Farther along that wall was my bed, a pallet covered with coarse-weave blankets. I bent to touch them; my coverlet at home was fine linen damask worked with gold and blue flowers that shone in the sunlight. My father had bought the cloth from Italy especially for me. I was here to forget my old life and I had longed for this rough lodging, but all was so new, so different.

I walked the length of my cell from the wall with two windows to my altar, counting my steps — nine paces; then across the narrower side, from my fireplace to my squint — seven paces. This would be my world. I touched the squint, a thin window about the length of my two hands from fingertips to heel and as wide as my wrist. I knelt and looked through. It was so narrow, and cut on such a sharp angle in the thick church wall, that I could see only the church's altar, its two lighted candles, and the crucifix above. I remembered, from the day before, that there was an arch into the chancel with paintings of angels around its curve, and that I'd thought then how much smaller and plainer this church was than my old church in Leeton. But I realised now that it made no difference; even if I moved closer to the slit or tilted my head, I would see nothing more than the crucifix and the candles.

I crossed myself and rested my arms on the ledge below the squint, set deep enough into the wall to hold my prayer book. Lower again, a small square had been cut through the wall so I could receive the body of Christ at Mass. I rubbed my fingers across the stone ledge and thought of those who had knelt here before me.

'My grandfather William carved that squint, Sister.'

I gasped with fright.

'Oh, 'scuse me, Sister, but I brought your food and saw you looking.'

'Louise, what of the women enclosed in this cell before me? I know of Sister Agnes, of course; she was such a holy woman. And Sister Isabella was enclosed here more lately, I think. You were here, in the village with them. Were they—?'

'Oh, yes, Sister Agnes was a very holy woman. As you say, she was well known all hereabouts and stories are still told of all she did. I came to her for counsel when my little girl died, and then when my Rob died. She said as how we all suffer, just like our Lord did, and she said she'd pray for me. I could feel her holiness, I could.'

Holiness. I hoped the village would speak of my holiness.

'It was sad when she died,' Louise said, 'but we were glad for her going to heaven. What she always longed for, to be with our Lord. She's buried here in this cell; her bones lie there, just where you're kneeling now. You're blessed, Sister, if I may say, to have the bones of such a holy woman to comfort you.'

I stood up and stepped back. Buried deep down, I thought, now just part of the dirt and stones, nothing more. Still, the hairs on my head lifted, the skin on my knees prickled.

At the maids' window I took the water and pottage from Louise: a mush of cabbage and parsnip. The smell turned my stomach so I put the food on my desk, thinking I might nibble at it later. I drank some water. 'And the other woman? Isabella?'

'I don't know so much of Sister Isabella. She came from the convent at Challingford and she was here only about five years or so. She was a widow, young, and I never had cause to visit her. But I did talk to Sister Agnes; strange to think, but I sat in the parlour, the other side of this wall, and now it's my duty to watch for those as want to visit you, especially those as would annoy you and interrupt your prayers. That's what Bishop

Michael said, "It's your special duty, Louise." And don't you worry, I can see out my door here to be sure of those as come.'

I moved to the parlour window, only a few steps away from the maids' window and set a little higher, but low enough that I would be able to sit at my chair to speak with visitors. I opened the shutters that covered it, though it revealed only a black cloth curtain. I touched it, felt the ridges of the white cross sewn onto it, and remembered Bishop Michael's words on the day he examined my request to be enclosed: 'The black cloth signifies that you're worthless to the world, and it to you. The white cross stitched on top is a sign of your virgin purity.'

He had stepped close, his voice low; I felt the hem of his robes brush against my shoes. 'Remember, child, your virginity is your fragile treasure, your jewel, the blossom of your body offered to the Lord. In your cell it is sealed, kept whole.' His words made my face redden. 'Enclosure is the only means by which your virginity may be assured.'

I felt again the heat in my face and thought instead of the curtain between my fingers. Despite its thickness, the folds were smooth. Close weave, I thought, well combed and new; Sir Geoffrey had bought good cloth for my window, if not for my bed. Had he ordered it from my father? Pa was furious about my enclosure, and even more that Sir Geoffrey was my patron, providing my living in this place, but I knew scant of what had passed between the two men: cloth, money, talk of loans and marriage, the bodies of women. The old anger at my father rose hot in my throat.

I pulled back the cloth, the only real opening between the world and me, though I knew the windows were not there for me to look through. Bishop Michael had told me severely that only women might look in on me, and only if needed, when I counselled them. 'There is to be no looking out and no letting men look in.' He stood tall and tipped his head back, in that manner he had. 'Lust prowls, it prowls,' he said roundly.

Anxiety curled in my belly at the thought of counselling women. Perhaps I knew more of prayer and reading than they did, but how would I, with my seventeen chaste years, speak to village women of their troubles, of husbands and babies and bodies? God had called me here to leave all that behind.

I held up my lamp to see into the gloom of the parlour and noticed a small opening cut into its door, enough to let in some light.

'That parlour ain't all it should be, Sister, and I be sorry for that.' Louise couldn't see me, but she must have guessed what I was doing. 'That door drags most of the time, and the little opening there lets in light, but when the wind gusts it blows through like a knife. I thought a village man might come and fix it, as it's Bishop Michael's custom to sit in comfort and some warmth. When he visits I can bring in a grander chair from the church, but that's all. And a man like that, he expects better.'

'Then the bishop's visits to me will be few and short,' I said, and let the curtain drop. I felt a creep across my skin when I thought of him sitting in my parlour, the words he would say. The flame from my lamp flickered and I looked around my cell. This would be all I knew now. I leaned on my desk, then pulled at my chair and sat down as my knees gave way. Louise must have heard the gasp I tried to stifle.

'Sister, are you all right? Sister, can I—?'

'Thank you, Louise, it's just weariness and an empty stomach. I'll be … I'll spend some time in prayer now.'

I closed and bolted the shutters and walked the nine steps to my altar, back to my desk, then there and back again, reciting my psalms. The words and the steps settled me and I breathed more calmly. I was alone, enclosed; the world would not reach me here.

I opened my Rule and read, but my eyes slipped from word to word, page to page, wanting what was to come before I had contemplated what was in front of me: these words written for me, words that understood my need. Then a passage made me pause because it was so serious, and also because I had heard it spoken:

> *I would advise no anchoress to take a vow except regarding three*
> *things: obedience, chastity, and stability of place; that she must*
> *never leave that place unless absolutely necessary; for example,*
> *if she were under threat of violence or fear for her life, or in*
> *obedience to her bishop or his superior. For whoever undertakes*
> *something, and vows to God to do it, binds herself to it and*
> *commits a deadly sin if she breaks it of her own free will.*

The day Bishop Michael examined my calling, his questions were many, and close. He needed to be sure of my faith, and also that I had a patron who would support my daily needs. Finally, satisfied with my answers, he had agreed, but with a warning.

'It is a laudable decision, Sarah, but you must know that whoever vows to God to be enclosed within four walls binds herself for the remainder of her earthly life. In that cell you become Christ's beloved, and it would be grievous sin against our Lord, and grievous sin against the Church, if you were to break that vow.' He spoke slowly, stressing each word. 'If you doubt that you can remain in your cell, Sarah, it were better that you did not enter at all.' He looked into my face. 'We must be grateful the people have agreed to welcome another anchoress to their village.'

I was certain I would remain; of course I would. But the warning frightened me. And here it was again. This was what I had longed for, to be alone in my cell, to love Christ and to share his suffering. I would pray for the people of the village, and in time, I hoped, counsel and comfort them. There was nothing the world could tempt me with anymore.

Something deep in my belly fluttered and lifted. Four stone walls to hold my body. I left my desk and pressed my hands against the stone beneath my parlour window. It was hard and solid.

FOR THOSE FIRST DAYS it was only me, the dull darkness, and my prayers. I felt I could finally let go the breath I had held for so long. I must have eaten and spoken with Louise, but it was as if my head was always bowed, seeing nothing beyond my altar or the words I read, hearing nothing but my prayer and the whisper of parchment. Christ listened to me, wrapped me in his love, kept my heart quiet. And the walls held me tight.

The walls began to crack the day my new maid arrived. I was at my desk reading and rose at the sound of Louise's muffled voice, her sharp knock on the shutter of the maids' room. She kept speaking as I undid the bolt.

'... And I've told her, Sister, we thought as she'd be here these past days.'

I could make out the shape of a young girl standing behind her, shadowy in the gloom. Warmth flushed through me; it was Emma, curling black hair straggling out from her cap, her head tilted, one hand on a hip, sighing loudly. Emma, my little sister, who lay cold and white in the ground. My fingers tingling with shock, I sat down on the end of my bed.

The girl spoke. 'I've said already as they wouldn't let me come till they found another to help in the kitchen.' She paused, looked back at Louise. 'And I'm Anna. Case you wanted to know.'

Louise refused to back down. 'Well, Father Simon said as you'd be here—'

'Like I said, they told me I was to wait,' Anna insisted. 'The steward Gwylim, he said as he was coming here from Friaston, and he'd get word to the priest here. Isn't that Father Simon?'

The first shock had passed, but heat still ran down into my fingers. She was so much like Emma: her way of standing untroubled in her own place; her edges not sharp but clear.

'Well, it be past time you arrived, girl,' Louise went on. 'Father Simon said nothing of you coming late. All he told me was that the anchoress should have a girl to do the fetching and cooking, specially as how he knew me as a good and faithful woman and I should have more time to pray.' She looked at me hopefully, wanting me to speak.

'Did he?' was all I could manage.

'You doubt that, Sister, that I'm known as good and faithful?'

'No, Louise, of course not. Now let me speak with the girl. Sit down, Anna.'

She answered my questions in single words. Yes, she would cook and carry, and yes, she would pray with us, and yes, she would be chaste and obedient.

'And Anna, will you be content to live here and to serve me?'

'Content, ma'am? I do as I'm told, don't I? What's content?' She looked into my eyes for a moment, then down. Emma would have used different words, but the tone, the angle of her head, were the same.

''Tis Sister to you, girl, and mind what you say to Sister, and how you say it,' Louise said from somewhere behind her. 'It's a blessing for you to be here; you can learn from such a holy woman. Beginning with manners.'

The way Anna lifted one shoulder, as Emma used to, made me want to bring her into my cell and tell her all, as I would have told my sister: to whisper to her that I didn't much like Louise; to complain about the rough blanket on my bed, the plain pages of my Rule, the dull food — and then to say no, no, that Louise took good care of me, that I was grateful I could pray and read, that I wanted to please God, to stay here, closed from the world. Emma would have listened to me and tried to understand.

But all that was gone. When they hammered in the nails, I left the memories behind. Who had planned this, to send this girl to me, to bring back my dead past? This was my new life, this cell. I couldn't do it; I wanted to send her out the door, away from me.

'Louise, you will tell the new maid her duties. She will join us for reading from my Rule, and for prayers at Prime, Terce, and Compline.'

I closed the shutters: I had found these walls and I would stay.

However many times I read them, the words always said the same thing.

There are many kinds of rule, but I shall speak of two: an inner rule that is love and directs the heart, and a second, the outer rule that teaches how people must behave outwardly: how they should eat, drink, dress, sing and wake. The first is like a lady, and this second one like her maid. Now, you ask which rule you anchoresses should keep. You should in every way, with all your might and strength, preserve well the inner rule and the outer, which may vary for the first's sake.

I read it again, knowing that it was merciful, but wanting clear directions that I could obey, that would bring back the calm of my first days here. Memories of home nagged at me now, old griefs and horrors and desires that I thought had quietened; they interrupted my prayers, walked through the pages of my Rule. If only someone would tell me how to behave, surely my heart would follow.

One part of my outer rule was clear, at least, and I knew the pattern of prayer from my months with the nuns when I was a child: Matins, Lauds, Prime, Terce, Sext, Nones, Vespers, Compline. The rhythm like sunrise and sunset, the beat of a heart. I was to rise each day in the dark for prayers at Matins, but the church bell would not ring to wake me. Martin, Father Simon's assistant, was diligent to ring all the other hours, but because Matins prayers were required only of religious houses, he slept until dawn, when he rang Lauds.

'The priory at Cramford rings the bell for Matins, and even though it's behind Cram Hill, you should be able to hear it,' my confessor told me during my period of instruction. 'But it doesn't matter if you miss Matins in the first weeks; simply wait for it to become a part of you, and you'll be waking before the bell rings. The body knows, eventually.'

But I wanted to wake on time every day; how could Father Peter tell me it didn't matter? For the first weeks I slept fitfully and sometimes rose to pray not long after I'd fallen asleep, part of me alert and listening for the priory bell. After a time, when it didn't ring, I'd lie down again and sleep on, so tired that I wouldn't hear the bell for Matins when finally it tolled, and would start awake near dawn at the heavy clanging for Lauds in the tower just above me. Some nights when I woke too early for

Matins the time was empty, left me unguarded, and my dreams seeped into my waking, dreams of holding Emma's hand, the pain clenching her fingers. When I opened my eyes into blackness, sure I was awake, I would see her hand in mine, as clearly as in daytime. No body, just a hand fading into darkness. I would will the priory to wake then, and ring the bell, to fill the night with prayer, to chase away my dreams. Only with the murky light of morning would they sink back into the cracks in the walls, leaving me shaking.

Wood scraping on stone, the drag of a door opening, scuffles, then … nothing. Was someone in the parlour? Someone wanting counsel? Where was Louise? More scuffling noises, then loud whispering.

'Do you think she's a witch?'

'Nah, Ma says 'tis a holy woman and we'd best not get too near. Let's go.'

'Scaredy. That's a story. I saw her just t'other day, an' she has three eyes and scales like a dragon.'

'Go away,' I shouted. 'I'm praying and not to be disturbed.'

Giggles, a sound of stumbling, a shout. 'Told ya! A dragon.' Then fading laughter.

Foolish children, but the silence in their wake was painful. A witch, a holy woman, a dragon: I was none of those, just a woman who had chosen to be alone. I cried, the tears burning my eyes.

I discovered quickly that the walls would not keep out the smell of food. It crept in through gaps in the shutters and lingered around me. And one day, not long after Anna arrived, the smell was particularly good. Vegetables, though I didn't know what kind, and meat, even though I'd told the maids that my food was to be simple: turnips, cabbages, onions, and, sometimes, fish. Brother Alain carried much of our food, basic and sufficient, from the priory — so why was Anna cooking meat?

'Folk about here brought it,' Anna said and smiled. 'Some food to share with you, to celebrate you coming: bread, milk, some eggs and peas, even dried meat. I've stored some, and I can cook—'

'I won't eat it and break my discipline.' I saw Louise was about to speak, but Anna went on.

'Sister, it be gifts, their way of saying welcome, to give alms. They say it's the only way they have, with you shut away like this. You can't—'

'Anna, don't presume to teach me. My Rule tells me to keep my body in some need; I've explained that.'

'But, Sister, you read to us not two days back as we should be grateful for the gifts of others. I heard it.'

I felt my face redden. Anna was right.

'Sister,' Louise put in, 'they're gifts, but not as they mean to make you sin. They hope you'll pray for them in return. An anchoress is special for the village and they want you to stay.'

I was ashamed; the village was welcoming me in the only way it could and I should be grateful. My confusion made me angry. 'Stay? Well, of course I will. There are nails in that door. I chose to be enclosed, it's what I want. They don't have to make me stay.'

'No, Sister, course not.'

'You may eat the stew yourselves, but I'll fast today, and pray for the villagers.'

I closed the shutters, bent down, brushed the straw away from beneath my squint and pressed my hands on the hard, bare soil. Agnes, wise woman, buried here in my cell, show me how to be an anchoress. Make me holy.

My knees prickled, the ground scratched at my skin, and a shudder ran through my hands and up into my arms. I flinched, fell to one side, pulled myself over to my desk and onto the chair. The sound of scraping bone followed me.

I shivered and touched my Rule. Looking for comfort, I turned to a page I often read, to words I knew almost by heart.

True anchoresses are like birds, for they leave the earth — that is, the love of all that is worldly — and, as a result of their hearts' desire for heavenly things, fly upwards toward heaven. And though they fly high with a high and holy life, yet they hold their heads low in mild humility, as a bird in flight bows its head, and they consider all their good actions to be worthless.

Swallow had flown like a bird, his arms stretched wide and his legs straight, then tucked in, to tumble in the air. His clothes had flashed red and grey, the stripes spinning, his head curled into his body. I wanted to fly like him, like an angel, to let go of my body and the longing that held me to the ground.

The stewed meat smelled rich; the fragrance wound around my head and sank into my clothes. My belly twisted with hunger. I shut my eyes, refused it, and thought of Swallow's leap. For a moment, it felt as if my narrow cell opened to the sky.

⟨◎⟩

Father Peter visited a few days later. He was my confessor, and I had been hoping he would visit to see that all was well.

The scrape of the stool, and he grunted as he sat down. 'Sister Sarah? God bless you, my child. Are you well, Sister?'

'Yes, Father, thank you.'

'I'm glad to hear it. You seemed weak at your enclosure, though, of course, it demanded much.'

His voice made me think of the river where it runs deepest, the silken sound of its slow eddies, but that seemed fanciful. His face had frightened me when I met him before my enclosure: the filaments in his watery eyes, foggy white rings on the blue, the red blotches on his sagging cheeks. He'd seemed weary, like a thick rug worn down. But he had smiled more quickly than I'd expected and there had been a gentle concern in his eyes. That was the last time I would see his face; from now on, it would be only his voice on the other side of the curtain.

'I'm sorry that I haven't come earlier, but I understand that Father Simon hears your confession when I cannot come. Have you warmth and sufficient food?'

'Yes, Father, though I eat sparingly. My Rule tells me that keeping my body in need will bring me to God.'

'Yes, it does. But it also says not to suffer needlessly. You must be strong enough to do God's work; it says that also.'

'And I'm teaching my maids from the Rule each day and making sure they pray.'

'Very good. There's a lot for you to get used to, child; don't rush at this new life. You have all the time you need to grow into it. I'm old, and slowing down; that's why I can't visit more often. The walk from the priory is pleasant, especially when the weather is fine, but my legs don't carry me as easily as they once did. Still, the slow walk makes me look around at the world. I've seen things I never noticed when I strode along as a young man. *You're* young, Sarah. Think of yourself as a child, still learning to walk, and that will be two of us, learning to lean on God together.' A chuckle. 'And now, would you make your confession?'

I submitted, wanting all the time to argue. A child? Me? I was no novice nun; I'd chosen this hardest life of all, and he called me a child! He was kind, but he was old, and perhaps he'd forgotten the strength of being young. He absolved me of my sin, though not the anger and argument in my heart.

'You will have read in your Rule that this life you've chosen is penance itself as you hang on the cross with our Lord. No need for me to add more, my child. God bless you, Sarah, and Mother Mary embrace you.'

I could hear the wheeze of his breath. 'Are you unwell, Father?'

''Tis the rheum that never really leaves me now.' He coughed, and sniffed loudly. 'Sister, I see your new maid has arrived. Anna, isn't it? I know it's customary for the younger maid to stay indoors praying, away from temptation, and for the older maid to spend more time outside the cell, fetching and cooking and washing, but I hear Louise is no longer able for such hard work. I understand how she feels.'

Another chuckle. 'I'm sure Anna's capable, having spent time in Lord Maunsell's manor at Friaston, but that isn't what concerns me. She's very young and I'm not sure that she wants this kind of life. A maid to an anchoress should be committed to God and to service, but it seems this is what the manor and Father Simon have decided, at least for now. It's a good living for a young girl but you will need to guide her well, Sister. Be sure she prays and reads; perhaps let her do some simple sewing. Not too much wandering about the village, mind.'

The bishop had told me I was to care for my maids, but not this, guiding a young girl who reminded me of Emma, of so much I'd left behind.

Again, the scrape of the stool and a grunt. 'But I'm sure you're wise on such matters,' Father Peter said. 'And your Rule has a section on the care of your maids. I'll come again, as soon as I'm able. God bless you, child.' Some shuffling, then the protest of my parlour door as he pushed it shut.

Noises outside — shouting, laughter, squeals, and curses. It was All Hallows Eve, and though I couldn't see the fires on the green just beyond the church, it seemed right that so soon after my enclosure I could pray for the dead, my dead. If I was to guide Anna as my Rule required, I needed first to commit Emma to God. I moved to my altar and knelt to pray, saying the words once more, willing my heart to let go of memories of my sister.

The squeak of metal close by, the sound of wood on wood as the church door shut. The smell of dirt floated in to me as it always did when someone entered the church. Muffled footsteps, a few soft thumps, and then quietness. The cough of a sick man, dry and rasping, the sound of breath dragged in and out. Perhaps he had come to pray, grieving for a wife or a son or a brother. I moved to my altar, knelt to pray for him, asking Christ to ease that hollow pain of loss I understood. The church bell began to ring, an insistent tolling, driving back time ...

I was with Ma and Emma, eight years past on All Hallows Eve, outside in the frosty night. Ma was telling us we had to keep away the angry spirits of the dead; they came with the chill winds that swept bare the trees, she said, when the earth was dying, when the boundary between the world of the dead and the world of the living was weakest. And so we built fires and rang bells. I imagined the dead floating in the air like smoke, with black misty holes for eyes and large wailing mouths, their legs stretching long and thin, hands over their ears, trying to get close to us but forced back by the rolling clangour of the bells. Father John urged us to give thanks for the food God had given us in the harvest, food to sustain us in the frozen winter, and on this night when life and death met, he asked us to pray for the souls of the dead.

It sounded so serious and frightening that after Mass I played at ghouls with Emma and the other children, shouting and whooping, and ate more than usual — nuts and apples and soul cakes — as my own way of warding off the dead.

A piercing screech and I startled, looked around, came back to my dark cell; the smell of smoke, flickers of orange high on my wall, coming in through gaps in the thatch. Outside, the crackle of burning wood, screams of merriment, drumbeats and bells. Children would be wearing masks, running, dancing, cackling, and whooping like monsters or ghosts, now shadow, now golden in the firelight. The sounds faded and then grew louder by turn as revellers ran up and down the village lanes.

This year, on this night of the dead, there was no one with me to see or touch, no one to reassure me that I was alive. But I wasn't; my Rule told me that I was dead to the world, that this cell was my grave. I looked around, wondered where they would dig the hole for my body. Agnes was here, just below my squint; had they buried Isabella there as well? A shiver ran from my hair all the way down my back, into my legs and through to my toes. Dread and excitement — in this place of life in death, what else could I feel, closed to the world and open to the unseen? Of a sudden I noticed I was cold, as if winter had walked in weeks before his time. I dragged a blanket from my bed and pulled it around my shoulders.

My candle cut shadows into Christ's face on the crucifix above me and for a moment I saw Ma, her cheeks thin, her eyes hollow. Perhaps she had lived an All Hallows vigil for the last few months of her life: half in the next world, where food and clothing and sleep mean nothing. At first she'd looked after the new baby with a distracted care, then she stopped eating. She would let Alfred cry on and on until one of us picked him up and took him to her to suckle, and after a few weeks his cries became higher and more desperate with hunger. When Madge, the midwife, told us she had found a wet nurse, Ma's smile was empty, as if she hadn't heard or grasped what Madge had said. Her face dull, looking at nothing, tears sometimes trickling onto the pillow; her body and heart worn out from what a baby demands in being born into this world.

'Despair is a sin,' Father John said to me when I told him of my mother's sadness. 'Her pain is the price of Eve's fall in Eden and all women pay for it. Your mother must pray and confess her despair, and God will hear her. She's a good woman.' He smiled at me. 'And you must pray for her, too, Sarah.'

I wanted to shout at him, to ask him: Are women made to bear the kind of pain that crushes them underfoot like grass trampled into the soil? It's easy then to call it despair and a sin. Alfred is grown now, stronger and taller than my father; he thrived where my mother sank, sucked under, drawn into the earth — but it's not for me to blame him.

'Holy Sister, a soul cake on this night of the dead?'

I blenched, fright jagged in my chest. My cell was black and I could see nothing but the yellow glow of my candle. The laughter and shouting outside were distant now. I held up my candle and peered around me. A man's voice. He must be in my parlour. I rose and took the few steps to the window.

'Who is it?'

'Just a traveller, Sister.'

I turned so quickly my candle flickered, guttered, nearly went out, then steadied. The voice hadn't come from my parlour; where was he?

'Ain't eaten for two days, Sister. Might you have a cake this vigil, or bread, maybe? P'rhaps ale?' The sound came from my squint. He coughed. Of course, he was in the church; it was the man I'd heard earlier.

'You're not to speak to me. I'm enclosed here. But I'm praying for you. What's your name?'

'I'm Harry, Sister, an' you might pray, but food is my need.'

I wanted him to leave. 'Ask for food in the village. They have—'

'Can't show this face, can I? Or these hands. They'd beat me out of town for it.'

My belly was suddenly hot. I stepped back into the wall, put my candle on the desk, both hands to my mouth.

'You are, you're a ...?'

'Leper, Sister, is the word you're after. Yes. An' you being holy, I know you'd—'

'Well, there's no food here for you.' I looked down at my desk to the cake Anna had brought me. I would not eat it, but I would not pass it to his tainted hands, even through my squint. 'This is a vigil and I fast. You must leave. You cannot be here. There are places for you to go.' In my mind I could see the ragged cloth binding his face and hands, hiding the horror beneath, the slow creep of death.

''Tis where I'm headed. But meanwhiles I must eat and sleep.'

'It's not for me to help you. Leave.' I was sure now that I could smell goats and their musky urine stink. How could he be here, so close to me? Would my cell keep away nothing of the world?

'You can't make me leave this church, you and your holiness that won't help. What's prayers when a man's stomach twists in pain? I thought you'd help me, you or the Father ... but no. 'Tis too holy for us, shut away, pure an' all ...' The squeak of the church door drowned his muttering.

I sank onto my chair, my legs shaking. I wanted to crawl into bed, but it was near my squint, near his disease. I watched the flame of my candle burn, its steady heart of gold, until finally it died. I went over and over the same thoughts: it was what my Rule demanded, what my life was to be — shut off from the world and its demands. That was right, I was sure. I would pray for Harry; that was my life now — to pray for others. And it was true, wasn't it, that lepers were sick because they had sinned? Yet whatever firm arguments I mustered, I knew I was simply afraid.

There was no noise from the church and I was shivering now, my blanket on the floor where I had dropped it at my altar. It was easy, by this time, to feel my way across to pick it up, pull it onto my bed and curl up, but I lay on the edge, keeping as far from the church wall as I could. My mother's face lingered in the dark.

Minutes later, sounds woke me: the squeak of the church door, fumbling, whispering. I recognised a voice, a man's, but younger than the leper's. It was Martin, the priest's assistant, speaking quietly. I crept to my squint, my ear turned to listen.

The smell was putrid, the fetid stink of rotting flesh, and I pulled back slightly, covered my nose.

''Tis warmer over here. Here's my robe and that's another blanket. They should keep you warm. There. And I'll come in the morning with some more bread … Father Simon won't be here until Terce. You won't be seen. Oh, but quiet, the anchoress, you know, is in there and we mustn't disturb her.'

The bang of the church door.

Jesus had healed lepers, had touched them with love, hadn't he?

I lay awake in the accusing silence, the rank smell in the air, remembering the night of my enclosure, the prayers for burial read over my body. How had Harry felt when they read the same rites for him and sent him away to a life he hadn't chosen? We two were dead to the world, though it looked on us so differently, and I had joined the world in shunning him.

I loved to read in my Rule that a virgin was just a little lower than the angels, but all I could hear now was the beating in my head like the throb of angels' wings, slowing, getting fainter, leaving me.

✤ RANAULF ✤

HIS FACE BURNED; HE felt he was being watched, though he was alone. His third mistake this morning. Ranaulf put down his quill, moved the knife from his left to his right hand, took a deep breath. Slowly, catching only the ink and the thinnest layer of parchment, he scraped away the *f* that should have been a *t*. His jaw ached; the muscles in his neck pulled tight. He set down the knife, gently brushed the page and slipped out from behind the desk. Standing, he stretched his left shoulder up and back, then his right. A muscle contracted as if tied with twine, tugging all the way down his right side. Gristly sounds echoed from his neck into his head as he turned it from side to side.

He glanced toward one of the windows. The autumn sun was gleaming weakly, but it would be hours before light would fall on his desk, and then only for a short time. The room was small; he had known it wouldn't be as grand or airy as the scriptorium at the abbey, and he was pleased to serve God at St Christopher's, taking charge of the young priory's manuscripts and no longer just one of many scribes ruling lines and copying. But on days like this, the room seemed to narrow and darken.

A noise at the door; Ranaulf recognised the familiar bustling and felt his body tense.

'Prior Walter.'

'Father Ranaulf, the corrody. Have you finished copying the corrody for the anchoress of Hartham? You know I'll be uneasy until we have a copy completed; if the original went missing, the danger to the priory would be immense! I don't think you appreciate, Father, tucked away as you are, how long it took me to negotiate, how significant is the agreement. Sir Geoffrey is shrewd, even if he does fear for his soul. Is it ready?'

Ranaulf nodded toward the shelves, stepped back to his desk, and restrained a sigh as the prior pushed past him. It had been a difficult day when he'd first arrived at the priory with his equipment, especially this awkward desk that had needed four men to carry and guide it through the narrow doorway of the scriptorium. Initially he had been inclined to complain about the size of the room and the poor light, but the prior's face had warned him against it. The priory was young, still a tender offshoot of Westmore Abbey, but Prior Walter's plans were ambitious; work on an additional building had begun, though a larger, brighter scriptorium would be seasons — perhaps years — away.

At the far end of the room, the prior glanced over the few books and scrolls on the shelves lining the raw stone wall. 'Here we are.' He lifted down and unwrapped a small bundle. Inside were quires of folded parchment, as yet unbound. 'Very important. The numbers must be copied correctly, and the details of the land, just as in the original. And the names of all the witnesses, not only the first line. If there are ever questions, Father, it must all be here.'

'Of course, Prior. I copy carefully. As you know.'

Usually he took little notice of the content of this type of document: numbers of acres, location of the land, amounts of money — but he had been surprised by this one; it betokened a remarkably good arrangement for the prior. Sir Geoffrey, Lord of Friaston and Hartham, had given valuable tracts of land to the priory in return for its physical and spiritual support of the anchoress of Hartham. What was the formulation? Acres of pasture and woodland, some cottages, meadow, three sheepfolds with foldage. And there was more, but he'd forgotten the detail. In return, the priory had to provide a confessor for the anchoress and make sure the anchorhold was maintained and repaired when necessary. In addition, it was to provide sustenance for the anchoress and her maids: basic foods like bread, ale, fish, flour — the amounts were specified, down to the type and number of fish — as well as oil, candles, and wood.

Ranaulf understood Prior Walter's delight: pasture for their sheep, rental money from the arable land, wood from the forest for building — he could see the advantages. All in return for the care of three devout women — how much time and trouble could that involve?

'Ah, yes, here's the corrody. Neatly copied, Father.' Prior Walter ran his fingers down the page, as if searching for a particular provision. 'Did you include Sir Thomas, the son? Most important, that part is. Sir Geoffrey won't live forever, you know, and … yes, here it is. Very good, Father Ranaulf.'

He straightened the documents, began reading again at the top, and turned the pages one by one, muttering contentedly to himself.

At his desk, Ranaulf looked down at the creamy parchment, the tiny shadows cast by its dimples in the weak morning sun, the ruled lines, the letters, even and black, standing one after another. A page well copied was a thing of beauty, especially when enhanced with illumination. The prior sought the written word as a tool only, as surety of his transactions, but it could be so much more. Marks on the page were signs that could communicate such complex ideas: precise dogma of creed and the rules of church discipline, or the deep love of God and the sacrifice of Christ's Passion. After all, the Gospels they read were written on sheepskin.

He pictured in his mind the library at Westmore, the shelves crammed with books, the pages and pages of words: Augustine, Anselm, Bernard, the great men standing behind each phrase he'd copied. Words that spoke to him again as he read. The priory held but a smattering of books and scrolls: some of them works Ranaulf had brought with him; some on loan from the mother house; one or two that he had copied himself.

He had thought it would be a pleasure to work alone, but what he missed most, he had begun to realise, and with surprise, were the conversations about the books and their ideas. Abbot Wulfrum, Stephen, Berenger: the brothers who copied alongside him and discussed, explained, and argued about what they had read. He smiled; even Ralph, with his irritating way of interrupting and talking over the top of everyone else — perhaps Ranaulf missed even him. Here at Cramford, Father Peter enjoyed talking with Ranaulf about whatever he was working on, and wanted especially to hear his opinion of all that he copied, but the man was often unwell, and if in good health seemed always to be walking out to the anchoress at Hartham, then recovering in bed from the effort. He should visit him.

A sudden flurry of clucking and honking and he started; the geese were attacking the hens again.

Ranaulf shook his head to rid it of wandering thoughts and tucked his long legs under the desk. The page was half full of steady, regular letters, and in the left margin of the line he was writing, a large red capital *A*. The surface was rough where he had scraped away his mistake and now his quill made a scratching sound as it crossed the parchment, but he could feel the ink flowing gently; the mistake would not be noticed. Next, the single stem of an *i*, and then the slight twist of the quill that made the small curve of the *a*, then — almost the same action — the larger curve at its right. The movements settled him into his work and at the end of the line he looked back: *Ave Maria, gratia plena, Dominus tecum*. Each letter becoming a word, giving body to an idea. He felt a gentle pulsing in his blood, a pleasing hum in his head. He was adding some simple decoration around the 'A' when gradually he became aware that the prior was speaking to him.

'... need to have these pages bound into a book. We have a number of charters now, Father Ranaulf, quite a collection. The priory should have a proper cartulary, one book to bind together the copies of our transactions. Important documents lying here in a bundle like this, it's—'

Ranaulf jerked up his head, turned to the prior, spoke quickly. 'We can't spare the parchment to bind a book of only those few pages, and the rest still blank. I need all our parchment for other work.' He tried to keep his voice even. 'These are only copies. You have the originals locked away, so there's no urgent need to bind these as a volume.'

'Yes, yes, I know that.' Still, the prior had set aside a piece of fine calfskin for a cover, whenever it should be needed. He folded the bundle together, wrapped it again, and placed it carefully on a shelf.

'I've been thinking that we might make it more than a collection of legal documents. It could include a chronicle of the priory: something that would show our importance, record our history, our growth, our influence in the area. The chronicle could be bound in the first part of the book and the charters in the second. Other monasteries have chronicles, and so should we. The Chronicle of St Christopher's Priory. You could begin the history, Father Ranaulf.'

The prior opened the door. 'That latest commission, the Breviary Sir Geoffrey ordered for his son's bride; have you sent it to Westmore?'

'I have. Brother Cuthbert will have already begun to work on it. It requires only a few illuminations so it should be ready by Yule.'

'Should be? It must be, Father.'

'I've done all I can.' Ranaulf's voice was strained. 'I had to wait for someone to carry the pages to Westmore. Now I must wait for Cuthbert to finish his work and then for it to be bound and returned to me. If I had an illuminator here, I could make sure the work was done as needed.'

'I've spoken to Abbot Wulfrum and he's considering sending someone. But you well know that he agrees with me — you must show some profit for your work. We cannot pay for parchment and ink without a return. If the priory is to survive and grow, it must have income: from rent for lands, from the sale of fleece, and from your books. The scriptorium will not survive unless you produce an income.'

'Yes, Prior, the abbot spoke to me, you know that. But he also appreciates that it takes time for word to spread. If the lord is happy with the Breviary, he'll show it to others, and more work will come.'

Ranaulf was caught between anger and weariness; it felt as if there was a warning every time the prior spoke to him. It was an honour that Abbot Wulfrum had thought him capable of starting a scriptorium, especially at so young an age, but he'd been given only three years to prove its worth. Now Ranaulf wondered if he was able, after all.

'Perhaps one day you'll recoup the cost of all this parchment and ink and ... and all this ...' Prior Walter waved his hand airily toward the room. 'We'll see if making "beautiful books", as the abbot calls them, proves successful, Father.' He paused, then spoke, almost to himself. 'But the chronicle should have some decoration. I'll speak to the abbot again about Cuthbert.'

Ranaulf felt his neck red and pounding. How could he work on commissions when there were always interruptions, charters to copy, letters to write for the prior? He looked down, noticed the ungainly curlicues he had sketched around the capital, and sighed. Letters he could form well and his hand was steady, but whenever he tried even the simplest decoration, his hand shook. These would have to be scraped away. He should have known better than to try them while the prior was fussing about.

And now a chronicle. He had seen the Westmore Chronicle, had dreamed about writing down his own words one day: choosing the right order, the right expression. But the priory was so young, there was scant worth telling. He had no idea where to begin, what to say.

⊰ SARAH ⊱

'Show your face to me,' he says, 'and to no one else. Look on
me if you wish to have clear sight with the eyes of your heart.
Look within where I am and do not seek me outside of your
heart.'

I LEFT MY RULE open and walked around my four walls,
touching their roughness, feeling the shallow gouges where
the masons had chipped them square and flat. When I held my
candle to them, their dull colour transformed, glowing yellow
even more strongly than it would in sunlight. It was five days,
maybe more, since All Hallows yet the smell of the leper still
hung in my cell, or so it seemed, and Martin's gentle words
clung to the stones. *Take my robe ... but quiet ... the anchoress is in*
there, and we mustn't ...

My Rule said I mustn't speak to men, but the leper hadn't
wanted words; he only wanted food, and I had kept it from him.
I argued with myself, on and on, quoting my Rule, my need to
be shut away, telling myself that it was for others to care for him,
until I was exhausted. I thought of a hand, what would be left of
it, taking my soul cake from the tiny opening in the wall where I

received the bread at Mass. I shivered and looked at my crucifix, my own white hands refusing death. Afraid.

You'll find a way to live with death, Sister Euphemia had said.

Emma had walked with me to Tarrant, but she would have nothing to do with Euphemia, the anchoress, locked away from the world, looking for holiness in the ground, my sister said. I wondered what she would say to see me now.

We were both grieving for Ma, but we were so different. Emma was angry at God, at Pa, at Father John, even sometimes at baby Alfred, but I needed to speak to a woman who knew about God, who could tell me why Ma had died. Yet when I sat in Euphemia's parlour, the morning sun drifting through an arched window, all I could do was cry. Behind her curtain, the anchoress said nothing. When I stopped, exhausted, and apologised for my tears, she told me to let them come, and when I asked her why Ma had died, she said that even though it felt so important, an answer to my question was not what I needed. *A few words from me won't touch your grief, and nor should they. Tend your grief like hard ground, and wait. One day, something will grow; there won't be an answer, but you will see you've found a way to live, and to live with death.* Then she was silent for some time, and finally she promised to pray for me.

On the way home, when Emma asked me what she had said, I told her I couldn't remember because I knew she would be scornful, would say that Euphemia had no answers to give. But I did say that the holy woman's silence was like a presence. Emma smiled and put her arm around me. I sniffed, wiped my eyes and nose. I didn't understand what Euphemia meant, but her stillness, her quiet acceptance of my tears, her certainty that God would help me — that was what I wanted. I could go home and face my father's sullen anger, the hungry baby Ma had left behind, even Father John's hard words of comfort.

At the time, I had not thought of becoming such as Euphemia; I hoped to be a nun, if my father would agree to pay the dowry. But the seed sat darkly in its soil. It took Emma's death to make me yearn for four walls and the wise silence Euphemia had learned.

My vows and my enclosure hadn't yet shown me what it meant to live with death, but the memory of Euphemia's assurance made me quiet enough to sit again to my reading. A scraping on stone, and my eyes and thoughts lifted from my Rule. I looked at my squint, at my parlour window, but there was no one. There it was again. Scratches, but not on stone. On wood. Probably children coming to laugh at me. 'Leave,' I called. The noise again. I looked toward my sealed door, and my chair trembled, the shudder running up into my legs, and I realised what it was: the scrape of fingernail on wood. Agnes, buried beneath my floor before I was born; her bones were cold, but not with silence. My breath came fast, and as I pulled away from my chair a shout flew through the shutters.

'Don't call me that. I'm not ill-bred, you brain-boiled hag!'

It was Anna, and was that my snort, a confused mixture of laughter and relief? I opened the shutters to see the two maids face to face, toe to toe, filling their small room with their anger. Louise turned to me, shock and triumph mingling in her shining eyes, her pursed mouth.

'I knew this girl was too crude and sinful to be your maid. I knew it! I hope, Sister, that you didn't hear that abomination from her mouth. She's been stealing food from gardens hereabout. I saw her do it, just then, trying to excuse herself to Avice, as lives a few houses up, a clump of her parsley in her hand.'

Anna looked to me. 'It's what I learned at the manor, from the cook, how to—'

'How to steal, girl?' Louise was shouting now.

'Louise, be quiet. This is an anchorhold.' My own voice was thin and high, my chest still thudding. The maids' words made no sense. 'Let me deal with this. Go and pray. Anna, come and explain yourself.'

Anna moved closer to the window, took a deep breath and let her hands drop from her hips. 'The cook at the manor showed me how to use herbs, so I collect them from the forest, and sometimes from a garden. But as I say to the villagers, it's for the holy woman walled in by the church, and can't they share a little? It's almost like giving herbs to God, so what be the trouble with that? And they agree. Most times.'

I smiled, glad that it was nothing more, but it was my duty to give the girl guidance. 'Anna, you know you can't take food that isn't offered. Use herbs you find in the forest or growing wild hereabouts, that's all.'

'Well, Sister, as I was trying to tell Louise before she called me stupid, Maud's given me a piece of rosemary as will get roots and grow, and I've already planted a clump of thyme, but Louise pulls it up, she does, and I've told her—'

'That's well, Anna, but I've told you to keep my meals simple, so—'

'But what harm is in a flavour, Sister? It's all food that God gives us.'

'To keep the body in some need brings us closer to God. We've talked about that.'

'But rosemary and parsley and fennel, they just grow in the ground. Gifts from God, that's what my mother always said.' She shrugged her shoulder, as if the argument was won.

'Your mother? Was she at the manor?'

She told me then that both her mother and father had died of the fever that ran through towns and country farther south two summers past. She and her brother had lived together for a time, but he had found a woman to marry and told Anna that she would have to find work. Sir Geoffrey had taken her in as a hand in the kitchen at Friaston Manor, but then decided she should come and work as my maid.

'Joan, she's the cook, she showed me how to make special food for the feasts, sauces and gravies for meat. She says good cooking is all in the flavours, spices and herbs, and knowing what's right for each meat. And for sweet food, too, like custards and tarts. She even let me help her make little flowers out of sugar.' Anna laughed. 'I wasn't very good, but she said I'd learn.'

'You must have been sad to leave,' I said.

'Oh, I liked working in the kitchen well enough, but I was glad to leave.'

'Glad to leave? But—'

'It wasn't the manor, Sister.'

'Then?'

'Sir Thomas said he wanted me to be Lady Cecilia's maid, but he looked at me like—'

'Sir Thomas?'

'Oh, I shouldn't have said, Sister. 'Twere nothing, just my fancy, most likes.'

Sir Thomas. A shiver ran through me.

The next day, as if the silence of my cell had been forever broken, a visitor came, and without warning. Where was Louise?

'Who is this?' My voice sounded thin and young in my ears.

'I'm Ellie, uh, Eleanor, and I live just down there a way. With my ma and pa, and there's Tom and Will, too, though he's only tiny still.'

I tried to remember what my Rule said about children: there was something about not teaching them, but nothing forbidding me from speaking to them.

'Eleanor, you can't just come into the parlour. You must ask first if—'

'Anna said I could slip in. You've lived here not as long as me, or Will, even. Why do you stay in your house all the time? I waited for you to come out one day but you stay here all the time.'

'Anna said you could visit?'

'Yes, she's nice, isn't she?'

'But she can't—'

'Do you stay here 'cause you're sick?'

'No, I'm not sick. I'm here to pray, not to chatter, so you must—'

'Ma says you're holy, like an angel, she says, and you just pray and pray all the time, even more than Father Simon or Martin.'

I wanted to be angry at this girl pushing her way in, but I found myself smiling and answering her. 'I do pray a lot, but I'm not an angel.'

'Why don't you come out for a bit? I'll show you my tree, and the place that's nearly always good mud, and I'll show you

Matilda, she's my friend, and Phil, and Tommy, and Warin.
Sometimes I see Alyce, and Christina, too. You'd probably like
them more than boys, but they're always busy helping their ma.
So can you come out?'

'I stay in here so I can pray.'

'Why? Does the sun stop you praying?'

'No, it doesn't stop me, but this way I can keep thinking of
God.'

A pause. I could hear her scratching. 'I can think of God in
the sun. It's easy. I just close my eyes. And sometimes I can do it
with 'em open, too. Like this.'

I pulled open the curtain just far enough to peer through and
see her face. Her hair was brown and tangled, and a red mark
like spilled wine spread across her face and down her neck, but
her eyes were as wide as she could make them, brown and clear.

'Won't you let me see your face?' she asked as I pulled the
cloth closed.

'You ask too many questions, Eleanor. You go outside now
and think of God in the sun, and I'll think of God in here.'

'All right, then. Bye, Sister. Oh! What's your real name?'

The autumn rain fell, chill and unceasing. I couldn't hear it, but
it began to seep through the tiny gaps in the edges of the thatch
above my fireplace and trickled down the crevices in the stones.
I moved my desk and books away from the wall, but I knew the
dampness would settle anyway.

'Maud says this rain's like a visitor that don't know when to
leave,' Anna said as she took away a grey bundle of soggy straw.

She glanced at me, then down again. 'Maud lives just over the main road a bit. She brought us the bread. But I didn't stop to talk much, Sister, I didn't.'

A cat jumped in through the maids' window as Anna spoke, strutted through my cell, sniffing at this and that, and scratched at the few dry strands of straw in front of the fireplace. She circled, lay down in the nest she had made, and began licking the rain off her legs and paws.

Anna laughed as she turned away. 'She knows where's like to be dry.'

I would not have a cat in here. How could a cat, a creature of the outside world, stay in this place, a place of death in life? Careful of her claws I picked her up, hissing 'Scat!' as I dropped her back through the window. A short time later I noticed her back by the fireplace, curled up asleep, her damp fur turning to orange fluff, her head on her paws but tilted toward me as if she had dozed off as she watched me read.

'Scat!' I threw her out again and again, and always she came back, through the maids' window or the parlour window, whichever was open, or squeezing tight through the narrow squint. For days I fought with her, making sure the doors and windows were closed, even asking Anna to be sure the church door stayed shut, determined that nothing would come inside my four walls to distract me. Still the cat found a way. In tears of frustration, I'd throw her out, then would look up from reading to see her asleep in her nest of straw.

When Father Peter next visited, the cat jumped past me and onto the ledge of the parlour window, poking her head through the curtain, her tail quivering with pleasure, orange against the black cloth.

'I won't let the cat stay, Father. I've tried and tried to …'

But, 'Hello puss,' I heard through the curtain, and then the hum of the cat's victory. 'You like to pray, do you? A holy cat, hmmm? Ah, child, a cat might be a gift, and you must have read in your Rule that a cat is permitted in an anchorhold. The priory has a family of cats that grows greater in number each year. We feed them scraps, they hang about the milking pails, gobble up the fish entrails, but most of all they catch the mice in the larder. Prior Walter shoos them from the chapel but they have ways of sneaking in under the seats. Does this one have a name?'

He laughed when I told him Scat suited her best, and she was used to it. He doesn't understand, I thought: the leper, Eleanor, and now Scat. Whether a cat was allowed or not, I wanted to keep the world out of my cell. But Scat had won.

Louise's voice was low and intent. 'It be Maud, Sister, as lives with Bill, and you mayn't want to see her. She's not as what you'd call pious. I've told her as you are a holy woman and have not time to waste with—'

'Thank you, Louise. Of course I'll see her; it's my duty, you know that. Tell her she may come. Then leave us, please.'

'Well, if she talks too much you must call me and I'll make her leave, I will.' She turned from her window with a cluck of her tongue.

My first true visitor, someone who sought my advice as a holy woman; I moved my chair closer to the parlour window and clasped my hands, wondering what she would say. The rustle of clothing, the smell of dirt and crushed grass wafted through my curtain.

'Good morning, Maud.'

'Sister Sarah, I've come to ask for your prayers. I'm not much for praying, though I try. Seems easier when I'm digging weeds or spinning wool. So, if you could pray for me, Sister, and my Billy. He works hard, he does.'

Her voice was softer than I had expected. 'I'm glad you came, Maud. And I'll pray for you and Billy.'

'Sister, most of all I wanted to meet you. And I thought you might want to meet me — or not me, special like, but someone from Hartham, you know, seeing as you come from another town.'

To meet someone? I would counsel her and pray for her, but how could she think I would be her friend? I'd told all my friends, everyone from my old life, not to visit me.

'I know, I know, Billy told me that you're supposed to be alone and quiet and that's why you're here, and so I didn't come at first. But I think, well, if it was me I'd want to meet someone. I mean, people are people, aren't they? Don't you feel lonely sometimes?'

'I came here to be with Christ, so I'm not lonely.'

'That's what Billy says to me, that you're not like us. You have God close by and we others don't. Still, don't you long for a good natter sometimes, Sister?'

'That's what an anchoress does, Maud: she leaves the world, denies herself the things she once enjoyed.'

'You know better than me, Sister,' Maud went on, 'but I know I couldn't do it, live in there all alone. And give up all those beautiful clothes like you did. Oh, Anna told me your father be a cloth merchant what gets silk and brocade and lace in ships from Venice. Those fancy dresses in purple and red like I see rich folk wear! Just two days back I saw Sir Thomas and Lady Cecilia ride past to the manor house. We all stared because it's not often the Maunsells stay here, except sometimes at harvest or Yule. Why would they, when Friaston Manor's so much bigger than the manor here? So we all watched Lady Cecilia on her grey pony, and she smiled at us, just a small smile.'

The grey pony, its eyes wide with fear. I took in a breath, put the picture out of my mind. Maud went on, unaware.

'But what does she wear? She has maids and money and jewels and she wears some colour puts me in mind of dirt, not purple and red like I'd wear. You must love God, Sister. I couldn't give them up, all those colours and silky clothes, if I had them.'

I promised Maud my prayers and told her she must leave, that it was time to say Vespers, but her chatter didn't leave with her. I stayed on my chair long after I heard the door shut, thinking on the awkward fall of a mast, splintered wood and bodies fat with water. Bolts of silk, gold and red and green, slowly unfurling and floating through the water, long coloured waves, enormous fish, beautiful monsters from the deep.

The past had found a way in with Maud. Pa, his head in his hands: the ship foundered, orders lost. 'All my money was in that shipment, all of it. Should as well be gold coins landing on the seabed. You owe it to me to help, girl. Be more friendly with men and we'll make a marriage, get a loan. I've seen Sir Thomas look at you. Forget this foolishness of God and purity.' His mouth was ugly with anger and fear. As he spoke, something hard began to form inside me, something that made my jaw tighten. I didn't say anything, but I would resist this man and his demands.

Winter was coming. The early cold hung in the air in drops that settled on me one by one, a damp, clinging blanket. At first I fought it, stamped my feet, rubbed my fingers, paced my nine steps and back again. This was too much attention to my body, I thought; I should defeat it by ignoring it. And so I would sit and read, forcing my mind time and again to focus on the words of my Rule, or I would kneel at my altar and recite my prayers aloud, only to find myself later — not knowing how much time had passed — huddled miserably on the straw.

How could I pray, how could I think of Christ, how could I think even of dying when every part of my body was howling with cold? My feet ached in the parts that weren't numb, there was no feeling in my fingers, my nose ran all the time, and I was too stiff to shiver. It wasn't as if I hadn't been cold at home sometimes. My toes had always become numb, even inside my boots and with a fire burning. On frosty mornings, Emma and I had huddled together under our blankets, slow to heed Ma's calls and leave our bed. And since I'd committed to being enclosed I'd lived more and more with the cold, letting it be my penance. But this was different, as if some creature had risen from a corner of my cell and taken over every part of me. It swallowed meaning. I hadn't thought suffering would be like this, so ordinary, so dull, and so endless.

I stared at the crucifix above my altar, Christ's body and cross carved from a single piece of wood, the lines of his pain deep gouges, his sinews stretched, his ribs tugging at his skin. I tried to place my coldness with him, in his pain, but all I saw was the futility and emptiness of my own. It led nowhere, only back to me, while Christ's agony meant rescue for every soul. My Rule, I thought, had given meaning to suffering, but the cold took it all away. The scratching and scraping went on, rattling the legs of my chair, shaking my altar. Claws at my knees when I prayed, marks on the skin of my feet.

Father Peter listened to me quietly.

'We'll fetch some more blankets for your bed. And wood, more wood.'

'But, Father, I should suffer.'

'Sister, you've just told me that your coldness and pain have no meaning. Why suffer for no reason?'

'I'm here to learn the meaning of suffering, Father. This must be the way.'

'You will learn in time, Sister, but don't seek meaning where it doesn't dwell. Do you remember what your Rule says? That the outer rule may change depending on each one, whether she is young or old or weak or strong, and that a confessor may change the outer rule because his wisdom understands how best an anchoress may keep the inner rule.' He paused. 'You must learn humility, child. Think of it as submission to me, the man you are sworn to obey. And continue to pray, recite the words, let them carry you.'

As he left, I heard him telling Anna that I must have sufficient warmth.

I was ashamed and angry. Did Father Peter think me weak? I had vowed to obey him, so I would, whether he be right or wrong. I ate the larger meals that Anna made for me, and the warmth from the fire loosened my arms and legs; slowly the aching let go of my body and I began to pray again. I confessed my doubt of Father Peter's counsel to him, but even though he told me to be patient with myself, I wanted to do as my Rule said, to overcome the demands of my wayward body. A shudder through the legs of my chair, a shiver to my womb. Agnes could feel my weakness.

The next morning, there it was: blood on my shift, the monthly rhythm of my old life refusing to let go. I remembered Emma growing up, discovering the trickle down her leg, holding up her fingers smeared with red, smiling. 'This means I can have babies.' Emma had her baby, and her blood, a red ribbon floating spirals in the water. Emma sinking away from me. I would have none of that. I knew of holy women so pure they had no flow of blood at all; they left behind their bodies, becoming more like men, or angels. Louise told me that Agnes lived only on communion bread. Surely her body would have dried, become whole, purged of this frailty?

I moved to my altar. In this place, kneeling where Agnes had knelt, I would be free of my old life and my grief for Emma, free of my body and its bleeding. After a time I found myself curled on the floor, the pain heavy in my belly. The earth was drawing me downward. The straw scratched at my ankle. I pushed it away with my other foot, but it scratched again, harder. I looked down at the thin pink lines, the skin torn in places and beginning to swell.

THE SHUTTERS RATTLED OF a sudden and I flinched.

'Sister Sarah, 'scuse me but I have news for you. Important news.' It was Louise at the maids' window and when I opened the shutters she rushed on. 'Sister, there's news from Friaston, from the manor. Sir Geoffrey, your patron and the one who—'

'I know who Sir Geoffrey is. What news?' My knees were still weak with fright, my chest thudding.

'Well, Sister, he took ill in the night, or worse than he'd been, as he's been in bed these past weeks, and they called the physician but he said there was no hope. Well, Father Simon just heard and told me as I was to be the one to tell you that he's gone, God bless his soul.'

I let out a long breath, felt my body sag. 'Yes, Louise, thank you.'

Louise clucked her tongue and spoke more quietly. 'I never thought he'd die, Sister, I didn't. We all die, but him with his power and all, it didn't seem he ever would.'

I'd been thinking the same thing.

Anna was standing behind Louise, her hands clasped on her chest.

'He was a stern man, but good,' she said. 'He was kind to me, taking me in, then letting me leave when … He told me to come here and not stay at the manor.'

'He left us to ourselves most of the time,' Louise said, 'but always gave us a Yule feast. A good man.'

I nodded and closed the shutters.

My patron was dead. I sat on the end of my bed and said the word. *Dead.* I looked at the squares of stone in front of me, cut smooth enough for building, but each one chipped and rough with the pointed marks of the chisel.

Thomas. Chips of flint in his eyes. *I will have you.* He was my patron now.

The funeral was at Friaston, but the village of Hartham held a special service to pray for their lord. The rumble of voices coming closer to the church made me look up, though there was nothing to see. God had set me apart from those people with their struggles and desires, sickness and decisions. I was dead to the world; I had escaped it, beaten death to the line. The church door banged, dirt floated past me, into my nose and mouth, the smell of dried sweat hung about me, seemed to stick to my skin, pull me from my prayers. Shuffling, voices, a child's whine, a thick cough; slowly the skein of noise unravelled into strands, single threads that were people, each with a name. I knew some of them, but I closed my eyes, whispered an *Ave Maria* to keep them away from me.

Father Simon cleared his throat and began the service. Three times he welcomed Sir Thomas Maunsell, the new lord, present among us, and each time my heart jolted. I ran my hand across the firm ledge beneath my squint.

Father Simon reminded the people of their debt to Sir Geoffrey. Louise and Anna had called him a good man and perhaps he was, but I could hear swearing and mutters of resentment. I knew of him first as a lover of fine cloth, through the custom he brought my father and the loan he had given him. Later, Thomas had told me more of him and his unyielding ways, though he had taken care to keep me from meeting his father.

The day of my enclosure was the first and only time I spoke to Sir Geoffrey. He asked to meet me, and I walked from the church with the bishop into the last light of day, my belly light with nerves and fasting. Sir Geoffrey stood so close that I could see the lines on his face, creased like the old leather belt-purse my father used to hold his coins.

His voice was strong, though his body was thin and bent, giving way to age: he sounded almost angry, whatever he said. Perhaps it was his habit, or perhaps he could see death coming. Anger or no, with his head for business and insurance, he had seen clearly the need to arrange for his soul, before and after death.

'You are Sarah, John of Leeton's daughter? Bishop Michael tells me you've freely chosen a life of enclosure. So, you've agreed to be a faithful woman and to pray for me each day in return for my provision of your cell and basic needs. I won't live much longer, so you agree to pray for me after my death, too.' He turned briefly and looked toward the cemetery and my anchorhold. 'And you'll pray for my son. I believe you know Thomas.' The trace of a smile. 'You need not worry. When

I die, the arrangement with St Christopher's will continue; all your needs, body and spirit, will be met by the priory. It's in the corrody we signed. And Thomas will become your patron.'

I nodded.

'God bless you, Sarah.' As he began to walk away, he hesitated and looked again at me, much as my father would judge a bolt of silk. He muttered to himself, though loudly enough for me to hear: 'So this was the problem. Who would have thought? Clearly unsuitable.'

Father Peter was at the service for Sir Geoffrey and he visited me afterwards to hear my confession and to reassure me that my living would continue. I confessed my failure to trust in Christ to protect me, but I realised later that we were both distracted. After giving me absolution, Father Peter sighed.

'Sarah, I must tell you that I can come to Hartham only once more. These old legs are worn out, and in this cold weather the walk here is more than I can manage. I'd hoped they'd last long enough for me to see you settled. I'll be sorry to leave you, my dear Sister. And I'll miss your cat.' He laughed and I heard Scat's hum; she would be curled, as usual, on his lap.

His voice, though old and weary, was blue-green behind the black curtain, like the quiet water where the river deepens beyond the mill. Sometimes I didn't hear the meaning of his words but let them float away, the murmur of flowing water calming me. He was kind and wise. Whatever my struggle — with visions of piety or the pain of failure — he listened, then brought me back to the simple things: my prayers, my reading, my confession. 'Say your prayers, child, that's all,' he would tell me over and over. 'Can you do that? Say your prayers.' He knew better than me, but that seemed too simple. I was an anchoress; there must be more I should do.

'Next time I'll bring Father Ranaulf, your new confessor. He's young and strong and he'll be able to visit you every week. He's a scribe and has a sharp mind. He's the one who copied your Rule with such care, so he understands your daily living and will benefit from … well, we all have much to learn, each one of us.'

When I heard the door close, I couldn't tell if it was anger or fear that ran hot through my body. A new confessor? I would miss the gentle wisdom of the old priest, especially now. I would not see my new patron, but still, the thought made me quail.

The muffled sound of voices just outside: Father Peter and Louise, no doubt. I felt like a child lost in a busy market.

The next day a woman came for counsel. I'd had visitors more than I wanted: a child, a cat, and Maud, who asked for my prayers, but seemed to think I needed a friend. This was the first one to ask for my counsel.

I waited, but there was only silence behind my curtain.

'I'm Sister Sarah, as you know.' I clasped my hands, unclasped them, put them flat on my knees, wondered what Agnes would have said. And Isabella: she'd been young like me, though she was a widow; she would have known more than me about the needs of these women. 'Louise tells me your name is Jocelyn. God bless you, Jocelyn.'

The rustle of clothes, a cough. I even thought I could hear her mouth opening and closing. She still didn't speak, and it was only when I offered my prayers that her words were loosened.

'Would you pray for me, Sister? Would you pray that I can find a way to please God?' Her voice made me think of a leaf in the wind.

'I will, Jocelyn, and you must pray, too. Your prayers are pleasing to God.'

'Yes, Sister,' she said dully.

I heard her shifting; perhaps she was about to leave.

'Jocelyn? Is there anything more?'

'I do pray, Sister. I try, but God won't hear me when I'm angry, I know.'

'You're right; anger does keep you from God.' I thought on what my Rule had said about it. 'Your anger is like a unicorn with a horn on its nose, and with that horn it gores everyone around it. Think what damage your anger can do and ask God to free you from it. And until you are stronger, stay away from anyone that makes you sin.' I felt my stomach settle; these were good words of counsel, clear and from my Rule.

'Sister, if only I could! It's my Hugh as makes me angry. Sometimes I think I won't cook for him, and I want to hit him when he sleeps, and then I think I'd never stop hitting, again and again. Such awful thoughts, Sister, they must be from the Devil!'

I sat back, alarmed. I hadn't expected this. 'Your husband, Jocelyn? You must obey your husband, you know that.'

'So Father Simon says. But I'm so angry when he buffets me about the head and pushes and kicks at me, all for what don't suit him: the bailiff demanding more wheat, saying the sheaf Hugh paid was mouldy, or the fire smoking because our only wood is damp, or the rain leaking in the roof he hasn't fixed, and then some days I can barely move for the bruises.'

Once she began, all her fears came pouring out like ale from a vat, until her words broke apart into sobs. What was I to say about marriage? I was the bride of Christ who died for love of me, but that wouldn't help Jocelyn, a woman married to a brute. I waited until her crying had stopped and promised to pray for her; my words of counsel lay shrivelled on the ledge between us.

'Good morning, Sir Thomas.'

Prickles danced through my hair. I looked toward the maids' room, as if I might see through the walls.

'May God rest your father's soul, sir,' Louise said. 'Such a good lord to his people, he was. And Lady Cecilia, she be well?'

'Yes, yes. I've come to look over the anchorhold.' A pause, a fumble at the parlour door.

'My lord, can I help you?' Louise's tone was sharper.

'Your name again? One of the anchoress's servants, aren't you?'

'Louise. I'm her helper and I make sure she's safe, my lord. Not so much a servant.'

'And the other, Anna? There you are. We miss you at the manor, girl. How is Sar— the anchoress?'

'She's well, sir.' Louise's voice again, protective.

'You understand I'm her patron now?' His voice was loud but somehow unconvincing. 'The priory might bring food and wood, but remember I pay for that arrangement, as my father did. Be mindful of your debt and tell me how she is. I've a thought to speak with her.'

I could imagine Thomas standing tall, his foot tapping, and Louise, her back straightening, her chin lifted, hands joined on her belly, the glint of pious defiance in her eyes.

'My lord, I vowed to defend Sister Sarah, to be sure she fulfils her vow that she see no man apart from the bishop and her confessor. A holy duty, is it not?'

'Listen, woman, I don't need you to lecture me on … ah, Father Simon, thank you for the comforting words about my father. I was just on my way to see you. That's all, then, Louise.'

A deep sigh, the cluck of Louise's tongue, muttering that faded. The curtain at my window billowed slightly, then settled; the wall wavered like water.

The crush of people bumping, pushing, the tangle of words and laughter, the smell of sheep's wool and ale, piss and sweat, carts loaded with fleece, stalls covered in cloth, sewing needs, vegetables, pots and pans. Emma swaggering and laughing more loudly than usual, boasting about Godric's ways in bed. She's missed a monthly bleed and thinks she might be with child. We stop at a stall to buy needles for Ma. Emma's whisper.

'He's looking at you, that lord over there.'

I pick up a thimble and slip it on my middle finger, then turn my head, a quick glance. He's on his horse, staring at me from the edge of the market. Blue cloak, ears that stick out, the first things I notice. His eyes meeting mine, my face flushing red.

Emma's excited voice. 'It's Sir Thomas. His father is Sir Geoffrey Maunsell of Friaston, and he has another manor somewhere else. I think he buys cloth from Pa. He must have money.'

The creep like hands on the back of my neck.

'Oi, you better buy that thimble. I'm watching you.' The rank smell of the stallholder's breath.

'I'm trying it for size,' I say. 'Do you want a sale or not?'

'Get away if you can't decide. I know thievery when I see it.'

I know the lord is still watching me. A millwheel turns inside my head, swishing water against my ears, sending heat crawling up my neck.

Sir Thomas, a man who offered me not heaven, but a manor house with tapestries; not the jewels of virtue, but rings and necklaces; not the white dress of a virgin, but red and blue embroidered with gold and pearls; not the embrace of Christ, but flames on my skin. Not spiritual children like patience, love, and humility, but bodies of flesh wrenched out of me, babies that would suck away my life. The man who had shown me how weak I was.

I looked up at the walls around me. At that moment, in the dullness of my cell, I was certain of the choice I had made. Then my heart lurched, hot and heavy, and all the fears I had held down boiled over. Thomas. He was now my patron. Responsibility passed from father to son, just as all possessions and debts had passed to him: houses, land, money, sheep. And me. He controlled my living, whether or not I could stay in this cell. I shook my head, steadied myself. Foolish woman. The agreement was made; the documents were signed and stored away. But parchment could be ignored, bought off, torn up, burned. I turned and touched the stones behind me. They were hard and cold; he would not reach me here. He would not.

⤳ RANAULF ⤲

SHORTLY AFTER PRAYERS AT Prime, Ranaulf let himself out through the larder door. It was a clear still day, but the sun had not yet risen above the cliff and he shuddered in the cold air. He looked across the duckpond and herb garden, then on to the river Cram, winding through an orchard of young fruit trees, their branches now bare. Chickens bustled past, but other noises drowned out their clucking: shouts, hammering, chipping and grinding came from the far side of the building. First the church nave was being extended to make more space for the villagers to come and worship, then the prior's lodgings and guesthouse were to be enlarged, then there would be an extension to the monks' dorter — room for more beds in anticipation that the fledgling community of six would grow.

Right now, the front entrance of the priory was a mass of carts, builders, donkeys, horses, piles of timber, and blocks of stone — mud covering almost all of it. Ranaulf knew he should be pleased that St Christopher's was prospering, but his jaw was clenched.

He peered up at the hill and took a deep breath, judging the difficulty of the path in front of him. Hartham wasn't far away if he could fly, but given two legs and no wings, he had to choose between the shorter route, up the rockface and over the hills, and the longer, easier route that followed the meanders of the river through the valley, skirted Cram Hill, and finally led through pastureland to the village. He had begun reading Gregory's *Dialogues*, and if he could get to the village and back quickly, he could justify taking a little time after Nones to read more. He decided on the shorter route.

The path was overgrown from lack of use and the ground rose more steeply than he had anticipated. Blackberry thorns pulled at his habit and he caught his feet in tangled loops of periwinkle and ivy. Father Peter wouldn't have come this way, given the weakness of his legs, and Ranaulf began to wonder if the longer way might have been quicker. He grabbed at a blackberry stem caught around his leg. Thorns scratched his hand and one lodged in the tender skin between two fingers. He cut short a curse and made himself stand still long enough to pull out the thorn, sucked at his hand, ran his tongue over the throbbing red skin. As he stamped down the vine, Prior Walter's soupy voice echoed in his head.

Pray that God will make you worthy of the calling ... he has ways of calling us beyond what we expect ... feelings of inadequacy will be the blessing that leads you to rely on our Lord ... we must not presume to discern always what is our duty before God.

Ranaulf had argued, reminded the prior of his duty to develop the scriptorium for the glory of God, but the appeal to God was useless, so he'd tried something equally close to the prior's heart: his copying would bring in money, the income needed to fund further building works.

'Indeed, Father Ranaulf, I appreciate your concern.' The prior's sympathy was worse than his piety. 'But remember the conditions of the corrody, the one that you so carefully copied: the anchoress of Hartham must have adequate counsel from a confessor who can attend her regularly. They are almost the exact words, I believe. If the conditions are not met, the agreement will lapse, the land will be lost.

'That corrody is an important part of our income. It enables the purchase of your parchment and inks. You are the only ordained priest in the priory with the time and the strength to fulfil the duties of a confessor. I must travel: the bishop, the court, the abbey. Your quill can wait, Father.'

Ranaulf scrambled a few last steps and stopped, panting and sweating, at the top of the ridge. Ahead, the track dropped gently, snaking back and forth down the eastern side of the hill. As he trudged, he thought back on the Rule he had copied for the anchoress. He had been impressed; it was wise and detailed, full of teaching on temptation, prayer, control of the senses and the emotions. But he had expected more specific rules for daily living. Surely a woman, even a godly woman, would need more guidance — though he wasn't sure what counsel he could offer. The words of the Fathers he knew well; perhaps they would be enough, along with confession and penance.

He sighed. Every week, the prior had said, though sometimes Father Peter had managed only every two or three weeks. He had spoken of her faithfulness, and had even thought she might be of some intelligence.

The path straightened as the land levelled out and turned to farmland. Gradually, Ranaulf's stride loosened, his shoulders relaxed and he looked outside his mind and into the day, to the grey, twig-still trees and miserable grasses. All around him was closing in for winter, but on his right, the crop — it looked like rye — was shining. A group of women was weeding, bent over, shuffling along row by row, plumes of white mist appearing and fading with their breath. One woman paused, straightened, tucked her hands into the small of her back and arched her body. A bag for the weeds was slung across her shoulder and bumped on her belly. She turned and looked at Ranaulf, smiled slowly, then even more slowly raised a hand to her forehead, her belly, her left breast and her right.

Ranaulf watched this languorous cross, felt the hairs of his groin prickle. He raised his hand in an awkward blessing and looked quickly away to some sheep grazing, a young boy near them throwing stones at a rock.

Women were strange creatures, a breed apart. They had never really crossed his path. At school he had been taught to see through the Devil's enticement, the beauty of the female form, to the true nature of woman as lustful and tempting; he had been told that if he touched a woman, he would feel his flesh burn like the fires of hell. After that, Ranaulf had flinched whenever his mother hugged him. Later, he had fought temptation by reciting to himself the words of the Fathers: 'daughters of Eve', 'gateway of sin', 'foul flesh', 'deformed male'.

He followed the track where it led on to the Leeton road and a simple bridge. The wood echoed dully under his boots and he might have noticed how quickly the river ran, but he was thinking of the unknown woman in her cell. Pious she must be, to seal herself away. What if she was young, or fierce? He wouldn't admit it, but he was nervous.

Shaking his head free of these thoughts, he began a familiar psalm, reciting it quietly in time with his steps: '*Deus in adjutorium meum intende…*' O God come to my assistance. He turned in to the village. People passed by, nodded, and mumbled 'Father', and he absently returned their greeting, his eyes ahead on the church, searching for its stone cell.

'Hello, Father, I'm Eleanor.'

Ranaulf quickened his stride. The young girl ran to keep up.

'I don't know you. But you've got the same robe as Father Peter. I like Father Peter. He comes to talk to Sister Sarah, like I do. But he walks real slow 'cause his legs are sick, Ma says. And you walk so fast! What's your name?'

Ranaulf looked down at the scrappy brown hair and the big eyes beneath. He noticed a red stain running down one side of the girl's face.

'Mmm,' he managed, and looked away as their eyes met; he couldn't think of anything to say to a child.

She tugged at his habit, then went on: 'I think your name's Father Finnegan. I like that name. Father Finnegan, you're so big, bigger than my pa. You're as big as a tree, you are.'

She skipped away, singing 'Father Finnegan' over and over again.

The anchorhold was smaller even than he had imagined. At first, all he could see were two doors in a humble building attached like a carbuncle to the side of the church, to the left of the front porch. The door closest to the church was ajar, and rattled as it opened fully, showing the skirts of a woman as she bundled through. This must be one of the maids.

'Father, good morning. Can I be of help? You seek our priest, Father Simon, this morning?'

'No, I come to visit the anchoress of Hartham.'

'The anchoress, Father?' She raised one eyebrow. 'The anchoress has no visitors that are men, apart from Bishop Michael and her confessor, Father Peter. I am Louise, her maid, and I guard who can see her, Father.'

'I am her confessor now, Louise.'

'Father, Sister Sarah has a confessor, Father Peter of St Christopher's Priory, though he tells me he may come soon with another priest to—'

'That's me. I'm her new confessor.'

'Oh, Father, I see. And you are ...?'

'I'm Sister Sarah's confessor.' Ranaulf moved toward the anchorhold.

'I'll introduce you to the anchoress, Father.' Louise pushed past him and stood, feet apart, barring the parlour door.

'That's not necessary. Thank you.' Ranaulf stepped forward, forcing Louise to move back toward the door of her own room.

He hesitated, telling himself he was catching his breath, but he realised, now he was standing by the cell, that beneath his frustration with this officious woman, he was anxious about what he would say. Words he understood, argument and reason with his fellow monks he enjoyed, among ink and parchment where he felt most comfortable — but none of that had prepared him for this, guiding a woman.

He peered around the corner to the external wall of the cell behind the parlour. It was tucked into the dank shadows of the church's northern wall, and water from yesterday's rain trickled down stones coated in green. A chill snaked down his back.

How would the enclosed woman continue here? What was he expected to do for her? He knew the ritual for confession, of course, but now that the moment had arrived, he wanted Father Peter with him, at least this first time. He murmured, '*Deus in adjutorium meum intende.*'

The parlour door had dropped and dragged on the ground as he pulled at it, grunting. Inside, he pulled it shut again. His heart was pounding in his ears. The parlour was bare, apart from a small opening to let in light, a candle set into a niche in the wall, and a stool placed just beneath a narrow window covered with a black curtain marked with a white cross. He stood next to it, lowered himself, then coughed to announce his presence.

'Greetings in the Lord,' he managed. Then, 'Sister, I am Father Ranaulf, your confessor. Father Peter cannot come today or ever again. He's too ill.' He looked down at his hands, picked at a line of ink under his thumbnail.

'Good morning, Father. I'm sorry to hear of Father Peter.'

He startled, a painful shiver ran through his chest, and he looked at the black curtain, almost expecting to see a face, reddening when he realised what he had done. She sounded young; the woman in the field and her slow sign of the cross flashed into his head. He scraped his knees against the stone wall, glad of the distraction of discomfort, then pushed the stool back. The white cross was in front of his face. She had spoken again, asked him something about Peter and he had answered, he thought, but he did not know how to go on. Of all things, he felt foolish.

'*In Nomine Patris, et Filii, et Spiritus Sancti.* Amen. God bless you, Sister.'

He could hear the slightest rustling behind the curtain. Perhaps she was kneeling? Yes, that would be it. Confession, that was all he needed to do now, hear her confession, and he could go back to his books. A whole chapter of her Rule was dedicated to confession, he remembered, though he had barely noticed the details; he would simply tell her to begin. But as the anchoress spoke, Ranaulf heard little of her sins, only the sound of her voice, clear and light, the steady rhythm of her words. He had not imagined this. This what? he asked himself. There was no special quality to her voice, no remarkable piety, but it was the voice of a real woman. Confession had its standard form, its rules and rubrics — it should make no difference that she was a woman — but as her words came through the curtain, one by one, he knew the order of his days was threatened.

～ SARAH ～

'GREETINGS IN THE LORD.' The voice was not as deep as Father Peter's. 'Sister, I am Father Ranaulf, your confessor. Father Peter cannot come today or ever again. He's too ill.'

I looked at my curtain, to where I used to imagine Father Peter's face would be, but this voice seemed to come from a somewhat higher point. I had heard the scrape of the stool as though he had sat down; he must be tall. I asked after Father Peter's health but this new priest muttered only a few words and told me to make my confession. I pulled at some dry skin on my thumb. This was not my custom. Would he not ask me about my daily prayers, my care for Louise and Anna, my thoughts and desires as Father Peter had? I stumbled with my words, forgot the sins I had planned to confess, but it didn't matter: he absolved me, *Ego te absolvo,* announced ten *Pater noster* for penance and left with a hurried blessing.

Was it because I had never seen his face that this new confessor felt distant? I knew Father Peter's face because I had met him before my enclosure. This new voice, rather flat and distracted — there was no mouth or face or body to go with it. And none of the reassurance Father Peter always brought to me.

I'd sometimes been angry when Father Peter hadn't come to visit me every week, ignoring what I knew of his painful, worn-out legs. A sulky child punishing a good father, I would answer him only in single words. But his laugh, his chat about all he had seen on his walk — a bright-coloured bird, a young boy who had stopped to talk with him — and my sulkiness slipped away. Now he was to come no more, and I began to recognise that it was fear, not anger, that I'd felt in the gaps between his visits.

I had thought that, dead to the world in my cell, I would not need anything, but just as I needed food and clothing and warmth for my body to survive, I needed Father Peter to help me — to help my heart survive. Now he had left me with the empty voice behind my curtain.

The sound that was my confessor continued to visit me each week, more regularly than Father Peter, but dry and distant. Even Scat stayed away from Father Ranaulf. At the sound of the door she would look up, but as soon as she heard his flat voice, her head would drop again, her eyes closed against him.

He brought with him in his mouth only the letters he had been copying. I heard the scratch of his quill, one letter and then the next, each angled like stalks of wheat obedient to the sun. His words did what he told them. One after the other they walked through my curtain like spirits and stood by the wall. I glanced at them because they required it. I knew them and their stern ways. They moved around and tidied my room: rushes shaken and laid flat, books squarely on the shelf, blankets smooth and square, firewood neatly stacked. But they had nothing to say to me.

Each time Father Ranaulf came, he asked for my confession and I listed my sins: my short words with Louise, my impatience with Anna, my failure in love for Christ, my wandering thoughts in prayer, my tendency to laziness. I wondered if he heard them at all before he announced *Ego te absolvo*. My penance was always the same, his admonition the same: to love Christ, to be faithful in prayer, to read my Rule diligently. After a time I was tempted to recite it with him.

Father Peter had also told me to pray and to read my Rule, and at first I couldn't understand why the same counsel from Father Ranaulf seemed so different. Slowly, I began to see that Father Peter's questions about my sins had enabled me to discern them more clearly; his counsel understood my weakness. He helped me to commit myself to my living death in this cell.

'God bless you, child,' he would say each time. 'And Mother Mary embrace you.' It was at those times that the walls of my cell felt most like warm arms holding me. When Father Ranaulf blessed me and shut the door, I felt alone, cold, no safe arms around me.

Winter. The cold had come early, and now the snow. Feeble light struggled at my horn window, and the sounds outside were hushed almost to silence. Scat lay curled by my fire most of the day, her tail wrapped against her face. I called her to me, hoping the warmth of her body would soothe me, but she would only open her eyes to slits and close them again. One day I bent to pick her up. She seemed so heavy, yet she ate only the food she could scrounge herself, mice and birds and beetles, and I could feel her ribs through her fur. This life without work and sun was making me weak. I had come here to deny my body, but I hadn't thought it would be like this.

Day by day it crept upon me. Grey, it was all grey: the walls, the straw, the cheap cloth I covered myself with. The words in my books, even the beautiful thoughts in 'The Orison of Our Lord', my favourite devotions, were but scrapings of ink — curve and line and dot — meaning nothing.

The scratches on my ankles began again, long pink lines crossing one another, tender to touch, spots of blood that turned to dark, tiny scabs.

The stones were faces that came out when my candle was alight, some laughing, some staring, some as sad as me. One in the corner by my squint had eyes like plates and could change its mouth from a howl to a jeer as my candle flickered; one just above my bed looked like my father, its hair curled, its mouth straight, and one over my desk was a skull, with sockets for a nose. I had to watch them. Day by day the walls crept closer, the faces came closer, such a tiny amount each day that no one else could see. But I knew. Some days they seemed to take away any space to walk and I sat still, pressing them back.

I saw how much Father Peter's visits had held me. Now I was falling.

Louise knocked on my shutters, but I told her to leave me alone. It was Jocelyn, she said, come to seek counsel. I knew Jocelyn well enough now. She visited often, most times sad, sometimes more cheerful when Hugh wasn't angry, and always wanting to hear me speak of Christ's love for her. I told Louise no, I wouldn't see her, but she called through the wood that Jocelyn was sickly. Shamed, I sighed and agreed.

Jocelyn's voice was thinner than usual. She told me Hugh had come home drunk, complained that the food she cooked was dull, and hit her so hard she'd fallen to the floor, unknowing. When she woke, cold and barely able to move, the fire was out and Hugh gone. Her shoulder was bruised and her head ached.

'I'll pray for you, Jocelyn, but I can do nothing more. You must speak to Father Simon,' I said.

'Father Simon? What will he do? Tell me it was my fault, he will.'

She was right. I could hear her sobs behind the curtain. She needed comfort, but I had no warm words. Everything was cold.

'Go and visit Maud, then. Or the healer. Stay away from Hugh, if you can. Now I need to pray.'

She left then, still crying, left me with my cold failure, more alone than ever.

But I wasn't alone. Scratching on wood, shivers in my legs. I moved my chair a little, settled it firmly and held on to one of the legs, but the shuddering ran up through my hand and into my arm. I pulled away. A quiet voice. I looked toward the parlour curtain, but it was still. Was it Jocelyn back again? Louise or Anna? Whispers that sounded like a stick dragged over stone. My name, a harsh sigh, scraping at the leg of my chair. Scat woke and stood, her back arched, tail whipping, teeth bared in a snarl. She stepped back, then turned, leaped to my squint and squeezed through. I stood up, crossed my chest with my arms.

Sarah, suffer. He loves us most when we suffer.

My heart echoed in my head, my legs shook. It must be Agnes; I'd prayed to her to help me. But these voices, were they from the Devil? I thought of the story of St Juliana painted on the wall in the church next door: Juliana with her fierce eyes and discernment, binding the Devil who came to her in the guise of an angel to tempt her away from Christ. But this was no temptation to pleasure. 'Christ, my Lord, protect me now from all the works of the Devil. Christ, give me discernment to see the works of your hands.' My prayer was quick, the words tripping over each other. 'Christ, my Lord, protect and guide me.'

I had heard some stories about Agnes, but after our prayers together at Compline, I asked Louise what more she knew of her.

Her eyes were bright, her voice serious: 'Oh, Agnes was very holy, Sister. She took her vows as a nun very young, being marked from a child as having a calling. There was no question of her not being enclosed when she got older. Lived here a long time, praying for the village and helping protect us all from the Devil. Her prayers could help get a woman with child, and she once cured a young girl of the fever, just by touching her.'

'Did she truly?' Anna lifted her head, eyes wide. 'A woman did that?'

'Shush, girl, and listen. No one ever saw her, except her maid at times, but there wasn't much reason to open her shutters, except to take some water and a little bread. They buried her where she fell, just there between her altar and the squint.'

Anna gasped and peered inside my cell, but said nothing.

'She was so thin, and word is the cell smelt not of a body but of flowers, like — sweet. She said this life was the trial, heaven the reward. If I may say, Sister, you're blessed to have her buried there beneath your feet, being such a holy presence. She'll pray for you. Her bones will pray for you, like relics, Sister.'

I closed the shutters and walked to my altar, took off my shoes and felt the rough straw beneath my feet.

Sarah, come to me in the earth, dark and quiet and still. Sarah. Scrape up the earth of your grave with your dainty white fingers.

She was quoting the words of my Rule, her Rule. I had thought this was death: my prayer, my reading, my dark cell, but I had not suffered enough. I had not committed myself to death. Agnes was right. That's why Father Peter left me, that's why Father Ranaulf would not counsel me. I undid the buckle of my belt, pulled off my robe, and slid to the floor.

The belt was snug in my right hand, the leather curved into my palm. I lifted it, flung it across my left shoulder, the cut like ice, like burning, a streak of life, sharp and bright like starlight. Another star, and another, then three from my left hand, my back like the sky on a clear winter night. Slashes of red. The warm trickle of blood. Mine. Christ's.

My robe was rough as I pulled it on, stinging, dragging at my torn skin, the smeared blood wet and warm. A creak of bone; I could hear Agnes smile.

⋇ RANAULF ⋇

'WE NEED TO PROVIDE what the customer asks for, Father Ranaulf.' The prior's tone was sharp. 'And Sir Thomas has asked that the Life of St Margaret be copied for the anchoress. For the sake of her soul, Father. It's his duty as her patron before God.'

'And I'm now her confessor, Prior. As you told me, it's my duty to care for her spiritual health,' Ranaulf said. 'Surely you or I should decide what books she reads? Sir Thomas is not qualified to judge her spiritual needs. She has her Rule, and long and detailed it is, some devotional works, and her Psalter: enough for any woman.'

'This is another commission, Father. A paying commission.' Prior Walter spoke slowly, emphasising each word. 'It's one way of ensuring more supplies of ink and parchment.' He turned abruptly and left.

His back speaks more eloquently than he does, thought Ranaulf. He opened the small volume the prior had given to him. So many of those stories, especially the lives of virgins, were exaggerated and fantastical. He had begun the Life of St Christopher for the chronicle, making sure it was plainly and simply told, with no unnecessary appeal to emotion. But the story of St Margaret: a woman killing a dragon? The Devil destroyed? If he must copy this virgin's life, he would add some clear teaching; he need not change the story, but would add some words appropriate to the anchoress and her situation. The saints who withdrew from the world — St Antony and St Cuthbert were two that came to mind — testified that temptation became more subtle, more difficult to discern, and no doubt Sister Sarah would find the same.

He scanned the pages: arrest, torture, prayer. He could add some teaching in the prayers. He continued to turn the pages, reaching the encounter with the dragon, then the demon. Perhaps ... yes, here: he could have the demon speak about temptation. He rubbed his forehead, picked at a scab until he felt it begin to bleed. It was not usual for teaching to come from the mouth of a demon, God's enemy. But what better way for a woman to identify temptation than to hear the wiles of the Devil directly from his mouth?

He had to admit that the tale began rightly, with a call to virgins to listen and to love the Lord. Margaret, the daughter of a pagan prince, was fifteen when she was sent to live with her stepmother in a village far from her father's palace. She chose virginity over marriage, seeking Christ as her lover and beloved. Ranaulf frowned, though he did not pause in forming each letter. He could see that women needed to think of God as a husband, given their natural desires, but such language, such words, 'lover' and 'beloved', they could as easily inflame a woman's desire as direct it toward Christ. How would the anchoress respond? He wondered if she would recognise such a conceit, that union with Christ paradoxically meant virginity.

On he wrote, letter after letter, carried into another world. The pagan sheriff Olibrius had seen Margaret as she tended sheep in a field, so beautiful that she shimmered and shone. The radiance of purity, Ranaulf thought, but will Sister Sarah see that, or just think of earthly beauty? The sheriff demanded that Margaret go with him, to be his wife or his concubine, to be decked in gold and treasure, surely a temptation. But Margaret refused him, praying to God to save her from the filth of the body, to protect her maidenhood, the precious jewel she had committed to Christ.

His quill was blunt so he set it down on the desk and stretched his arms wide. He could hear the familiar gristly crackling in his neck and shoulders. Knife in his left hand, the quill flat on his desk, he trimmed the tip square and sharp, dipped it into the ink pot and watched the blackness turn grey as it crept into the hollowness of the shaft. The smell was strong high in his nostrils.

'Small.'

Ranaulf looked up to see someone standing in the doorway. 'Brother Cuthbert! Welcome! At last.'

Cuthbert took three steps inside and stopped, as if there were no space to walk farther. 'Father Ranaulf, here I am, and indeed at last, after that tedious journey from Westmore.' He shivered and looked around. 'Small and cold. And the light …?'

'This is the only place we have to work. The prior isn't interested in books, except for his chronicle. But we have parchment and ink — and a little less than three years to prove we can bring in sufficient income, just like the sheep and the crops and the peasants paying their rent. But now you're here, all will be well.' Ranaulf stood. 'We'll put your desk here, below this window, in front of mine. It's in the best light.' He paused and looked at Cuthbert's face, at the frown shading his intelligent eyes, and realised how much he wanted the illuminator to stay. For the books, and for his company. He rushed on. 'And there are plans for a proper scriptorium in the new building, the abbot made sure of that. He wants us to continue here, that's why he sent you. You remember his chant: "The most glorious books —"'

'"Glorious books to the glory of God, spread across the land"? Of course. How could I forget?' Cuthbert smiled. 'But here? A bit out of the way, isn't it? No town; only this scrap of a village, this tiny priory. Six brothers, and I make seven. Are you sure you want to stay here? More important, do I want to stay here?'

'Earl Wyckham donated this land for the priory. It's not a wealthy area, but Prior Walter has stabilised the priory's income — that's why the abbot was able to send me here. And now you.'

'Maybe so, Father, but what's the point of our talent, hidden away here? Even if—'

'We can make beautiful books of prayers for families hereabout. We already have orders for another Book of Hours and a Breviary, and once word spreads there will be more. Sir Geoffrey Maunsell of Friaston recently bought one for his son's bride … though Sir Geoffrey died recently.' Ranaulf reddened. 'And I'm finishing another for —'

'Oh yes, the prior mentioned them as we walked here. Three whole days of the prior's company, Father. Think of it. I listened long enough to hear that the Maunsells plan to eventually rid themselves of the village and turn the land to pasture. More money in wool, apparently. Then he got onto acreage and foldage and the like, so I stopped listening. A long three days, it was, just to end up here, this scattering of houses. Surely you don't really want to stay?'

'Yes, I do. I do. Our own scriptorium, our own books. And the prior has asked me to write a chronicle. I'm sure he's told you he wants it illuminated. Memories are frail, Brother, but I can put ideas and events into writing; it might be useful to our brothers in years to come. Maybe the Church, too.'

'Oh, and the prior said something about you counselling a woman, an anchoress, is it? At another village nearby. I hadn't thought you'd be interested. And a woman, Father.'

'Prior Walter's instructions. Of course, I'd rather be here.'

'Tell me, Father, how is it, really?' Cuthbert stepped closer, smiling. 'Is she young? Does she have a sweet voice? If I were a priest, I'd do it for you. Is it enjoyable, talking to a woman, even if it is about God?'

'We don't talk, Brother Cuthbert. I hear her confession, give her penance, that's all.'

'But a woman locked away like that, she must want company, someone to tell her secrets to. She might be holy, but even so—'

'She has maids to talk to. My duty is to hear her confession.' Ranaulf could feel the warmth creeping up his neck.

'I can see it's not an easy task, talking to a holy woman. And all that time away from your books. The answer seems simple to me: leave here. If we don't make it pay, we can go back to Westmore, back to a decent town.'

Cuthbert moved to the worktable, looking over the tools and inks.

Ranaulf opened his mouth to speak, but said nothing.

'But I've missed my brushes,' Cuthbert said. 'You have some work for me?'

Ranaulf gathered his thoughts and turned to the table. He cleared his throat. 'This is for a Book of Hours. I've finished copying these pages, and I've left plenty of space around the prayers.' He unfolded the parchment from a small bundle. The quires were still unbound and the top two or three slipped from the pile. He opened the top one and pointed at the first page. 'I've outlined the spaces and scribbled a description. One full-page illustration of the Virgin here, and a decorated capital, here. It's all written clearly enough for you to follow.'

'Yes, easily done. I'll start once my desk is carried in here.'

Ranaulf hesitated, then picked up the bundle. 'This being a Book of Hours, the illustrations should be ... well, the marginal decoration need not be ... I think that the lord who ordered it would be happier with holy images, flourishes and such. No need for griffins or monkeys.' He laughed weakly.

Cuthbert held out his hands for the manuscript. 'All part of God's great design, aren't they, Father? All suitable for our contemplation.' He leaned forward but Ranaulf tucked the bundle under his arm.

'Monsters with a man's head, a dragon's tail, and a cockerel's feet? God's design? They mock God's order!' Ranaulf could feel the redness continuing up to his face and lost the thread of his words.

'But who knows what creatures exist in the world?' Cuthbert smiled, his tone easy. 'You must know reports of amazing creatures that live in other lands. I've seen pictures of them, drawn by men who've travelled, who —'

'Not suitable for women, whether men say they've seen them or not.' Ranaulf's voice caught in his throat. He had charge of the scriptorium, but the illuminator was talented and knew it;

nothing unsettled him. He feared Cuthbert would be laughing at him.

'I hear that ladies use the drawings to help them find their place, help them remember where the prayers are.'

'A blackbird or a swan or a rose can do that, Brother. No need for monsters, or crudity.'

Cuthbert bowed slightly, hints of a smile around his mouth, and stepped forward to take the bundle from Ranaulf. 'Of course, Father. For this book, no monsters or crudity. Only holiness.'

Ranaulf passed him the manuscript and looked for a moment as if he had nowhere to put his hands; he tucked them into his sleeves. 'But colour, of course, Brother Cuthbert. Colour and beauty for the glory of God.'

Virginity, the brightest blossom in the body, a precious gemstone. The words from the Life of St Margaret followed him along the cloisters and into the church for Chapter. Listening to the minute details of priory business and the prior's warnings about discipline took time he would rather spend on his copying and reading, but he was required to be there.

The monks were already seated on their benches, and Prior Walter on his chair facing them, when Ranaulf slipped in. Before sitting, he set his hands behind his hips and stretched his back, then settled in, his eyes quickly glazing, as usual.

'Three of our sheep got stuck in mud. At the edge of the river where it turns swampy. Nearly dead in the frost. So far gone we had to knock 'em on their heads. Kindest thing.'

Ranaulf looked up at Brother Hugo, the man's large eyes shining in the dim light of afternoon. It was the longest speech Ranaulf had heard him make, though he had no idea really what he had said. Sheep, wasn't it ... he had just written those words ...

'And we've salted some of the meat already,' Brother Alain added, pleased.

'It's all very well to have meat, Brother, but we need all the wool we can get.' Prior Walter refused to be appeased. 'Three sheep are a significant loss. They could have yielded years of wool. Sir Thomas is sure that this land is best suited to grazing sheep. He'd like nothing more than to turn all his land into pasture. Much less trouble than crops and rents from tenants, he told me.'

Sheep, Ranaulf thought; Margaret had called herself a lamb among wolves — the sheriff, his soldiers ...

'But Sir Geoffrey gave us the land. Surely he wouldn't have done that if he wanted to increase his own pastures?' Alain said.

'He didn't give it to us, Brother. That land is payment for our care of the anchoress of Hartham and her maids. And that was Sir Geoffrey. His son has different plans.'

Ranaulf startled at the word 'anchoress'. Would Sir Thomas close the anchorhold, move Sister Sarah? There was the corrody, that carefully worded agreement that promised to care for her. No doubt a man of his power could work his way around that, though. But surely he couldn't take over the land and houses of everyone in the village, turn them all out; there must be laws. He pictured the bent backs of people working in the fields, the faces of those who greeted him on the village road, the big eyes of the little girl who always ran to talk to him.

The meeting wound its way through the weary business of accounts, mould in the apple trees, restocking the fishpond, Christoph's penance for breaking the great silence, and finished with prayer. Ranaulf heard none of it.

❧ SARAH ❧

YULE AND ITS CELEBRATIONS were nothing to me. The villagers took a holiday for the whole twelve days until Epiphany; whether they prayed or drank or slept, the ground was too frozen to dig, so they did no work in the fields. Snatches of song, laughter, brawls, and shouting floated past my cell, but I took scant notice. Maud came to see me and told me of the feast for the villagers at the manor house.

'They were both there, Lady Cecilia and Sir Thomas. She spoke to us all, quiet like, but friendly. And Sister, she wore colourful clothes this time, a blue dress with red trimming. Mutton and pork, we had, Sister, such a feast! My Bill's so drunk he'll sleep for days,' she exclaimed.

I told her I would pray for her, hoping she would leave, but she chatted on, as if unaware. When finally she left, Louise asked me if she could visit her son, Wymer the blacksmith, who lived on the village road, and if Anna could go with her, to be part of a proper family celebration. I was glad to hear them walk away. I wanted only my dull, quiet cell with Agnes, and to banish memories of festive Yules when Emma was alive to relish the season.

I prayed Vespers, knowing I loved Christ but feeling nothing. Scraping on my ankle. I sat on the straw and looked at my legs, the scratches deeper, the trace of fingernails. *He loves us most when we suffer*, Agnes whispered. I smiled and touched a drop of blood. A rustle at the door and the scrape of the stool being moved in my parlour. I looked up at the swaying curtain. I hadn't closed my shutters when Maud left.

'Good evening, Sarah.'

Warmth swept my face and scalp. I stood up, took a few steps, and stopped.

'I hope I didn't scare you. I'm visiting the manor for the Yule season and wanted—'

'Sir Thomas ... I cannot ... '

'I want to talk to you, Sarah, to make sure you have all you need. Are you well? This cell is so cold, almost colder than outside.' His voice was soft, concerned. 'Can I send more wood? Or blankets? A woollen cloak?'

I breathed in and out deeply and spoke. 'I'm well. I have all I need, thank you. But you must not visit.' I stayed by my bed. He couldn't see me, I told myself, though I turned my head away. My chest hurt.

'Sarah, I want to apologise. The last time I saw you, in the stables ...'

I was alone with him, as I had been then. But this time there was a stone wall between us.

He paused, then continued. 'I was angry, but it was not because—'

'That was my old life. It's gone from me now. I pray each day that God will bless you and Lady Cecilia.'

'Cecilia! That's why I was angry; you must know that, Sarah. This ridiculous marriage my father organised. You know I wanted you.'

There were some things the stones couldn't keep out. Memories of him and me, warmth, the smell of the stables. I took a step back.

'Please, I'll call—' My voice was high, my head pounding.

'Call who? There is no one here but you and me, Sarah. Don't you understand what I'm telling you?'

'This is all I want, this cell.' I was shouting. 'Only this.'

'Well, you have it.' His voice was jagged. 'Everything you want. But don't think it was all your victory, all your way. Too holy for me, you were, but not for my father. Did you think he was giving you this place, this living, because he thought you holy and pure? Yes, he wanted someone to pray for him, but you had even greater uses. You were what he needed to punish me. Because I resisted him, said I wanted you, not Cecilia. He used you, Sarah ...' his voice a whisper now '... like a whore.'

That last word hit me across the head. A sound like gasping — was that him or me? I backed away, barely breathing, until I felt something solid behind me.

'Do you see how he would have smiled, Sarah, at his perfect solution?' The words came quietly, one after the other, like steady footprints. 'I never had you, but you're my father's whore.'

Then the scrape of the door, and nothing but the wheeze of my breath. The curtain shifted and Scat jumped lightly down from the window, a bird in her mouth. She strutted to her favourite nest in front of the fireplace, lay down and began to delicately pull feathers from flesh.

I stayed by the wall that held me.

The stones shifted and blurred, their eyes black holes, their mouths wide and ugly: you wanted, you wanted, foolish girl. They laughed, their mouths stretching long. Foolish girl. I shook my head, felt for my body. It wasn't the wall behind me; I was standing with my back to wood, my hands flat against the door with its nails that kept me safe. No way out, no way in. Here I would be always: so close yet always out of reach for Thomas. *He used you like a whore.* Scratching at my ankle, the sharp tearing of my skin, nail on bone.

His voice in my head, whatever I did, louder even than Agnes. *I wanted you, not Cecilia.* It was my habit to read psalms after Terce, but this day, breath by breath, stitch by stitch, I was keeping away the voice in my head. *Don't think it was all your way.* I was working at a cloth for the credence table in the church; it needed to be hemmed, a simple blanket stitch. I folded the cloth, looped thread over its edge. *Used you, like a whore.* I pushed the needle through. *Wanted you.* I pulled the thread taut. *Whore.*

Sewing was usually a comfort, the familiar activity stilling my mind. I had thought to leave it behind but Father Peter told me that plain stitching would be a service to the church. Its rhythm so much like prayer, it was one part of my old life that I could bring inside my cell, and make new. This day, though, the stitches were uneven, the thread pulled too tight, and I caught my finger with the needle. *Wanted you.* I gasped, watched the blood well at the tip of my finger, relieved that the pain made me cry at last.

Two nights later, the dull clunk of the church door cut into my sleep. I opened my eyes, startled, looked into the blackness: no flicker of candle. Was it Thomas? Thick pulsing in my throat. Muffled words, laughter, a girl's short squeal, a boy's reply. I breathed out; it was a couple looking for somewhere private and dry.

The ale had made them clumsy and noisy. I shut my eyes and began to recite Compline, whispering, praying the words would take my mind from the scene in my head. 'The Lord Almighty grant us a quiet night ...' He pulls her against him, kissing her mouth, her neck, sliding his hand under her skirts. Warmth in my belly. She wraps her arms around his neck and slips to the floor, pulling at his breeches, and they giggle when he loses his balance. It's freezing tonight, but there's heat between them. Burning. Where was Agnes?

Thomas. His touch on my chin, lifting my face to his. Heat in his fingers. The silent hum in my neck, my breasts, my legs. His arm warm across my back, protective. Disappearing into the touch of lips.

I pulled off my blankets, knelt in the cold, prayed psalms, tried to smother it all: my memories of Thomas, the laughter and grunting and sighing in the church. Back in bed, shivering, I heard their whispers, the gossip about the Yule feast at the manor. 'She were like a mouse, Lady Cecilia. And Sir Thomas, he never looked at her once. Do you think they do it, these rich folk?' 'Not likely. Still, they have to make an heir or two.' 'He don't want her. Word is, he had to marry. His father made him.'

I opened my eyes, sat up in bed and crossed myself. *Veni creator spiritus* ... I would pray until the bell for Matins rang across Cram Hill. *Wanted you, not Cecilia.*

Thomas comes to choose cloth for a coat. My father is anxious, offering wine, protesting that he could have brought samples to the manor. The wave of a hand, Sir Thomas decides quickly on deep blue linen, asks to speak to me. My face flushing, noticing his ears. At the corner of my eye I see my father backing out the door, nodding to me. Thomas tells me of his recent return from London, steps toward me and asks about my embroidery, whether I make my own designs. The warm, sour smell of him, like my brother and my father. I answer briefly, pour more wine, confused. He takes the cup, touches my hand. I feel warmth run up my arm like honey. I step aside, awkward, my body making me weak. All I had hoped to avoid. He speaks again, moves closer. I don't know what he says, but I look up. I smell the wine on his breath. His eyes are brown, flecked with yellow.

The next days fell into one, cold and prayers and reading, memories of Thomas that crept through the cracks, the moans from the church, the grunts and sighs, shudders in my chair, scratches at my ankles, weary light from my oil lamp.

> *The spark that flies up does not set the house on fire straight away: it lies still and nurses the flames and grows larger and larger until it sets the whole house on fire, before it is in the least suspected.*

The words of my Rule. I had chosen four walls, but the spark was not gone, a sin I needed to confess.

'At night, Father, I'm pursued by demons that come to me and dance in my cell, touching one another with lust; I burn with desire, I long for them, to join with them in their wanton acts. The spark flew through the window and I've allowed the fire to grow in me.'

I stopped, shocked at my own words. I had thought to confess my failure to subdue my body the night of the couple in the church, my failure to leave behind my past life. I'd always confessed my impure thoughts, of course — women are by nature drawn to lust — but I'd never before described such a scene. Where had these ideas come from? I had learned some of them from a travelling friar who preached about St Antony overcoming severe temptations. And from Emma, though she said *swive*, made crude gestures, and laughed.

My head close to my window, I heard a sharp intake of breath behind the curtain. A reaction. I smiled; I had shocked Father Ranaulf as much as myself.

'*Ego te absolvo*. For penance you will meditate upon the purity of the Virgin Mary, Sister. Remember her obedience and her chaste life. Say the *Ave Maria* ten times at each of your prayers. Ask her for mercy and for the strength to resist your sin. Fast for three days.' Father Ranaulf spoke quietly, quickly.

'Yes, Father, I will, but I need guidance. How can I leave behind the memories of my past life? A sound, a smell, and they return. Can you help me to—'

'Pray and read, Sister. As I've told you. Pray and read, that is all. And call on the Virgin Mary. God bless you.' The dull sound of the door pushed shut behind him; he was gone.

MY PENANCE REMINDED ME of my body. My stomach grumbled then gnawed at itself, turning around and around in spirals like a worm, drawing every thought and prayer back to it; perhaps one of those that crawled around Agnes's bones had now found me. Hunger, emptiness, longing. And the memories stayed. Thomas, the couple in the church, Emma's words about Godric — they became a single longing for the warmth of another against my body, a longing for skin, hair, breath, sweat. Desires that I wanted to leave behind took over my prayers.

Agnes's voice scraped and called.

Sarah, listen to me. Protect your heart by protecting the senses. Deny your body. Deny its pleasures. Deny your belly.

Part of this was from my Rule. Agnes was a holy woman; she would guide me. I prayed in the dark, I knelt on the ground that sucked at my warmth. Agnes smiled at me. Memories crowded in, my body called to me, fighting all that Agnes told me to do. Kneeling at my squint, I felt the touch of the worn stone ledge under my hands. I am at home, my mother's hand resting on my cheek, holding me, the throb of life beneath her skin, her familiar scent of roses, my body softening with pleasure.

She is gone, Sarah. Let me hold you now. The past is dead. Come to me in the ground.

The tug of my robe, the scratch of fingernails, bone tearing skin.

Sitting at my desk to sew, white cloth and thread, blanket stitch. I felt silk beneath my hands, sliding like water between my fingers, stitches taking shape and colour: a face, a flower, a bird, tiny pearls, gold thread glinting, the gentle hum flowing through my fingers.

Deny the senses, Sarah: touch and sight. Look only within.

Praying at my altar, I heard the grind of a cartwheel outside my cell. I could see it in my mind: Friaston Market busy, bodies pressing, bumping as they pass me. I am there, my arm tucked into Emma's. So many people, their skin warm, mouths smiling, laughing, shouting, tongue and teeth and spit, the stench of sweat. Over here, we buy pies, the smell thick and rich; I feel the crunch of pastry, meat and gristle between my teeth, gravy sliding hot down my chin, Emma teasing me; she brings ale, its bitter tingle on my tongue. Our stomachs full, still we buy steaming baked apples, the skin tough and tart, the quick burn then the fluff of its sweet flesh, sharp spices weaving flavours in my mouth. My stomach rumbled.

Deny the belly. Agnes's teeth ground together. *The belly. Closest to your sinful organs, the belly heats your blood, inflames the flesh. Burning, burning.*

Agnes knew the words of my Rule. Her eyeless sockets peered into my heart, saw my desires.

Day followed day. What did it matter if I never saw the sun, here in this grave?

Sarah, you sleep too long. Get up and pray. Dig your grave with your words of penance. The clack of Agnes's jaws. *You deserve to be*

cold and hungry, you sinner. Kneel on the bare earth, your bridal bed.
The ground was icy beneath me, pulling me into itself, wrapping
its arms around me, sucking at my mouth.

Anna brought my food; I could smell the herbs she'd added to
tempt me.

'Just vegetables, Sister. Only a little. Father Ranaulf said you
were to have bread and milk, but you ate none of that. It's been
more than a week now. You must eat.' The tilt of her head,
reminding me of Emma, of all I had left behind.

'Leave me alone. I won't eat. Sister Agnes lived only on
communion bread. That's your lesson for today, Anna. Pray on
that.'

She brought more. The smell of steamed fish made my stomach
heave. I took a piece of bread but it was dry: I couldn't swallow
it, spat it out. I agreed to take some ale.

My body felt lighter, sealed. I had not bled when I was due last
month. I was losing my woman's body, leaky and desiring.

Father Ranaulf came. I heard Louise whisper to him, words
like *sickly, fasting, weak.* He told me to take some food. 'As your
confessor,' he said, and I smiled; I have my guide. I was silent,
listening to his thin words. *Ego te absolvo.*

'Sister Sarah, here be your supper. Only some bread and sop.
Best you eat a little.' Anna was at the maids' window.

'Leave me, Anna. I'm fasting.'

'Sister, you must eat something.' Now it was Louise. 'It's been weeks now. Father Ranaulf says—'

'Father Ranaulf? Dry Father Ranaulf? What would he know?'

A mouthful of bread, a gulp of water, heavy in my stomach. The claws of hunger clutched at my belly, its teeth gnawed when I moved, pain stretching through me, hard labour, bands of fire. The cluck of Louise's tongue, then silence.

I could see the shape of my bones in my arms, traced them with my fingers, thought of their dry whiteness. At my altar, I felt my ribs, one by one, the skin hung over them my shoulders sharp, like Christ on the crucifix above me.

I was light, empty of food, that stuff of earth. My flesh could not hold me down and I floated above the ground. This must be purity. My body cool, clean, emptied of heaviness and sin, alive and light, the beginning of union with Christ. The creak of Agnes's smile.

I knelt at my altar, gazed on Christ's broken feet, watched the blood gather, the drop grow a little bigger, then bigger again, a red tear so large that it broke, at last.

The walls blurred, I fell backwards onto the straw. I was as light as air now, floating up into the corner. There I was, spinning slowly, one of the motes of dust in sunlight. I floated close to where the crossbeam sat on stone. One spot of light and all around me was black. I saw what no one else had known. Not Father Ranaulf or Father Simon, maybe not even Father Peter. Only Agnes. There was nothing of my body but emptiness, pure and open like sky; I was a bird drifting on the breeze. Swallow. I could learn never to touch the ground.

We flew inside the cell, Swallow and I. The roof was sky and the walls were air. I leaped and turned, once, twice, then swooped. My feet came close to the ground but didn't touch it; I was too light, I was made of air, my body left behind. Swallow looked at me and smiled, then frowned.

'Sarah. Sarah. Come down now. You can't stay up here. Sarah. You must land.'

I turned to look around, to lift my arms, but I couldn't move. Swallow opened his silent mouth.

'Sister Sarah. Sister Sarah. Are you all right, Sister? Can you get up? I'm to come in and tend you if you're too ill to move. Sister.' The voice was heavy, nagging. I shook my head, tried to shake it away, but it kept on until I opened my eyes.

'Oh, Sister Sarah, I was so worried seeing you lying there. I told Father Simon as I should come in, that they should open up your door, but he said first to see if I could call out. Well, I said, of course I'd called out to you, as if I hadn't thought to do that already. That was the first thing I did. But now you've ...'

I lifted my head to see Louise's face peering at me through the parlour window. I would have smiled at her double chin squashed onto the ledge, but I was angry that she had called me back to this cell, to her, to this dragging body. I lifted my head from the straw and managed to sit up, the walls and windows spinning past me, again and again.

'I'm all right, Louise. You can see that. Now leave me.'

'I have some bread and milk here that Anna warmed. Just bland enough for your poor starved belly. Father Simon says you must eat. If you don't, or can't, help yourself, he's to call a man to pull out the nails in your door so's I can come in and tend you.'

'All right, Louise. All right. Let me gather some strength and I'll call you.'

'Sister, here's the food. I'm to see you eat it, Father Simon ordered.'

I wanted to lie down again, wanted Swallow to take me flying. Instead, while Louise looked on and talked, I ate some dull lumps of bread, tears sliding down my face. My body tingled at the taste of their salt. I listened for the sound of nail on wood, the grind of bone, but there was nothing.

Father Ranaulf visited sooner than usual, and though his greeting was the same as always, there was some change in his voice, as if he had looked up at my curtain for the first time. Perhaps it was concern.

'Father Simon sent word that you've been unwell, Sister, and I've come to speak with you. Louise says you've been fasting to excess. Is that so?'

'I should deny my desires, my memories of the past, my lust for food, my constant watching for my next meal, however plain or small it may be. My Rule warns me about letting my blood be heated with food.' I spoke quickly. 'I've confessed often, as you know, but it's not enough. And Agnes, the holy woman who's buried here, she's been guiding me, teaching me how to subdue my body.' I was excited, the chance now to tell him everything.

'Agnes? Guiding you? What do you mean?' His voice had the edge of a plough blade, blunt but cutting.

His sudden interest made me nervous. We had never talked like this, had never really talked at all. But he would be pleased, he would praise me now, he would say, 'Well done, child.' Wouldn't he?

'Agnes was holy, very holy; her bones are buried here.'

'Yes. And what of guidance?'

'Her bones are blessed, and they speak to me, they tell me what to do: when to pray, how to pray without sleep, what I should not eat … she tells me, her bones speak. She helped me to fast.'

'Sister, I'm your confessor and guide. You are to obey me in all things, as your Rule says. I told you to eat. Now let go of this foolishness of bones. You can't discern God's will as I can. Take no heed of any idea you have of words from the bones of a dead woman.'

'Father, Louise says they're relics. The village knows … She's a holy guide, she—'

'Sarah, it's nonsense. What would the village know? Or Louise? You have your Rule and your prayers, words that will lead you to God. Pray and read. And continue to eat as your Rule instructs you. Ask me if you wish to fast. Now, you will make your confession, beginning with wilfulness.'

And so I did, but knowing little of what I said. I felt the ground give way beneath me; I was a child being punished by a parent. No, this was something else. My mother would have been stern but forgiving; my father would have shouted and most likely hit me; Father Peter would have gently eased me back to the right path, perhaps with a sigh of disappointment that stung more than my father's slaps. Father Ranaulf's anger was like a blade flashing in sunlight, blinding my eyes. But one thing I heard most clearly: in the midst of it all, he'd called me Sarah. Just Sarah. For the first time. As if he'd finally noticed me. A tiny leap in my belly.

When he left, I stayed on my chair by the window, feeling the space he left on the other side of the wall. A low humming and I felt warmth against my leg. I started, looked down; it was Scat, her eyes closed into slits, her tail twitching gently. I bent to pat her and realised I had not seen her since … well, not since Agnes began to speak. She jumped onto my lap and curled up as if to settle my doubts.

I looked around my cell, at my books lined up on my desk, at my quiet altar, at my squint, at my bed. Where was Agnes? Slowly, slowly, I searched for her. I called in silence. No answer. The sounds of scraping; it was Anna cleaning a pot.

⊰ RANAULF ⊱

RANAULF RETURNED TO THE priory a little late for Terce. He slipped quietly into his seat next to Alain and joined the steady monotone of the brothers, his mouth reciting every word by rote. The anchoress needed his prayers, but his head was full of questions. He tried to recall the teachings of the Church on women and visions. The page was blank.

With his brothers he filed from the chapel and along the cloister. Cuthbert and Alain were laughing quietly, sharing a joke. As the little procession reached the infirmary, Ambrose pushed open the door to ask Father Peter if he needed anything. The old monk was bedridden now and when Ranaulf was free, he visited him to discuss a manuscript, or a teaching of one of the Fathers. Peter always asked about Sister Sarah but the scribe felt uneasy about his lack of experience in counselling and would say little more than that she was praying and reading. Today, though, he knew he needed Peter's advice. When Ambrose walked on, he put a hand to the door, hesitated, then pushed it open and bent to step inside the room.

'Father Ranaulf! Will you sit? I've been hoping you would visit. Brother Ambrose is so good to me, and Brother Alain stops and chats in his cheerful way ... though sometimes it's more cheer than I can manage. But our talks about your manuscripts, brother scribe, they're what I most enjoy. What are you working on?'

'I'm finishing a Breviary, and I've begun work on a saint's Life for the anchoress. Cuthbert is illustrating a Book of Hours, and we have an order for another. I have Anselm's *Cur Deus Homo* on loan from Westmore; the prior brought it with him after his last visit. I could bring it for you to read until I begin copying. What with my visits to the anchoress ...'

'Ah, a blessing for the anchoress, you are. It's a hard life she's chosen. I'm sure she appreciates your learning, all the ideas you must discuss, eh, Father?'

Ranaulf covered his confusion with silence, relieved when Peter continued.

'How is Sister Sarah?'

'She's in fair health, Father. She's been somewhat troubled this Lent and Easter, but I've been to visit her this morning. She ... well, she's been fasting without my permission and collapsed. The young maid is preparing food she can eat easily, and Louise is ready to step in with firm words.'

Peter half grunted, half laughed in recognition. His eyes were tired, but soft, their deep blue startling in his gaunt face.

'Sister Sarah believes that a previous anchoress told her not to eat ... something about her bones speaking ...' Ranaulf's voice seemed to lose its strength.

'Ah, that would be Sister Agnes. Father Simon is very proud that she's buried there. Prior Walter tells me that some time ago Simon applied to the bishop to have the bones officially recognised as relics. He was denied, but he encourages the idea of her sanctity in the village. And now a new anchoress: they feel there's something blessed about the place. But you'd know that, the way they go on about it.'

Ranaulf remembered faces that had become familiar, but he only spoke to Louise and Simon. Oh, and the young girl who chattered to him as he walked along the village road. 'If Father Simon is so proud of the old woman's remains, why is he worried about Sister Sarah? As I left the anchorhold he stopped me, told me I must take special care with the anchoress. I had no idea what he meant. He mentioned visions, said I must discern if they are from God or the Devil, and spoke of foolish women alone — someone called Isabella.'

'Ah, Sister Isabella. She was the anchoress some years ago, apparently. Before our time here, of course. Father Simon was her confessor, but she left her enclosed life. There were stories. I don't take much heed, though that's one of the reasons Bishop Michael insisted the new anchoress have a confessor from here, the priory, to be sure she's faithful to her vows, and stays.'

'Stays?'

'It's a serious sin for an anchoress to leave her cell. The bishop was furious when Isabella left. There was some question of her commitment to God, some foolishness about the Devil ...'

Silence sat between the two men. Ranaulf rubbed his hands together between his knees. A woman sealed in a cell, that was all. How could it become so complicated?

'Well, Father, I'll leave you to rest—' he began, but Peter cut in, his voice stronger than before.

'It's a responsibility, you know, being confessor to an anchoress. You must help her remain, Father, and encourage her love for God, but most of all take care of her.'

Ranaulf pushed through the door, walked the length of the cloister, his swirling thoughts blinding him to a nod from a passing brother. Relics, voices, talk of the Devil, a froward anchoress, a warning from Simon ... He strode on. *Help her remain ... take care of her* ... Could he do that?

❧ SARAH ❧

IN THE DAYS AFTER I swooned, a strange quiet sat inside my cell. I prayed and read, but mostly I waited to begin to understand that place between life and death where Agnes had dwelt, eating only bread and living so close to death that it was days before her maid realised she had breathed her last. I had tried to find that place Agnes called me to, where Christ would love me most, where Father Ranaulf would be pleased, but I had failed.

The chill in my cell had lessened and I gradually realised that the season had turned from winter to spring while I had been with Agnes. I ate as little as I could, and only very plain food, though even then it seemed against nature to swallow a piece of bread or a mouthful of pottage. I refused the egg and milk Anna gave me, the smell thick and heavy, sure to weigh me to the ground, complaining that it made my belly twist in pain and sent me rushing to the night bucket.

Anna sighed at all I left uneaten and the concern on her face surprised me. It was a comfort I had not expected. One day she brought me some pear sweetened with honey and a flavour I didn't know, that flowed from my tongue to the ends of my fingers. Three small mouthfuls and it was gone. When I told

Anna that this was what I needed, and I would take more, she shook her head. There would be no more until tomorrow, she said. I was angry that she would keep food from me, until her careful words explained that my body could manage no more. I was slow to also understand what she had seen: that I must learn to want the food. Day by day, I began to look forward to her smile as she described each ingredient of the meals she brought to me. And when she sat with us to read and pray, I no longer resisted the sight of her stray curls.

I prayed quietly, trusting Christ to hear me, though I scarcely knew what I said and sat most of the day at my desk. The cell was still: no faces, no voices. I looked for the skull in the stones by my desk, but it had hidden itself inside the rock. I moved the legs of my chair to feel the shudder, looking for the fear, like digging at a scab, and I called for Agnes, but there was nothing. She's dying, or dead, I thought, and laughed out loud. I wanted her company, yet I was afraid she would come back.

Between Nones and Vespers each day it was my habit to read, but the words, clear enough on the page, floated away and past me, so I went on with my sewing instead. The linen for the altar was easy work, hemming that needed little concentration, and the rhythm of the stitches held me. The cloth was a good weave, fine and well cut, and the thread slid through gently, time after time, into a straight line of feather stitch.

I'm eight years old and watching carefully as Ma leans towards me, teaching me how to do split stitch, my awkward fingers struggling to pass the needle through the thread. Ma guiding my hand, mending my mistakes. My mouth tight, trying until I have a meandering line of threaded loops.

Even though I was growing stronger in my body, the memories came unbidden and my heart could not resist. They gathered and held my raggedness, and sometimes they seemed to deepen my prayers. At Matins, in the groundless night, the metallic echoes of the bell faded quickly, lost to the wind. All was black, but without the need for thought or sight I pulled my blanket around me and sank to my knees by the bed. 'Mother Mary, full of grace ...' The words were a nest and I burrowed down. My illness had softened my soul a little, and now I looked for Mary's embrace. Mother. The smell of newly dyed cloth, of bread with its dusting of flour, her breath yeasty with ale and the rose of her scented water; the swell of her belly between us.

'... have mercy on us sinners ...' Was this a deceit, to let the memory of my mother draw me closer to Mary? I knew what Agnes would say, but I could not hear her.

The rhythm of stitch after stitch had always felt so much like prayer that I began to think it would be a way to teach Anna stillness. She had sewn a little, she said, but only rough darning and mending of her clothes. We began with taking up the hem of Father Simon's alb to hide the places it had worn ragged.

Anna laughed. 'Now we'll need to repair his shoes, as they'll be showing underneath.'

She bent her head over her work, holding it up now and then to check if the stitches were even, sometimes sighing as she took out a mistake. We worked together in silence. When the hem was finished she asked if she could fix the tear in the sleeve of the alb. The mending would show, so I taught her how to work a small cross in satin stitch over the top. I watched the thin creases in her forehead as she focused.

'Not as even as it should be. Next time I'll do better,' she said. But I could tell she was pleased.

Father Ranaulf continued to visit every week. His voice was still distant, but he now asked if I was well and getting stronger, and invited me to make my confession, rather than demanding it. Sometimes he would ask if I had questions about my Rule, or my devotional reading. I said no. The time since he had first visited seemed like wild weather that had begun as flurries of unease between us and strengthened each week till stormy winds blew about us. The day we spoke about Agnes was a black tempest, rain and gales so loud I could hardly hear. Now there was only the quietness of the ravaged world, and I wanted nothing more — neither his attention nor his approval. I would obey him, as I must, and I would listen to his words and accept whatever penance he imposed. I had longed for his attention and praise, some conversation, some advice, but now, when he offered that, I wanted nothing from him but his refrain, *Ego te absolvo*.

'Sister Sarah, morning to you. Louise said you've agreed to talk to me.'

The woman's voice made me think of a round wooden bowl, sturdy, plain, practical.

'Yes, Lizzie.' I was seated by my desk and turned the chair toward my window, though I decided not to open my curtains. Even so, the mingled scent of herbs felt almost as strong as a body. I had never seen her, but in my mind she had long hair, a brown face.

'Sister, Anna told me, and only as I be a healer she told me, that you'd been taken ill and I thought it only right as I should come and visit. To see if I could help. I've been thinking a long time as how living here, without doing work but with all your praying and kneeling and fasting, you'd get to be ill. It's a half year or more that you've been in this cell, and you're bound to be poorly.'

She paused, waiting for something from me. What was I to say? I sought to be one with Christ, to suffer with him; illness was part of that.

'Thank you, Lizzie. I feel well enough.'

'Sister Sarah, it may be well enough for holy men like Father Simon and Father Peter, and now the new priest who comes to see you, to talk of prayer and suffering and God's matters, but they know nothing of women. Nothing.' Lizzie's voice was more certain now. 'Well, Father Simon might a little, seeing as Martha sleeps so much at his house, but they know nothing of women and their conditions, and they'd as like let you suffer here in ways they do not understand. How can they, being men and keeping away from women as they do?'

I heard the stool shift.

'Sister, I can talk to you through this window, but if I could come in and bring you some oils and herbs as will help—'

'Lizzie, thank you, but I won't need oils or herbs. A little more rest and I will be well.'

'Sister, no. Your condition's not one as will change with rest. It's too much rest as is the problem. Anna tells me that you haven't had your flowers for some time. Every month a woman needs her flowers, as you would know, to clean out the waste inside. And for a woman such as you, not working in the fields or standing cooking or scrubbing at clothes, it stands to reason you won't have your flowers. It's work as helps them come on.'

'I know, Lizzie. But that's part of my enclosure, it brings me closer to Christ. I need not care for my health, it's—'

'Being close to Christ is what you know about, Sister, and what you chose. But you know too that a woman as has no man can have problems. We all have desires; it's how God made us, to lie with a man.'

'Lizzie, you mistake God's creation. It was Eve's first sin that made women desire to lie with men. It's sin, not how God made us. That's why I live like this, to be with Christ alone, to stay away from men, to deny those desires. Women are lustful because they are sinful.'

'Whether it be sin or no, Sister, a body is a body, created by God. And a woman must have certain ways, outlets for her longings, or she becomes ill. As you have. I leave the talk of God to holy people, but I know the ways of bodies, and if you don't lie with a man some time, you become ill.'

I said nothing.

'So, Sister, even though I think it would be best for me to bleed you from the foot, we can begin with some herbs in wine or as tea, as you're not sure. Fennel, cumin, cowbane, spikenard — nothing very strong; and with some honey to make it easier to drink. I'll mix it up and give it to Anna to heat up for you. Will you agree, Sister? Nothing too much, but a beginning. You might find that you piss a bit more, that's all, but it should bring your flowers on again, and that's what you need.'

I was tired of being told what I should do: pray, eat, stop eating, suffer, stop suffering, read, listen, stop listening. And here was another voice, certain that she knew what I needed.

'So, I'll do that, Sister.' Her healing advice given, Lizzie again sounded hesitant. 'I'll come back in a few days, and see.'

I was too tired to argue.

Would I take the herbs? Being without a monthly bleed meant that I had been shedding my weak woman's body. Holy women, virgins like Agnes, had denied their bodies and become like men. I thought again of Swallow and his leap, his flight, his neat spinning in the air. I wanted no blood, no leaking seed, but I drank the tea, still waiting to understand what it meant – this living death.

The women who usually visited me had mostly stayed away since my illness. I was glad not to hear Jocelyn's voice, so thin and sad, and Louise had probably told Winifred to keep away, thinking her loud and merry ways would overwhelm me. In church, her prayers were louder than anyone else's, and sometimes in the evening I could hear her shouting at Roger in their garden, even though she lived across the village road and well towards Colley's Hill. Despite all that, when she had come to me for counsel she had been subdued and thoughtful, asking how the crucifixion could make a difference to those like her who brewed ale for a living. I spoke about love and suffering, but I knew I hadn't really answered her question.

Eleanor had not been to visit; no doubt her mother told her to leave me be until I was well again, and though I missed her, I was glad to have a pause from her questions.

Only Maud came, and more often than usual, but for a short visit each time.

''S not for me to say, Sister,' she said, 'but those as get so ill need us living ones to be sure they come right back to life, you know. Right back, not just a little way. And I like to visit anyways, just as being company.'

I had no strength to argue or to be offended by the idea that I might need her to help me heal, so I let her stay and chat. Each time she came she told me about her work in the fields, and slowly I recognised that she was teaching me all that she knew.

'Not having enough oxen to pull the plough, we had to use cows in the team, though it may as well be ducks or pigs for all the use they are. Slows down the work so as the men get angry.

'S'pose I don't think of it much, just go out and work in the fields like always, but telling you, Sister, as don't know about it, makes me think of the sense of it. The first plough turns under the weeds and straw and they rot, give the soil food, and then a second one is shallow and not so hard, so it's quicker. And then the harrowing, breaking up the clods so it's easier for the seeds to grow. Breaks my back, too, it does. Sometimes I think it'd be easier to be an ox dragging that plough than following behind it like we do.' I could smell the soil, rich and dark, so different from the dry dust that floated in from the church porch.

By the following visit, the beans had been planted: 'Careful like, so's not to waste any. Though this year the rain's made the soil like mud so the mounds where we plant collapse and the soil slips down into the ditches and we have to dig it all up and put it back. Sister, you need to pray as it don't rain any more now, not till the roots get a hold.'

It felt strange, but I prayed for the crops, and I imagined the hard, shiny beans softening and swelling in the dark. On the visit after that, Maud pronounced the beans were shooting: 'And now they're coming up, thin stalks, and with this sun you can almost watch 'em grow ... and the weeds, of course, they never go away; no matter what we do, they grow just as fast.'

I thought of the tiny green shoots, twisting around sticks, or each other, climbing upwards and unfurling each leaf. Maud's chatter was drawing me back into life.

I worried then that I was no longer helping her but instead, I was drawing deep on her goodness when she had scant time to sit with me. Apart from work in the fields, she had a family to tend, vegetables to cultivate, a cow to milk, cheese to make, and much more. Even with those thoughts of Maud my mind was straying beyond my four walls, the cracks opening up again. But whether I prayed for the women or the crops, my prayers were no longer empty words.

Avice had visited me only once or twice, but she came to see me after church at Whitsun, confused by the day's reading. Her voice was light, seeming to float through the curtain to me. It was confusing, she said, the Holy Ghost coming from the sky like that, in tongues of fire on the heads of the disciples, and all of them talking in different languages.

'That shows us that God calls to everyone, whatever language they speak,' I said.

'I see that, Sister. But it's the words I mean. All those languages, all those strange words people use. How is it we use a word for something, like *tree*, and someone in another land uses a different word?' She paused. 'After all, a tree is always a tree, a pot is always a pot, however we say or think on it.'

She was right; at first I was surprised at such thoughts from a woman who couldn't read. But we all use words to think. Why shouldn't Avice have such ideas, even without books?

She asked me to pray for her husband, Sam, weak with a sickness that wouldn't leave.

'Lizzie gives us some herbs that help for a time, and then he sickens again. But I'm glad you're well now, Sister. Each time I go past this cell I think of you inside praying.'

I was pleased to see the women again, though I had begun to feel ashamed of how I had spoken to Jocelyn, and to worry about her. I asked Louise how she was faring.

'Well, Sister, Jocelyn is poorly.'

'Is it a fever? Or Hugh, did he do something?'

'A fire it was, in her house. Jocelyn says she was careless of her skirts by the open fire and they caught alight. It's common enough. Some years back, five houses burned down over Colley's Lane, all from one spark in the straw.'

'But Jocelyn, is she all right? Is she badly burned?'

'One leg and her hand. Lizzie says they will heal in time. Jocelyn says it was a blessing Hugh was nearby to beat out the flames. But Sister, you know as I don't like to gossip, but I saw her the next day and her face and shoulder were bruised, like she fell as well. Or were pushed.'

'Oh, no! Louise, if you see her, tell her ...'

A silence fell.

'Yes, Sister. I'll do that,' she said quietly.

'Thank you, Louise.'

I was surprised that Louise had said very little about my collapse, but she knocked on the shutters sometimes in the evening.

'Sister, there's a sunset as might cheer you,' she would say.

The door to the maids' room was on the opposite wall to the window into my cell, but set to one side of it, so that I could not see through it to the world outside. Even so, in the warmer months some light from the setting sun would flow into the room and reach my cell. I'd open the shutters and let the gold of the sun colour the walls while I sat at my desk. Sometimes Scat came in through the window and curled up on my knee, sleepy after a day roaming outdoors. Louise would sit outside her door, watching the sun sinking through the tangle of trees on Cram Hill, and once or twice Anna sat with us. In my mind I would see the tangle of her curls, the full roundness of her chin, still with its trace of childhood, the tilt of her head and shoulder.

The scratches on my ankles and feet had almost healed and I ran my fingers over the raised criss-crossing of pink lines. I listened for Agnes; she was always there, a restless scraping and shuffling beneath me, but her voice was quiet. I knew, though I wouldn't admit it, that whatever Agnes said about death and suffering, I had hung on to life. The sunsets glowed like fire on the straw above her grave.

WATCHING THE SUN CAST its orange radiance into the back corner of my cell, onto my altar and crucifix, had seemed harmless, but I had let in more than I knew.

As the weather warmed I moved more easily, and the price of my ease was restlessness. Though I was still weak and ached with the effort, I walked the short span of my cell, nine paces from windows to door, and back again, my legs wanting to continue outside. I opened my Rule, found the chapter on protecting the heart from the senses, and read, wishing it were Father Peter talking to me, his voice soothing.

> *Disturbance only comes into the heart from something that has*
> *been seen or heard, tasted or smelled, and felt outwardly. And*
> *know this to be true, that the more these senses fly outwards, the*
> *less they travel inwards. The more the recluse gazes outwards,*
> *the less light she has from our Lord inwardly.*

I understood the words, but it seemed that in my weakened state I could no longer resist the demands made by my senses. I'd had no idea that sounds and smells could separate themselves; as if unravelling a piece of cloth, day by day, thread by thread, I began to recognise them. This is mill wheel, this is cartwheel, this is dragging a sack, this is throwing a bucket of water, this is digging, scything, ploughing, and even, sometimes, whispered seed scatter. These are Louise's tired and heavy footsteps, this is Anna's laugh, that is Eleanor's chatter; these are curses, sighs, laughter, the moans and gasps of bodies joining, grunts of tiredness, frustration, sadness. This is wind on a warm day; this is a breeze that barely moves the leaves; this is rain on dirt, on stone, on thatch; this is the silence of falling snow.

The smells took longer to recognise: all kinds of shit and mouldering, hay and corn and dried rushes, parsnips freshly dug, ale spilled and stale, drying blood, drying fish, the sweat and dirt that seeped into everything. Of all the smells, what I missed the most was my scented water. It had been a part of my life, the jug in my room that Elsbeth filled each day with water and violet petals, or rosemary and orange. The smell would float around me whenever I poured it, linger on my hands and neck, caress my clothes and bedclothes. Now it was gone, I discovered how much I had loved it. Anna brought bunches of wormwood and rue, occasionally rosemary, to hang in my cell to keep away moths, but the scent was harsh. I longed to tell her to collect some violet or rose petals, and she would have, gladly, telling me they were all given by God.

On church feast days, the smell of incense wafted through my squint, though it soon faded. Louise and Anna carried it faintly on their clothes when I opened the shutters to read with them, and it was then that my own loss felt sharp and strong. For the first time, I felt how silky was Scat's orange fur, how she smelled sometimes of death, or of straw, or of wet grass. I recognised my own thick smell and washed more often.

*

Even inside my cell, with work that Father Ranaulf gave me, the touch of my fingers drew me outward. My Rule said that I should sew only simple cloths for the church and for the poor, so when Father Ranaulf suggested I embroider a panel for the altar cloth at St Christopher's Priory, I was startled. Perhaps he thought it would take my mind from Agnes and her guidance. He passed through my window a scrap of parchment with a design the priory illuminator had sketched in lead. The moment was awkward: his hand pushing through the curtain, the chance of seeing each other, me looking away then glancing back to see his long fingers stained with ink.

I traced the drawing with my fingertip, feeling delight in each curve and straight line, each dot and flourish. It was St Christopher, the priory's patron saint, who had served God by carrying people safely across a deep river. One day he carried a child, but this child was so heavy that Christopher felt he was carrying the whole world on his shoulders and was afraid he and the child would drown. He staggered to the other side, exhausted. Only then did the child reveal himself as Christ, and that in carrying him Christopher had indeed carried the whole world. In the drawing, the saint was tall, standing knee deep in water, holding the child gently and easily in one arm, a staff in the other, his face strong with a long, straight nose.

I decided on each colour and type of stitch, excitement pounding in my head, memories of Ma's words about the way each stitch would produce a different effect. The saint's robe would be brown in stem stitch, shaded to show the folds, and where the water covered it I could mingle brown and blue threads. Chain stitch for the staff, or perhaps feather stitch, in shades of gold and brown, and in the four corners of the panel, white flowers to tell of his staff that blossomed. Gold thread for the haloes, of course, and silver to mingle with the green of the water in the river; some tiny pearls for the fish, orange with green fins. I thought of the river, the deep flowing water, long sleek fish, red and purple and yellow, floating and weaving like lengths of silk, coils of gold and silver braid, some sinking, some rising.

When I began to sew, each stitch, each coloured thread, made my fingers tingle, a warmth that flowed through my arms and chest, down into my belly. I would ask Anna to help me; we could sew the water and the fish together.

Even though I knew I should limit the amount of time I worked on the cloth each day, so that I kept my rhythm of prayer and reading, my thoughts would wander to it, my eyes would look across to where it was folded on my desk, and sometimes I found myself working on it, unaware I had put down my book, or even that I had made a decision.

A stifled laugh, muted footfalls on the grass and they were gone: young girls running past my cell on the way to the river. May Day, and they were up before dawn to collect flowers when they were freshest, their perfume strongest.

As I finished praying Prime, snatches of laughter and words blew in on the breeze. There was the pungent smell of borage, then thyme, even stronger. I could see it: the grass, the sunrise, the bunches of flowers — daisies, gillyflowers, mallow, comfrey, and cowslip. I could imagine the games: boys' names shouted, cries of delight, disgust, anger, whistles and lewd words, prophecies of couplings, weddings, babies.

Emma, a plaited crown of periwinkle on her head, had been the most excited of them all, collecting flowers, organising the games, giving instructions, arranging the girls in a circle to throw balls made of cowslip, calling to me to join in. I always shook my head; I didn't want a husband, and offered instead to take bundles of flowers to decorate the houses of our neighbours. Once Emma was married, she no longer joined the games of finding a husband, but put on a crown of flowers and pulled Godric out to dance.

I used to frown when she laughed at crudity, drank too much mead, or kissed Godric under the maypole and told him to give her a baby. But that May Day morning at my altar, I no longer saw the lines of pain on her face as she died, but her laugh, the curve of her back, the lift of her feet as she danced, her hair curling with sweat, and I realised, with a shock like being slapped, that in truth I had wanted to do that, to wind around the maypole, to sing and laugh with the others; I had watched on, longing and afraid. A foolish idea; I had always wanted only to pray and serve God. My prayers finished, I stayed on my knees, my face throbbing at the thought. Was it a temptation sent by the Devil? The clack of teeth, a scrape on my ankle, and I felt the tender skin opening once more, the warmth of blood trickling across my foot.

When I heard Louise's voice at my parlour window, I dabbed at my foot with my robe and stood. Maud had come to see me on her way to church, to wish me happy May Day. She told me then of an argument between her Bill and Winifred's Roger about the plough.

'It's ploughing for the wheat now, Sister, and Roger had agreed that he'd finish with the plough in three days, but it rained so hard one day that the ox couldn't get a foothold, so by the time his three days were up, his fields weren't ploughed, were they? My Bill, he had such a set-to with Roger. Both said they were in the right, and they were. Were just the weather, but could they see it? Finally Roger waited till our Bill was done, even agreed to help him out, so I told Bill he was to do the same. Good thing it's May Day and they can get drunk together, eh, Sister?' She laughed. 'Though I worry, drunk men anywhere near Sir Thomas. We saw him ride in a day or so past and no doubt he'll visit the feast today. Brave or foolish, he is, the men are so angry with him. Word is he's a mind to get more sheep and take more of the common land for their pasture. We've bare enough as it is, the land's so worked and starved, without he takes more.'

I knew enough now to see what she meant: that Thomas would be taking away some of the land set aside for the whole village to use. 'Oh, Maud, you must be worried. But can he do that?' I knew how hard they struggled.

'Laws are made by the rich, aren't they, Sister? For the rich.' A bitter laugh. The scrape of wood as she stood to leave. 'Ah, but this misery isn't right on May Day. Forgive me and my woes, Sister. And you, you'll sit here alone. Such a shame, a day like today with food and dancing. Sister Isabella used to laugh and say she could join in even from her cell, though there wasn't much room. Someone like her, pretty and full of life, a cell was no place to be shut in. Oh, beg pardon, Sister, I didn't mean to offend.'

'It's all right, Maud. Go on.' I sat forward.

'It's just she was a holy woman, and she prayed for us. I loved her, but it was best that she left. Must have been hard, though, after making her vows.'

'Left, Maud? I thought Isabella died here. She was here five years, Louise said.'

'She was, a bit more than five years, and she said she couldn't stay no more in this cell. It was sad.' She sighed. 'I'd best go. I've said too much.'

I moved to my squint. The church was noisy with excitement and relief that seeding was finally finished, children whined to be allowed to leave, there was talk of the weather, plans for the feast, complaints about the oxen — but all I could hear were Maud's words about Isabella. An anchoress can't leave; that must be Maud's fancy. Louise had said she was here five years and I'd thought her body must have been weak: the cold, the damp, and the dark all too hard for her. What woman would make her vows and then turn from them?

When church had finished, the laughter and shouting outside my cell reminded me that I must make a decision about Anna. During my long fast and illness I had paid scant attention to my maids, but lately I'd begun to think of them again, especially Anna, contemplating how much time she should spend in prayer and reading. Despite my decision when she'd arrived that she should join Louise and me when I read from the Rule, and to say Prime, Terce, and Compline with us, she was often busy outside the anchorhold at those times.

'It all takes longer because she stops to talk, she does,' Louise had told me. 'I see her laughing with the young girls in the village. And, not as I like to gossip, but she's very friendly with that boy Fulke, Maud's son.'

When I'd told Anna she would need to organise her time so she could pray and read with us, she'd spoken quietly, but her eyes had argued.

'I came here as your maid, Sister, and I do my work, don't I? Why make me holy as well? You're the holy one. I work, you pray.'

I saw Emma in the twitch of her mouth, the sharp lift of her shoulder. My sister had questioned everything — the need for this or that stitch in embroidery, the fear of demons, the fear of God, the purpose of prayer, the truth of Father John's sermons, the need to bend our knee to any lord or baron — all without anger; it was all open to question for her.

I'd remembered Father Peter's words when I was first enclosed, that I should move slowly into this new life, and had thought it good advice for my guidance of Anna. I had lessened the times she must sit and listen to me reading until she felt she could do more.

Now May Day was another problem. It was not right for the maid of an anchoress to dance at the celebrations, but as I read to Anna and Louise from my Rule, the smells and sounds, ale and woodsmoke, cooked meat and pastry, music and laughter and shouting from the green drifted past us in enticing gusts. Anna tapped with her foot, sighed, turned around again and again, as if she might see through the closed door, until I gave in and told her she could go to the feast if it was just to watch, and she was to be sure to stay with Louise. This was the kind of duty that Louise enjoyed, and she clicked her tongue in anticipation.

'And Anna, you know you must not be friendly with the village boys. You may speak with the girls from time to time, but not with the boys.'

'Sister, you can't make me ...' She stopped and turned away.

I wondered again about how much I asked of her, but remembered Father Peter's warning to take care with my young maid.

Even if the weather was still cool, with prayers to the Virgin Mary, with maypole, fires, dancing, rituals, and feasting on the green outside the church, the village coaxed their seeds to grow. The excitement of holiday, the relief from work, the games and singing going on close to my cell, the sense of hope that ale and food and the touch of bodies gave to people, all of these seemed to take away the fear of my cell, of me, and what the women called my 'sickness'. Eleanor rushed in as soon as church was over, pulling her friend Alyce by the hand, excited for her to meet me at last, but the girl was shy, nodded to me, and ducked out the door again.

One by one the women dropped by: Maud, Avice, Winifred, Jocelyn, Lizzie, and others, to tell a story or to bring something small for me to eat — a pie, a piece of cheese, a honey cake. I thanked them, though I would not eat the food and, remembering the leper, put it on the ledge of the maids' window to give to others who needed it. Even a few women who had not previously come for counsel opened the door to quickly wish me happy May Day.

I had made it my habit to keep the curtain closed when I spoke to the women who came to me, but that day I opened it to take the food they offered. We women looked at one another, smiled awkwardly, each seeing a face unveiled in the dimness of my parlour. From the sound of their voices I had given each woman behind my curtain a face, but that day I found I had to change them. Winifred was big, as I had expected, but her hair was fine and fair, not black, and her green eyes were not bold but a little uncertain. I had thought of Lizzie with a brown face and long brown hair, but her pale skin was covered with freckles, and as she pulled back her hair I noticed her fingers tapered long and fine, though they were stained with the powders and unguents of her trade. She sat for a time, seeming content, as I was, with our silence.

A short while later when I heard Jocelyn's quiet call from the parlour doorway, I looked up, afraid to meet her eyes. Her hair was lank as I had imagined, her face worn, but she looked straight at me with clear blue eyes and a nervous smile, almost like a child, grateful for any kindness. And Maud, who had told me so much about her life: I had always thought of her in the fields, strong and capable, so I was surprised that she was small and wiry, not even as tall as me. Her face was as brown and lined as I'd thought it would be, her smile warm, and I was pleased to see her, above all the others. She told me about the dances and her Fulke: 'Brawny lad as he is, he can still dance enough to please the girls.'

And finally Avice, her voice quiet and thoughtful, as if suited to reading and learning, was as I had thought: even through the worry around her mouth and eyes, she was beautiful in the way that I think a queen must be — her face fine, her lips red. When she left I wondered at the strangeness of the world, and whether she chafed at the narrowness of her life.

My Rule did not forbid opening my curtain to women, but I knew that I would not do it if they came seeking counsel; that day it was as if my sealing in stone had also taken a holiday. I had worried about the ways the world crept through my walls, but on May Day I opened my curtain for it to come in. I thought of the bishop's warning, not to become snared in the web of women's gossip, and I remembered, with a jolt of curiosity, Maud's few words about Isabella, the anchoress who had left.

The drag of the door again and I looked up in surprise at the sound of Anna's laugh as she rushed into the parlour. I had said she was to stay with Louise.

'Sister, I bought you a baked apple.' She was out of breath, her hair tangled, her cheeks red, the dance still alive in the movements of her shoulders and head. 'It's not fair you miss out, but I'm glad you can hear the music. There'll be music in heaven, too, won't there? So God must like it and it can't hurt you to enjoy the singing and drumming then.' She slid the apple onto the ledge.

I should have asked her what she had been doing, whether Louise was waiting for her, but I was suddenly awkward, for a moment seeing myself as she must see me, dull and serious, the holy woman who demanded such discipline. The flame of my oil lamp was reflected in her eyes and for a moment she became shy, darting a glance at me and then away. I thought of the spiced pear she had made for me in my illness, that quiet wisdom.

'Thank you for the apple, Anna.'

She laughed, too excited to be still for long. 'Enjoy it. Eat it, Sister, eat it,' she called as she pushed the door shut.

I had come to recognise that she didn't look very much like Emma; her eyes were more hooded and her lips thinner, but they both seemed to move as if they liked the body they had. Foolish thoughts; I hardly knew what they meant. I closed my curtain. Should I ask so much discipline of Anna, when she didn't want this life that others had chosen? I would never have thought of Emma as maid to an anchoress. But it was a good living for a poor girl, and Anna had small chance of anything else.

The dull sheen of the apple she had brought me glinted and shifted as the flame of my lamp flickered. I stretched out a finger, stroked at the honey, licked its sweetness. My body stirred. Sounds of scratching, shudderings in the leg of my chair. I ignored them, pulled at the apple's skin, bit down on its firmness, let the sweet tartness flow through me. Mouthful by slow mouthful, I scooped out the fluff of apple flesh with my fingers, felt the sudden tang of a currant, the resistance of sticky apple peel between my teeth. It seemed I had never tasted an apple before.

THE SCRAPE OF THE parlour door and the sound of the stool falling. Was it Winifred, drunk already?

'Sarah, are you well?'

Fright prickled through my arms and chest, down to my toes. 'Who is this?' I asked, my voice thin and strange, though I knew well enough. 'You must leave.'

'It's Thomas.' His voice was slightly slurred. 'A shame you can't come out and dance with me instead of burying yourself in this darkness you chose. Word is you've been unwell.'

I could smell ale and dried sweat. Had the village men seen him? I wondered.

'I'm well now. Please leave.' I hadn't closed my shutters and now it was too late.

'They said you collapsed, that you haven't been eating. Is this really what you want? All this punishing yourself, dark and cold and lonely.'

'I can't speak to you.'

'That's not true, Sarah, you can talk.' He stumbled a little with the words. 'You speak to, speak to ... villagers who—'

'I cannot speak to men. Apart from the bishop and my confessor.' I stepped back, away from his voice. I would not break my rule.

'Ah, Father Ranaulf, that silent, serious man. He must be punishment enough. All I want, all I ever wanted ... I could have saved you from this harsh life. I think of you often, closed in the dark here, eating your bread and sop. I could help you, take you out of here.'

'Please leave, I'll call ...' My voice was ragged, a pounding in my head. His sounds of concern made me nervous.

'Who will you call, Sarah? The door's shut, there's music and noise outside ...' I could hear the sharp edge in his words; I knew how close his desire was to anger.

The back of my legs bumped the bed and my knees buckled. As I fell, I scraped my hand on the wall. The pain made anger flare in my chest. 'You make me sin.' Blood welled on the graze.

'Whatever you've done, you've chosen. I can't make you do anything.'

But he could — he could make me. My face was hot. 'Then leave me.'

'No, Sarah, I choose to stay.'

My mouth was dry. I moved farther back in my cell, my legs shaking.

'Why move away, Sarah? You know I can't touch you, unless you choose. Silly to creep to the end of the cell like that, all ten steps or so.'

How did he know? Could he hear me? I crossed my hands on my chest. Could he see me? Scat had been watching me, but as Thomas's voice became louder she looked toward the parlour window. Slowly, more quietly than I could manage, she stood, arched her back, shook herself, and padded a few steps before springing up to hover between the curtains, facing Thomas, her tail curling toward me. I could hear him murmuring quietly to her, and Scat began her contented humming. The curtain moved; that smell of him — sourness, leather, ale.

I shuddered. 'Leave!' I said as firmly as I could.

'But, Sarah, your cat likes me; she likes to be patted. Listen to her purring.'

I could sense the smile on his face, that slight narrowing of his eyes when he was pleased. 'Go! Please!'

Scat disappeared through the curtain and it parted, wrenched back, Thomas's face in the opening: knowing, triumphant. My legs gave way. I sank into the corner by my altar but I noticed his ears, for all my terror.

He pushed the curtain open further. I flinched as if struck, put my hands up to fend it off, that face. My cell was my body, my skin began and ended with these walls. No longer whole. I stretched out my hand, felt my way along the familiar stones, moved until I could touch my squint, press the warm curve, worn smooth by hands, mine and others'. Agnes. Isabella.

'Is that the best you can manage, Thomas?' My voice was low.

His smile tightened, his lips thin and stretched. He opened his mouth to speak but I knew he wanted to strike. His face disappeared and he left without a word. In my mind the stables, the sound of the stable boy falling, Thomas looking beaten, angry. I cowered away from the memory, refused to see it through to the end.

I stayed on the floor until the shaking stopped. The stones around me were no longer firm. When I touched them they shifted like water, gave way beneath my fingers. I'd been so sure they were solid, sealing me in, sealing out the world, but now I could see right through them. The world could thrust its way in.

A flickering behind me. I glanced up at the dull orange flashes of fire in my horn window. Some shouts, a raucous laugh, snatches of song: outside, the dancing and feasting went on, though I had heard none of it while Thomas was in the parlour.

My Rule was on my desk. There was comfort in turning the pages I knew so well, in reading familiar words, though I knew they would condemn me. I knew where to open it, just near the beginning, the section on how to protect the heart by protecting the senses. The eyes make us leap into sin, just as Lucifer and Eve leaped after sin because of what they had seen; it was looking at the apple that made Eve long to eat. That was why I had a narrow window covered with a thick curtain, so that I could not see out and no one could see in.

I do not wish anyone to see you, unless he has special permission from your confessor. See to it that the parlour curtain be fastened and well attached on both sides, and guard your eyes lest your heart escape and go out, and your soul grow sick as soon as it is outside, for all that comes of it is evil, especially to the young. Not one evil, nor two, but all woe that there is now and ever yet has been and ever shall be in time to come — all came from sight. Eve, our original mother, beheld the forbidden apple and saw it to be beautiful and began to delight in beholding it, and bent her desire towards it, and took it and ate of it, and gave it to her lord. Thus sight went ahead and made a path for evil desire, and then followed the deed that affects all mankind. This apple, dear sister, betokens all the things that desire and delight in sin lead to. When you gaze on a man, you are in Eve's position, you are looking on the apple.

I knew the words. I knew the sin. I closed the book.

But I had tried to keep Thomas away. This curtain, my Rule, my cell. I'd asked him to leave, again and again. Could I have closed my shutters on my patron's face? The words were there, unmoving, unmoved. I had let him stay, I had looked at him; I hadn't turned away my face. Even when I denied him, I looked. I was uncovered.

I stayed at my desk long into the night, until the sounds of the celebrations faded. My curtain shifted, the night was restless, the flame of my candle bent, hovered, a yellow glow no larger than the wick, and went out. A scent lingered in my cell, the ghost of tree roots, soft dirt, and brought with it the faintest pictures that flickered and disappeared as soon as I looked at them. There was no keeping my body together now, no keeping it enclosed. *Isabella*. The sound tumbled out of my mouth, the sound of a song. Edges shuddered and wavered.

I RAN MY FINGERS along the edge of my desk, flicked at a stray piece of straw on my robe, kicked at the wall. My mind was like a bird in a cage, wings flapping, unable to stop even though it is futile. How could I have prevented Thomas seeing me? My cell was not sealed, though they'd told me it was. My body was whole, but I felt undone, violated. Was it because I had looked out at the women, and let them look in? I opened my Rule and scanned the careful lines; Father Ranaulf did not decide on the words, but he copied them, told me to obey them. What did he know of women? What did he understand of my life? I paused, surprised; I sounded just like Emma.

I turned to the parlour window and pulled back the curtain, let it fall, walked to the door and back again, moved my chair closer to the window. Father Ranaulf would be coming. I looked again at my curtain, two pieces of black cloth meeting in the centre. It was as if I watched myself as I lifted one, adjusted it so that it looked like it had caught on the stone ledge. A tiny opening, that was all, probably not enough to see through, but I went on with it. I called Anna, asked her to be sure to light the candle in the parlour for Father Ranaulf, and when she was sure he had arrived to fetch some water. She was always happy when her chores took her outside the anchorhold, but that day she merely nodded and kept her gaze downwards.

'Are you sickening, Anna?' I asked.

'Just tired, is all.'

'What's that on the side of your face? Have you hurt yourself?'

'No, Sister, not that matters. I fell in the dark. 'Tis nothing.' I thought I saw tears in her eyes. She rubbed her face with the sleeve of her robe. I watched the shift of her shoulder as she turned, the soft curve just below her ear.

A chattering was coming closer, Eleanor's voice bubbling like water over pebbles, talking about a Father Finnegan, then Father Ranaulf's brief words. I smiled; the girl would not be ignored, but how did the serious man cope with her? The door opening, a step and the creak of the stool. I kept my head bent, my heart beating hard, excited and ashamed at the gap in the curtain, at what I had planned.

I could not knowingly sin as I confessed, and I kept my eyes closed the whole time. I admitted to having my curtain open more than was wise on May Day, though I said nothing about Thomas looking in. How could I explain that to Father Ranaulf? But as I heard the words '*Ego te absolvo*' I looked through the slit separating the flaps of black cloth. I could see the pink of his face, his nose, long and thin, and the side of his mouth. His lips were red and fuller than I had expected; I had thought, with his dry words, he would have thin lips, pale and sad. I started and ducked, pulled away, my face burning as if he had seen me, but he blessed me as usual. Ashamed, I became aware that my belly was warm, liquid.

'Sister, do you have any questions from your reading?' he asked. Since my fasting, this had become his custom but I had not wanted to talk. That day, however, I wanted to keep him in my parlour.

'I do have a question, Father, though not from my reading. It's about Sir Thomas and his plans for the land hereabouts.' I peeked again; he raised his eyebrows, his eyes intent.

'Yes?' He sounded uncertain.

'Maud, she's one of the village women, she tells me that Sir Thomas wants to take land from the common fields to pasture his sheep. That's land the villagers need for their own animals, their hay crops and the like. She seems to think there's little they can do, but surely there are laws, something to protect the common land. And with your reading, I thought you might know.'

'I heard of this some time ago, yes. There are laws to do with common land, but I know nothing of the detail. I'll ask, Sister. God bless you.'

He would leave, I knew, so I rushed on. 'Father, I've been thinking of the lives of saints, and St Catherine, especially.' I peeked again, saw one eye, brown, the skin around it dark with weariness, and forgot what I was saying. He moved his head and I saw a pimple on his cheek, the edge of his ear.

'St Catherine?' He sounded surprised.

'Her story is such an example for women ... she stood against the pagan king and defeated the arguments of the wisest men in the land.' Suddenly I couldn't see his face at all; he had sat up straighter.

'It's a sign of God's blessing that she rose above her nature, Sister.'

I sighed; this was a man with a pimple on his cheek. 'Yes, Father, my Rule tells me and you tell me and Father Simon tells me that women are made for bearing children and cannot grasp the truths of God as men do. But virginity is the highest ...' I spoke too loudly, especially for such words; a docile question would be better. 'But I wonder, Father, if virginity is the highest order for women, and we defeat our bodies, as St Catherine did, then perhaps ...' I began to lose courage.

'Sister, beware the sin of pride.' I could see his mouth again, the purse of his lips. 'It's true that St Augustine says virginity is the highest estate, above that of widows or wives, but you were not created in the image of God as man was. It is man who is mind and soul, woman who is body.'

'Yes, Father.' I leaned away from the curtain, took a deep breath, wanting to argue, afraid to speak. Then I heard him move. I rushed on before he could think of leaving.

'But St Catherine used her mind to argue for God and defeat pagan philosophers — fifty men assembled against her. How was that possible?' I spoke quickly.

'With God's grace, Sister, that is all.'

God's grace. I smiled to myself. 'Then with God's grace and strength, it seems all virgins can learn to think as she did.' I was pleased with my answer, but nervous, and tried to make it a question when it wasn't.

His voice was serious, focused. 'There were virgins in the first centuries who thought as you do, who claimed that because they were virgins and no longer women they need not cover their heads in church, as women should. But Tertullian warns against such false reasoning: he says a virgin always remains a woman, otherwise she would be a third kind, a monstrosity. Unlike a man, her body, the fragility of her virginity, makes her always vulnerable, always at the edge of sin. That's why you're enclosed.' He paused. 'Remember, Sister, that virginity is not simply of the body, it is purity of spirit. Pride can make a virgin fall from her high estate.' I heard him stand up. 'God bless you, Sister.' The scrape of the door.

I opened the curtain, looked into the parlour at the stool where he had been sitting. What I had seen changed things: he had become a man, flesh like me, not just a voice and words. I'd known he would tell me I was wrong, but there had been pleasure in trying out my words, ideas that I barely knew were in my mind. My Rule said that an anchoress should not match her confessor word for word, should not teach him who had come to teach her, but I would not think yet about whether my words were sin.

I was too restless to sit, even to sew, and I walked the length of my cell again and again. At the door I stopped, touched its wood. *Isabella*: the name hung in my mind like a chant. When it became dark I asked Louise to open the door to my parlour, telling her that my cell still smelled thick of a dead mouse I couldn't find.

'And Louise, what more do you know of Isabella? I thought you told me she died. But I've heard ... or did she leave?'

'Isabella, Sister?' She seemed surprised. 'Yes, she left. She was here five years and she asked to leave.'

'Why? Do you know?'

'No, Sister.'

'You know nothing more? But you must! You were here in the village, weren't you?'

Louise clicked her tongue. 'Isabella was young and I didn't come to her for counsel.'

'But you must have heard talk of her, from others.'

'Truth be, Sister, that Father Simon told us that once she chose to leave, we were not to talk about her. Best to let the sinner go, he said. And he told me especially I wasn't to speak of her, for your sake, he said, so as not to unsettle you. They were his words. I'll open the door, as you ask, Sister.'

There was no light from the moon but the darkness outside the parlour door seemed shifting, different from the constant dullness in my cell. Who was the woman who had sat on this chair and prayed at this stone? And then left. What woman is once so holy and so disobedient? A dog's bark, high and lonely. Isabella. I said her name aloud, the sound of a breeze. It should have sounded like sin. Is-a-bella. The leaves in the oak tree by my cell rustled; they would be thick and green now. My curtain swayed a little, the hint of a fragrance entered my cell. My mind reached after it: soil, perhaps, that mixture of sweetness and richness when leaves rot away; the crumble of tree bark; the velvet of moss. She was there, in the parlour, a rustle of robe, a footfall, the sound of my name. Then the scent was gone and the stench of rotting mouse took over.

⤁ RANAULF ⤂

THE RHYTHM OF HIS steps had the same reassuring steadiness as the stroke of his quill when his writing was going well. He had chosen the longer route to Hartham, following the meandering line of the river through the floor of the valley and around Cram Hill, but Ranaulf scarcely noticed the time passing, caught in memories of his conversation with Peter a few days earlier. He couldn't decide if the priest had become wise or fanciful in his old age.

He had told Ambrose, the physician, that he would take Peter his meal of pottage and bread, in truth as an excuse to speak with him. The copying of the Life of St Margaret was nearly finished, and Ranaulf was uneasy.

'Father Ranaulf, what a surprise,' Peter had said. 'And a pleasure. Kind of you to bring my meal, though I eat very little these days. What I need is company. Sit down; stay, if you have time. What are you copying now, brother scribe? What jewels, eh?' Peter had asked.

'I've almost finished copying the story of St Margaret of Antioch for the anchoress. It's a special request of Sir Thomas. Though I wonder about the wisdom of a story for a woman, even if it is the Life of a virgin martyr.'

Ranaulf rubbed at some ink on his fingers. 'She's courageous, St Margaret; her belief is clear. It's not the story that's the problem but the words the writer chose, the language, given it's to be for a woman, enclosed. A woman's mind might make of the words more than it ought.' Ranaulf had felt like he was wading in mud.

'Ah, yes, I see what you mean. These stories have so much in common with romances. I read some of the Lives of virgin martyrs when I was confessor for an anchoress at Deerfold. I had those doubts, too, at first. But she told me, Sister Claudine, that she could imagine the saint — St Margaret, St Juliana, St Catherine — in her own cell, in her anchorhold, feeling afraid and praying. And so she could begin to see herself being brave ...' Peter's words had tailed off as he coughed heavily.

Ranaulf had stood to fetch Ambrose, but the older priest had waved him down, the cough subsiding.

'We all need stories, don't we?' He'd looked up at Ranaulf. 'For our hearts, I think.'

Ranaulf had nodded, but he was uneasy. Such slippery things, stories, so different from theology or devotions. But he was pleased with the teaching he had added to the story of St Margaret; it was clever, he thought, to have the demon itself reveal its wiles, all the ways it would tempt a woman.

'I've often wondered at the men who wrote the stories,' Peter had continued, 'of what was in their minds when they saw this saint or that stripped naked. Perhaps we should be more worried about them, eh?' He'd chuckled. 'But Sister Sarah is not foolish, you know. You find her thoughtful?'

'She's begun to speak her mind, yes, though at times she becomes ... proud, perhaps. I've been forced to remind her of

Tertullian's teaching on the veiling of virgins, how a virgin is still a woman.'

'Oh, Tertullian, yes, he's very intent on that subject.' Peter had tried another laugh, but it turned into a cough. 'He was clever, but in matters like this he's inclined to be harsh ... severe on those holy women. Their commitment to God is greater, perhaps, than that of men. Take St Margaret, her suffering.'

Ranaulf had hesitated in confusion. His head was light with pleasure at the flow of ideas. How he'd missed conversation like this! But under the gentle gaze of Father Peter he'd felt ashamed of how angry he'd been at Sarah's comments about virgins. He'd cleared his throat. 'Perhaps, but Augustine himself tells us that woman was created as body, and man as mind, in the image of God.'

'Indeed he does, but he also says, and I can almost repeat it word for word, that even in those who are women in body, the manliness of their souls hides the sex of their flesh. I used to quote that to Sister Claudine. A woman can almost become a man. Remarkable.'

Ranaulf had wanted to argue, to defend his position, to quote some more Augustine, or Jerome, but he hadn't the words. He'd merely stood to leave. 'I must let you rest now, Father. It's like the grand days at the abbey, the chance to talk like this.'

That had been three days ago, but Peter's words still echoed in Ranaulf's mind. *Manliness of their souls. Can almost become a man.*

The rumble of wheels made him look up. The manor house was on the other side of the valley, ahead and to his left, rising above the village. An empty cart was rolling out of the gates, two men walking alongside the horse, heading toward the main road through the village. Spreading to the right and beyond the Hartham road were the virgates, some strips yellow with tall, swaying wheat, some the deep brown of ploughed earth.

More movement from the manor house and a single rider on a horse turned onto the river road. Ranaulf could tell from the clothes that it was Sir Thomas, and he recalled then Sarah's question about the lord usurping the common land. He could see some sheep on the pasture beyond the village, and he'd passed some grazing on the road around Cram Hill, but he had no idea which tracts of land were threatened.

His steps slowed, then stopped. Still looking out across the fields, he remembered: it was Ralph at Westmore Abbey, Ralph who needed to tell everyone in detail about the work he was copying, on and on in his monotonous voice. But Ranaulf remembered this particular occasion because Ralph had been angry, his face reddening, his voice expressive. The law had been in place for twenty years or so, but Ralph had noticed it for the first time as he'd copied it. One part of the statute he was transcribing allowed lords to enclose common land, the only protection for tenants being the requirement that the lord leave them sufficient land for their needs. *It's a law made for landholders and Devil take the poor like my old parents. You see if I'm right*, Ralph had said.

Now, almost level with Ranaulf was the man himself: Sir Thomas. Ranaulf breathed in deeply, straightened his shoulders.

'Father Ranaulf, good morning. You are visiting our dear anchoress?'

'Sir Thomas. God be with you.' Ranaulf looked up at him briefly and then away.

'You have chosen a pleasant way to walk, Father. '

The silence that grew between them seemed like a third person.

'Sir Thomas, I hear you have plans to enclose some of the common land that is already in use by your tenants.'

'Father Ranaulf, I didn't think you would be interested in such matters.' Sir Thomas smiled down at him.

'If it affects the villagers, their crops—'

'Ah, Father, don't be concerned. They need to make better use of the land they have.'

The Merton Statute, that was it. The name he had been searching for. 'The Merton Statute requires there be sufficient access for free tenants. Sufficient access to common land, Sir Thomas.'

'I will, of course, make sure of that, Father. You need not trouble yourself.' Sir Thomas shifted in his saddle. 'But on a matter that concerns you more closely: how does your copying of the Life of the blessed St Margaret progress? I imagine it must be near to complete. Yes?'

Ranaulf nodded. 'It progresses well.'

'Good. I'll come for it soon.'

'But it's for Sister Sarah, isn't it?' Ranaulf's words were sharp.

'It is, yes, my gift to Sister Sarah. My duty and my pleasure to provide for her, as her patron. I'm committed to her education.'

'You do know you can't see her? It's forbidden.'

'I'm her patron, intending to deliver a book that will assist her path to God. I see no problem.' Thomas shrugged.

'It is a problem, I'm afraid, Sir Thomas. I have care of the anchoress's welfare. No man may visit her, unless he is her bishop or her confessor. Her Rule is very clear. The sister is a godly woman, committed to her enclosure and to following her

Rule of life, and I'm committed to care for her. You cannot go to her. It would cause great harm—'

'Ah, then I'm confused, Father Ranaulf.' Thomas sounded almost bored. 'I understood from Prior Walter that as I ordered and paid for the book, it's mine. When I take it from you, I will do with it as I choose. By the way, as part of my payment, I'll be providing some ink and parchment for the priory. Prior Walter tells me you are running low. So I'm sure you'll agree there's no harm.'

'Sir Thomas, you have placed me … you are …' Ranaulf stumbled after words.

'Good, then. We're agreed. Ten days will be enough time? God be with you, Father. And with dear Sister Sarah.'

Too disturbed to visit the anchoress immediately, Ranaulf wandered into the forest behind the manor grounds; he would pray, he thought, commit the matter to God. Instead, he held a stick in his right hand and swiped at the trees as he passed. Sir Thomas, that smug man, taking control, threatening, bribing. Not only the book for the anchoress, but dismissing his questions about the land as if a scribe would know nothing. The day was hot and he could feel the sweat gathering under his arms, but the whiplike sound and the flutter of leaves released some of the pressure in his chest. Where the track narrowed, he attacked the trees on both sides, swinging the stick in large arcs across his body. He was looking down at the tattered leaves on the ground when he hit the branch of a willow that swung back and whipped across his face. He cried out, cursed, cringed as if he had been attacked, then struggled with the branch to break it off, but it was too supple and all he could do was bend it and twist it until some of the outer fibres gave way to reveal white-green pulp underneath. Tiring, he became aware of himself, a foolish man fighting a tree, a foolish man who couldn't stand his ground, who had failed in his duty. Panting, he dropped the stick; the willow branch swayed. His face was throbbing with pain, his ears were ringing, and he had blasphemed.

❧ SARAH ❧

I HAD THOUGHT WINTER was hard, but summer brought the kind of struggle that would not be overcome with blankets or fire. My Rule had warned me that the longer I stayed in my cell, the more intensely the Devil would attack me, but I hadn't expected a demon in such a guise.

In the morning, before sunrise, I heard murmurs, footsteps going out to the fields, and at sunset, the weary walk home. In my mind I followed the villagers, listened to their words, watched the rhythm of the scythe sweeping through the yellow, the children running behind, tossing the grass for drying. But Avice reminded me how hard it really was, asking prayers for her husband, Sam, who was still unwell.

'We've mown the hay all right, but it near killed my Sam, and we've hardly anything left for making bread till harvest. I sent our Christina into the forest for berries and whatever nuts she could find, but how do they feed an ailing man? Wheat harvest can't come soon enough, though how we'll manage that I don't know.'

I could offer nothing more than my prayers, yet that was all Avice wanted from me. And when I prayed for others, it was more often, those midsummer days, for a sore back, a bleeding arm, an exhausted body, than for an obedient soul.

Maud came as usual, but instead of listening, I found myself asking questions: how were the new lambs I could hear bleating; what were the weeds the women pulled out; when would the wheat harvest begin? She answered each one patiently, though her voice was tired.

'I should be glad of this sun at last, but it's so hot out there, Sister. I drink more ale and more water and I still don't piss. I've got so many prickles in my hands and they won't come out. Have to leave 'em to swell and pus, then Bill squeezes 'em out. Get home at night, aching to lie down, but my back hurts to straighten it, though that's all I want, so I have to lie curled until the pain lets go.'

I thought then about my own sore back, my knees that shot with pain when I tried to stand. I was just like Maud, though our work was so different. I was feeling stronger since my illness, but I knew that I would never fully recover; it was a part of this life that I could no longer ignore, and it frightened me. My joints ached, two of my teeth were loose, each twinge or graze now called for attention, each bump became an ugly purple bruise, each cut reddened and healed slowly. My Rule told me I was to forget my body and I longed to do that; I looked for the feeling of lightness, of floating and flying, that fasting had given me — often in prayer I could feel free of the earth. Yet as much as I told myself this weakness was the suffering my Rule counselled, it took me further into my body, not away from it.

A few days earlier I had fallen when I'd tried to stand from praying. I'd stayed on the floor and looked up at the crucifix, at the skin pulled across Christ's face, his arms stretched wide, and

I knew again that I wanted to join with his pain and his love. I was a woman stretched between life and death, this world and heaven. But however much I committed myself to hang with Christ, my desires resisted; my aches wanted sun, a day in the fields. I was caught between my cell and the world outside it.

I was reading when I heard him, a cold stab in my chest.

'Ah, Louise. And Anna. Good afternoon.' His voice was the familiar blend of power and goodwill, the kind that left people without a means to answer. Except Louise. She spoke more quietly than Thomas, so that I couldn't make out her words, but her tone was clear; he was not a welcome visitor for the anchoress.

'Louise, I'm her patron and I will see her.' He called to me, 'Sister Sarah, I've come to you on a matter of business. Send your maids away.'

The pounding in my head, the dim cell, the wrenched curtain, and me alone; the memory was all around me. I stood, but said nothing. It was daytime, my maids were close by. Louise would protect me. I took a breath, tried to steady my legs.

'Sister, Father Ranaulf sent me to you. Now ask your maids to leave.'

Father Ranaulf? Would he? Perhaps he was unwell. I looked toward the maids' room. From my desk I could see only Anna's knees; she seemed to be hunched on her bed against the wall. Louise would be at the door, arms crossed, sturdy feet planted firmly on the threshold. Thomas was my patron, I owed him my living; I couldn't send him away, especially if he was visiting at Father Ranaulf's bidding.

'My maids will stay in their room with the shutter closed.' I was surprised; I sounded certain, though I had to hold onto my desk to remain standing. I stayed by the wall, close to the window's edge so that he would barely be able to see me if he pulled open the curtain.

He began quietly. 'Sarah, I want to apologise …' His voice was warm. 'Sarah? Are you there?' He laughed. 'But of course you're there. You have no choice, unless perhaps you float through your tiny window.'

My back hurt where a jutting stone pressed into my skin, but I didn't move, tried not to make a sound.

'This was what you wanted above all else: holiness and solitude above comfort, a man's love, decent food, children.' That familiar scorn, the glittering edge of anger. A pause. 'But let's not argue today.' I could hear his indrawn breath, a deep sigh. 'Sarah, I've brought you a gift.'

'Thank you, but I cannot accept gifts.'

'You've already taken gifts from me. It's my money and my land that make possible your life here. And I'm sure you'll want this gift. Come, have a look. It's here, in my hands.'

I turned my head toward the window so close to me, to the swaying curtain. Remembering the wrench, his face I pulled back.

'It isn't to eat; it isn't to wear. Well, what else is there? It's to read. I know you love books.'

I felt like one of the mice Scat had brought into my cell, half-frozen with fear, and taunted until they died, exhausted but barely marked. I shuffled my feet closer to the window.

'Sarah, I lose patience. You were always like this. I offer you friendship, or more, and you treat me like a leper.' His voice had hardened. 'I continue the agreement with the priory so that you may live this ridiculous life and you behave as though I wish you ill. I wonder what it is you want the walls to keep out? Now, do you want the book or shall I take it away?'

'Thank you.' I tried to still the quaver in my voice. 'Would you leave it on the ledge, please?' I sounded like a child.

'No, it's a gift. I'll give it into your hands.' Again, he sighed. 'Sarah, I want to give you something that will help you endure this life. It's the story of St Margaret, copied by the hand of your confessor, intended for your soul's health. All I want is to give it into your hands.'

A book, pages to turn. And a story about a woman. Like me, perhaps. I had no stories of people doing things, losing things, discovering things. The tightness in my chest, wanting it — my own book, a new one. I waited, listening to the rich creak of his leather boots as he shifted position. I wondered if he could hear my fast breath.

'Come, Sarah,' he said, more quietly.

I told myself I had no choice. I pushed my hands through the cloth, keeping my eyes down, but after a time, when I'd felt nothing, I raised my eyes and looked through the gap I had made. His face was just below mine; he was sitting. And smiling. He touched my fingers gently and I pulled back, shocked at the warmth of flesh. The curtain fell closed between us.

'Please, leave the book on the ledge,' I said.

'I'll give it into your hands, as I said.' His voice sharp.

I pushed my hands through the curtain again, my eyes once more looking at the floor. The bundle was small and I wrapped my fingers around it, but before I could move he pressed my hands between his. A thin flame ran through my arms, into my chest, along my neck, and down into my belly. He said nothing. I should have felt only revulsion, the touch of sin. I wanted to feel it, my shunning of this man, but the warmth of skin on skin was an embrace. I staggered with longing.

'There, now. A frightened bird, you are. But why be afraid of me?' His voice comforting and threatening at once.

I moved back against the wall, the bundle clutched to my chest like a small animal. I heard the door pushed shut, then nothing more. My heart was still beating hard. I had the book, I had what I wanted. And so did he. The cracks in the cell were wide now; I couldn't keep away the memory any longer.

There's a chill in the north wind, though it's still summer. I wrap my arms around myself, avoid the puddles and mud from the previous night's rain. His voice beside me is quiet, almost nervous: *Sarah, I've wanted to speak—* My words cut him off as if I haven't heard. I ask him to tell me more about London, Earl Markham's grand house, the tapestries. He ignores my questions. *You know my father wants me to marry Lady Cecilia, but Sarah ...* We step into the stables, the drop of wind, sudden silence, only horses shifting, muffled by hay. Afraid of this stillness, of being alone, I talk again, too fast, of my embroidery, the work I've finished, silly details of sewing for nobles, a purse, a collar, beginning designs for vestments. I stop at the stall of his favourite black horse and he steps in front of me. I know what he wants to say and I rush on, I'd always thought of Compton, St Catherine's, to take the veil, if my father will agree, the dowry, if ... He touches my cheek, tries again, *Yes, I know, but you need not, Sarah. I want to —* I look down, speak again: But now it's changed. Since my sister died, I've prayed and fasted, waited on God, sought guidance. Now I'm sure that I'm called to be enclosed — and the bishop agrees — as an anchoress, if there's a patron to support me … it's what I've … His hand drops and I look up, run out of words. *Anchoress? That's* … tightness in his voice, a thread pulled, linen puckered. I love God, and I've always, since I was small … So I … that's … I can't find ways to explain. I look around. And is this the new horse? I walk toward it, a pretty pony, fine and grey, too dainty for me. Thomas muttering, moving away, speaking to the stablehand. The pony's eyes large, its head thrown up. I start at the sound of shouting, the slap of skin on skin, the boy falling, his hand to his cheek. And Thomas again, near me, his face raw, as if it were the one that had been slapped.

Enough, I thought. No more. I had the book, a new story; I would not finish mine, the one in the stables.

I loved the story. And I wished I'd never seen it. I wanted a story too much to think about where it had come from, at least at first. I slipped off the soft covering Father Ranaulf had wrapped around it and sat for some time. The dull smell of parchment floated around me, and then the sharpness of ink. I saw a man bending toward the page, the quill in his hand moving back and forward, his head turning to the book nearby to read the next lines, then back again to the words he made, letter by letter. Now it lay still in my hands, and though it wasn't heavy I felt its weight against my skin, and the slight dimpling of the pig's hide. I thought of the stone ledge under my squint, worn smooth and curved as if to fit my body, the ripples of wood grain in my desk, the hard-baked clay of my oil lamp – I had begun to comprehend objects by the way they felt. The few books I had held in my old life had never touched my skin this way.

The first page with its lines of words and, above them, the title, its lettering slightly larger: *Saint Margaret, maiden and martyr,* the capital S largest of all, in red, and coiled around it leaves and flowers as if from a plant, and emerging from inside the bottom curve of the letter a dragon, its tail a sharp point, its mouth wide and lined with teeth. I touched it lightly with a fingertip, felt the slight ridges of ink that reminded me of the roof of my mouth.

I opened the shutters to the maids' room, but I said nothing to Anna and Louise. They would be wondering what had happened with Thomas, and they would hear the story as I read it, but at that moment I wished to be at my desk, alone.

The story was happening in my cell: I could see the sheep in the fields, spots of white against the green, and Margaret nearby, tending them. The pagan sheriff Olibrius rides past on his fine black horse and notices her beauty, the way she shines like the sun, and decides he will have her. He offers her marriage and riches, the honour of his bed, but the faithful maid denies him, declares her love for Christ. At the sheriff's command, soldiers with swords and ugly faces surround her, grab her roughly, bind her, and take her to the city. I could see people coming into the streets to look at the captive, chattering and pointing and sighing at the young girl's beauty. Among the clamour there is one voice, clear and ringing. Margaret doesn't seem to think about her safety; she argues with the sheriff, who snarls as he looks down at her from his horse.

Even after a night in a prison cell, alone among the threat of racks and wheels, of curved and sharpened metal, she denies the sheriff and his vicious bullying. When they drag her into the town square, she becomes even more determined, proclaiming the power of God, who rules the winds and the storms and all that the sun shines upon, to whom everything above and below the earth must submit. And more: she says that Christ is most fragrant and most beautiful to behold. She avows that she has given him her maidenhood and loves him as a lover. All this to the man who threatens to marry her or torture her; it seems that both appeal to him. But Margaret won't believe in his power and she won't believe in his so-called love. She almost asks to be tortured, so that she might be with Christ in heaven.

So they strip her naked, hang her high, beat her with rods, then attack her with flesh-hooks, the kind they use to hold up the carcasses of dead animals. Her skin is soft and tears easily; the blood runs in rivers until even the ghouls who've come to watch can't look anymore. But the torturers know, I suppose, how to keep her alive to suffer more the next day.

I stopped reading. She was a woman just like me, wanting to love Christ above all, though unlike me, she was brave and certain.

I closed the book and wrapped it in its cover: skin on my skin. I had brushed away the feeling of Thomas as I'd pulled my hand back, but it hadn't gone. The presence of a man in front of me, a face so close to mine that I could feel his breath murmur, our lips almost touching. All my time here, all my praying and fasting and reading, and the touch of skin made me feel I had never entered this narrow place at all.

~ RANAULF ~

THE ANCHORESS LISTED HER sins, among them fear, anger, and disobeying her Rule. There was silence for some moments. Ranaulf heard the words but not the voice behind them; instead he studied the intersection of threads in the curtain in front of his face, horizontal and vertical, crossing one another at a multitude of places. He thought of Cuthbert copying interlacing designs, one single line wrapping around itself again and again, circling and looping. He had always admired the way those images showed such ordered complexity; all he could see at this moment was the way a single strand became a knotted tangle allowing no way out. One short tale of a virgin martyr, a chance meeting on the river road, and he had been caught.

He kept his absolution brief and stood to leave without asking Sarah if she had any questions concerning her reading.

'Father Ranaulf, would you stay a moment? I need to speak with you.'

He sighed as if it were a word. 'I must return to the priory, Sister. Can you speak quickly?'

'Father ...' He could hear irony slice that single word. 'Sir Thomas came to visit me a few days ago. He said that you sent him.'

Ranaulf could hear the expectation of an answer and he struggled for words. 'I knew that he would come, though ... it's wrong to say that I asked him to visit you.'

Sarah's voice was light, but her words were pointed. 'Sir Thomas delivered the book that you copied.'

Ranaulf searched for authority. 'Sir Thomas ordered the book to be copied and told me that he would deliver it.'

'Father, you know that I cannot ... that my Rule says ... you yourself say—'

'Enough! You have your book now, the one that I copied for you. But he's your patron and he has the right to—'

'To what? To tease me, to make me open my curtain, to hold my hand? Not even you, not even the bishop—'

Ranaulf winced. 'You let him touch you? Why didn't you close your shutters, tell him to leave, to give the book to your maids?'

The curtain swayed. I did not ask for this; I am a scribe, nothing more, he thought. He pictured his empty desk, the small scriptorium he had begun to inhabit, the silence that sat there with him.

'Because he's my patron. He agrees to support me here.' The voice behind the curtain was louder now. 'You know that it's not my place to say what he can do. He owns this village and this cell. I must be grateful to him and pray for him.' A fleck of anger in her voice. 'But you sent him, you let him come.'

'Sarah, I had no choice. I wanted to ...' His words ran out.

'It was me that had no choice, not you. I am supposed to be safe here, and you let him—'

'None of us is safe,' Ranaulf cut in. His face was red and throbbing, his voice louder than he'd wanted. 'Don't come to God and ask to be safe, Sister. Now say your penance and think about why you want this life. God bless you.'

The door was too swollen to slam so he left it open. He didn't want to meet Louise or, God forbid, Simon. The young maid was walking up from the river carrying a bundle of washing; she had slowed to watch a group of children on the green playing a game, probably marbles. The flex of muscle in her arm where she held the basket, the curve of her neck as she looked across to her right; she seemed less a child. She was smiling as she turned toward the anchorhold but bent her head when she noticed him looking at her. All this was none of his business; it simply wasn't. He was a scribe, that was his duty.

Eleanor was waiting for him under a tree at the side of the road. 'Father Finnegan, you going home now? You been to see Sister?' She ran to him and held on to a fold in his habit, as she always did. She didn't expect an answer. 'Do you like her face? I think she's beautiful, like an angel. Ma says she must be an angel, she's so holy. But Tommy says she's a witch with warts and gooby eyes and she makes spells, she does, and that's what she really looks like when no one can see her. What do you think, Father Finnegan?' She stopped to bend and scratch her leg, still holding his habit with her left hand. As it pulled against his neck, Ranaulf turned, wrenching the cloth free of her hand.

'I'm Father Ranaulf. Now let go.'

Eleanor watched him walk away, through the village and around the bend of the river.

'It's Father Finnegan,' she said as she stamped away, wiping at her face.

❧ SARAH ❧

I LEFT THE BOOK on my desk. Some days I would pick it up, unwrap it, and look at the painting of the dragon, but that was all I would allow myself. *Don't ask God to keep you safe.* Father Ranaulf had visited twice since he'd shouted that, and had said nothing more about it, but I hadn't expected he would. My mind wandered around that day, those few words.

My cell was to keep me safe from men, so what did Father Ranaulf mean? Every time I thought on St Margaret in her prison cell, the answer was there, but I would not look. I would not read.

'Sister Sarah, Louise says today is the feast of St Margaret. Will you read from her story today?' Anna asked as she passed my bucket through the window. 'You've had that book so long, and I wonder about it.'

I looked up. Hair was curling from the edges of her cap, as usual, but her face was pale and thin. For all that, her lips showed red as she spoke. I hadn't noticed before how delicate she seemed.

'We heard you reading the beginning, how she was captured and tortured, and I want to hear what comes next. God saves her, doesn't he?'

'You know he does. Say Prime with Louise and me and then I'll read some more,' I said. 'And Anna, you look pale. Are you sick?'

'Not as is special, Sister. Tired, is all.' She turned away.

'Margaret is thrown back into her cell, barely alive. The soldiers have covered her wounds and her nakedness with a dirty robe, and even though they laugh they must be nervous near this woman who is braver than any man they know. The cell is dark and narrow, the floor cold, and Margaret lies where they drop her. Slowly she stirs; there are voices outside, some scuffling and a sound she recognises, her stepmother's anxious call. The door opens wide enough for a soldier to throw in a flask of water and a chunk of bread, what's left after they've taken their share from the loaf as payment. The water helps her dry throat, though it stings the cuts around her mouth; she isn't hungry, but she tries to swallow a mouthful of moistened bread, mostly to comfort her stepmother.

'After a time the two women pray together — one outside the door, one inside — though the older woman can really only sob. She looks up suddenly as she hears Margaret praying to see her enemy. Doesn't she have enemies enough — soldiers with swords, a vicious sheriff, bloodthirsty townsfolk — without asking for more? By now, onlookers have arrived, curious mostly, craning to see through the bars of the window, to get a sight of this girl, foolish or brave or blessed, or maybe all three.

'It's difficult to tell where it comes from, simply emerging from the darkness in the corner, lumbering forward as if it's always been there, at home among the slime on the walls. A dragon. Its eyes are enormous, glittering as if they're made of gemstones, throwing light that makes its scaly body glimmer in the shadows. As if all the jewels of Sheriff Olibrius have come to attack her, as if this is what his riches really look like.

'Margaret falls to her knees and prays again, this time praising God for creating the world, dividing the waters, putting the sun and moon in the sky, controlling all things. The dragon draws closer, opening its massive mouth, a maw that seems to be bigger than its body, and worst of all it stretches out a long, purple, snakelike tongue. Margaret stumbles to her feet, steps back, but the cell is small and there is nowhere to go. She looks into the open mouth and wonders how it could be any blacker than the cell, but it is. The tongue comes closer, wraps around her feet, and, in one quick swipe, the dragon throws her down its gullet.'

I stopped.

Anna gasped and Louise clucked with concern. We all knew the story, of course, and those words were not the exact ones that Father Ranaulf had copied, but that is how the story felt. It took shape in my cell as I read, the words on the page transforming as in a dream. In the silence we looked at the dragon's mouth and gleaming eyes; we stood as near as Margaret's stepmother.

'The crowd outside the door gasps in horror, takes a breath as if one. No one moves and silence falls. The brave woman has disappeared. Then the sound of tearing flesh and a violent cry of pain cut short. In a moment, before the dragon has even managed to swallow all of her robe — some of it still hangs foolishly from its mouth — the woman bursts through its back, her hands clasped in prayer.'

'But how did she, how could—?' Anna began.

'Sssshhh. Listen, girl,' Louise cut her off.

'And she proclaims, "I am a *kempe*, a hero, a dragon slayer,"' I read. I knew that my timing and expression were as good as anything Swallow could have done and I smiled. I wasn't a jongleur, but who would have thought I could be a storyteller, here in this cell? It was one of the few times Anna asked a question: she had really listened. Stories have a life, I thought, even beyond the man who writes them.

The mystery plays told stories like St Margaret's. I'd seen the dragon in the Harrowing of Hell at Friaston. It was terrifying, even though I knew it was made of wood and straw and paint. There was an entrance to hell, an enormous mouth built on a wagon, rounded like a cave and lined with long, pointy teeth. Flames were painted at the back of the mouth, and above it was a big flattened nose, a bit like the snout of a dog, and two bulging eyes. We could hear Satan cursing from down below. First Jesus came out, proclaiming that he had broken the gates of hell and freed the captives, then one by one people emerged praising God. I didn't notice those who were freed, or even Jesus, who stood by the side of the mouth, calling to the remaining prisoners. And I didn't laugh with everyone else when a prisoner stumbled and broke off one of the teeth. Instead, I watched the darkness inside the mouth and imagined how it would be to go down to hell, into the blackness. It was the place of death and endless pain, but I could feel a pounding in my chest and in my neck, excitement edged with fear, wanting to see it, to know death and then return; to die and be freed. Was that possible, I'd wondered?

I thought of Isabella. Had she burst from this cell like St Margaret? I looked at my door; on the other side were grass and trees and the road — one way leading to the manor, the other way to Leeton and my old life. *Isabella*. It was a word that could never stand still.

⁕

'Sister, can I hear the story about the dragon?' Eleanor visited more than anyone, if she could creep past Louise. She always asked questions, but this was the first time she had asked for a story. 'Anna says you've a story about a dragon that swallows people whole. He's big and shiny and has a long tongue. That story, Sister.'

'The one about St Margaret.'

'Anna says you tell it real well. She says the lord brought the story here, a man as don't come ordinary, not Father Finnegan as comes mostly. I talk to him.'

'Who's Father Finnegan? I don't know him.'

'Yes, you do! The man as comes here in a long robe. He's as tall as the trees.' Eleanor ran her fingers down the weave of the curtain, then poked at it, watching it billow and fall back. I smiled at Father Ranaulf's new name and this little girl who must test his patience. In the silence, the faintest rustling near the roof of my cell.

'Is that a mouse, there in your roof?'

'No, Ellie, that's a bird making a nest. If I look carefully, sometimes I can see the shadow of it flying and landing, tucking in the twigs and flying away again.'

'So one day you'll have baby birds. They might fly around inside for you.'

Another pause.

'I walk to the bridge with him most times.'

'Who?'

'Father Finnegan, like I said. He don't say much and sometimes he's cross. Is he cross with you, too, Sister?'

'I don't know, Ellie. He thinks a lot, you know. And he reads and writes. He writes down books for me. He wrote down the dragon story.'

'In a book? Can I see it, Sister?'

Eleanor was kneeling on the stool and I pushed the curtain back further so she could see. Her brown eyes were bright and sharp with interest. I pulled off the loose cover and lay the book flat on the stone ledge between us so that the words would face her, as if for reading, though she wouldn't know the difference. She stretched out her fingers to touch the page, but I stopped her and her days of gathered dirt.

'You can look but best not to touch. See, what's here at the beginning?'

Eleanor bent to look closer, glanced up at me, back to the page then up at me again.

'That's the dragon, the dragon in the story, isn't it? Look at his mouth, and he's got tiny wings, too, and big claws on his feet. Look how big. And that lady's standing on his back. Is that the story?'

'Well, it's part of it, but these marks tell us what the words are. Look.' I read the first sentence, running my finger above each sound as near as I could. '*In the name of the Father and of the Son and of the Holy Ghost, here begins the life and the passion of St Margaret.* See? All those marks tell us what to say.'

'Did Father Finnegan make it up?'

'No, it's a true story, told by a man who saw it happen. Father copied it from another book.'

'So can you use those marks to say any word? Any word at all? Is my name there?' she asked.

'No, not Eleanor, nor Sarah. But I can show you the letters of your name.'

I showed her a letter *e*, and we looked at its curls. Was this teaching? My Rule told me not to teach children, and this was more than I had done for my maids. But how could I not show a child who asked, whatever my Rule said? I pointed out each of the letters in her name. We turned the pages, looked at the rows of letters lined up straight. Eleanor thought they looked like rows of barley just coming up, before they grow tall with their long, floppy leaves.

'How do you know what to say when you read a word?' she asked.

I knew no other way than to make the sounds of each letter. 'Hold out your hand, palm up, like this,' I said, 'and I'll show you your name.' I closed the book and put it on my desk, and began to make the shape of a letter 'e' on her palm, making its sound at the same time. She stopped me, licked her palm four or five times — wide, full-tongue licks like a mother dog would give a newborn pup — rubbed it hard on her tunic and offered it again. I smiled, but her face was still, eyes waiting. I held her hand flat on mine and carefully traced the shapes onto her palm with my finger, one at a time, saying each sound slowly. It was tiny and thin, her hand, the skin still soft, her fingers fluttering at the new sensation, a little bird between my palms. The feeling of skin on skin, the life of another body so close to mine. Warmth tingled into my arms and up into my chest, the familiar longing. I moved past the different sounds for 'e' in her name, the one in the middle so different and almost swallowed by the 'a' next to it; she didn't notice, though I knew she soon would. She wanted to try herself, so I traced one letter onto her palm and she copied it, then the next, a thin finger spinning and flicking. She was entranced, caught whole into the thought of her name being made of shapes. Bodies and words; I was breathing fast, more excited than I could remember in this cell.

She left, letters in her palm, though I told her not to tell anyone — not her ma, nor Louise, not even Anna, and especially not Father Finnegan; the shapes were to be our secret. What would she do with letters when she worked in the fields or stood over a pot? I tried out the argument in my head. Why should I have letters and not Eleanor? She didn't need to do anything with them; discovering her name, making the shapes of the letters, repeating each sound — it all, somehow, made more of her world.

'The dragon destroyed and split in two, Margaret praises Jesus, the brightest face of all, the blossom that bloomed on a virgin's breast. As she prays, a demon comes crawling to her and clasps her feet in misery, pleading with her to torture it no longer with her prayers. It is ugly and gruesome, its hands bound fast to its gnarled knees. "You are so strong," it says, "that you killed my brother who came to you as a dragon, and now your prayers are killing me. My lady, I beg you, let me go."

'Margaret is not afraid at all. She grabs the grisly thing by its terrible hair, lifts it up, and dashes it to the ground. Her right foot heavy on its neck, she commands it to be quiet. With each word she speaks, she stamps her foot down time and again;

the sound is gruesome, flesh and sinew crushed. Each time she presses harder. "Never strike down Christ's chosen again, you disgusting thing! Your stench makes me sick. I am Christ's lamb and he is my shepherd; I am his slave to do his will. Now tell me who you are."

"'But I cannot speak," the demon wheezes. "Please, loosen your foot from my neck."

'The blessed lady lifts her heel just enough and the demon declares that, after Beelzebub, it is the worst bane of mankind, and has been defeated by no one, until this day. "You are not like other women. You shine brighter than the sun, especially your body that blazes with light, and your fingers with which you blessed yourself and made the mark of the cross."

'But Margaret is wise, aware of its temptations; she demands that it stop flattering her and confess its ways. The demon says its kin live in the sky, their paths on the wind. They are devoured continually with envy of the righteous, especially virgins who have been raised so high. They make war on them, tempting those who fly from the flesh and from sex.

"'My ways are not to attack," it confesses. "Instead, I leave them alone, a man and a woman, let them sit chastely together speaking of God and debating the nature of goodness until they feel secure in being so close. Then, secretly, I shoot poison at them as they look at each other, but they don't discern the danger, because they think their words are safe. Through their eyes I spark in them the flames of lust so that they burn and are blinded with fire until they fall into the foul mire of that dirty sin. The only way to avoid me is to fight the lusts of the flesh with prayer, with eating and drinking simply and never being idle. But you, Margaret, you have overthrown me. I would be shamed if it was through a man, but even more since it is through a girl; you have broken the bonds of your kind by which we had you tied. And now you have defeated me, we are worth nothing at all."

'At last Margaret has had enough of its words and commands it to fly from her sight. The earth parts and swallows the demon as it falls, roaring backwards into hell.'

The story wasn't finished, but that seemed a good place to stop, so I closed the book and we sat quietly, the two maids and I. There was nothing to say. I knew the story of Margaret and the dragon, but I had never before heard of the demon speaking; it was as if the words had been written for me, for a virgin, an anchoress in her cell.

In her nest by the fireplace, Scat looked up at the sudden silence, stretched her legs long, settled her head again in the straw, and went back to sleep.

Some hours later at the time for Compline, Louise and I waited for Anna. Summer was ending and the evening air was chill. Though my cell was dull, as always, some light still glimmered in my horn window.

'That girl, oh, she's slow. She said she were off to collect some herbs, was all.' Louise never had to look far for a reason to chastise Anna. 'I'll go see.'

As she pushed the door shut behind her, I thought of May Day. Louise had tried time and again to tell me that Anna hadn't stayed with her, to demand that I punish her, but I knew I could not. I had traded her disobedience for her gift, the baked apple.

It was some time before Louise returned, grunting with effort. 'I have her, Sister,' she called through the window. 'I found her at Winifred's. She'd been there to gather some of that plant she likes to put in the food, but Winifred saw her fall and managed to get her to the house. White as a goose she was. So I've brought her back to her bed.'

I remembered my own sickness and how Anna had cared for me, making sure I ate, speaking to Lizzie about remedies and infusions.

Later, Louise knocked at the shutter and spoke quietly.

'Sister, there's a thing I must needs tell you. It's important, Sister. A dreadful sin, I must tell.'

'What's wrong, Louise?' I couldn't keep the surprise from my voice — and perhaps a touch of delight at the thought of Louise sinning so badly.

'Oh, it's not me, Sister. It's the girl. I had suspected as much but not being one to gossip, Sister, I kept my silence. But now it seems you must know I was right.'

'Of course, Louise,' I said, with a foreboding twist in my stomach.

'The girl is … well, Sister, the girl is, it seems, with child. Now there.'

*A*NGER, *WHILE IT LASTS, so blinds the heart that it is unable to discern the truth. It is a kind of enchanter, which can transform human nature. Anger is a shape-shifter, as stories tell us, for it strips people of their reason and totally changes their appearance, and transforms them from a human into the likeness of a beast. An angry woman is a she-wolf; though she recites her Hours, Aves, Pater Nosters, she does nothing but howl.*

I slept a dark sleep crowded with faces long and thin, stern and scolding, awoke before the bell for Matins and began to pray. Each time I paused I could hear Louise saying 'with child', and so I prayed on and on, a psalm and then another, until the bell rang for Lauds, then I prayed Prime of the Holy Ghost, Prime of Our Lady, and more psalms, more words to make sure silence never settled. *Though she says her Hours, Aves, Pater Nosters, she is only howling.* Scratching on my ankle, the tear of skin. I stood, stamped at the ground, rubbed at the dirt. Leave me alone, Agnes.

My cell was becoming lighter, my horn window glowing orange, and despite the endless words from my mouth I could hear Louise moving around in her room, her quiet tap on the shutters. I drew a deep breath and held it, tried to let it out slowly. I didn't want to know what was happening behind the shutters, but I opened them enough to allow Louise to speak.

'The girl has slept the night and she's tired, but not too sickly. I thought to get Lizzie, though, and ask for some tea or such.'

'Yes, thank you, Louise.'

'You look pale, Sister. Could I bring you some food?'

'Some water and bread is all.'

I closed the shutters and sank onto my bed and then to the floor. All of this, all my prayers, all my vows, had failed. This was my disgrace. I was meant to have a pure cell, obedient maids. The bishop, Father Ranaulf, Maud, Avice, Lizzie, Winifred, even Jocelyn, the whole village would see my failure. Thomas as well: he had never wanted me to be here; he would smile. The holy anchoress unable to teach her maids, keep them safe. God had called me to this high place and now I was thrown down.

And all because of a silly girl and some boy. Probably behind the church, so close to me, in the dark while I was praying, his hand on the side of her face, sliding into her hair, down onto her breast. Why had I been patient with her, tried to give her time to get used to this life, when all she did was flirt and swive? She'd have to be gone. Reject sin, banish the world, be aware of demons that long to seduce you. Thomas and now Anna; my Rule had warned me and now the Devil was attacking, trying every window to enter and defile me.

Lizzie spoke quietly through the parlour curtain. 'As you know, Sister, the girl is with child.'

'She'll be leaving here. I have a small amount of money. I'll pay for your care, but she cannot stay. I'm an anchoress, enclosed from the world. I can't tend to girls who open their legs for anyone.'

'Sister, she's told me—'

'I don't care who he is. Her rules were clear, that she was to live a clean life. This is no ordinary position, maid to an anchoress. I've looked after her and now I'm disgraced. I've no doubt I'll be thrown out myself. She *cannot* stay. Give her what's needed and find her a bed somewhere.'

'She'll hear you, Sister. Please. You need to listen. She has things to say to you.'

An angry woman is a she-wolf. 'I don't want to hear them.'

'You will, in time. I think she's been taking rue to try to rid herself of the child, but all it's done is make her weak. Today she's too sick to move, that's clear.' Lizzie's voice was sharp. 'She's sleeping now. I'll come back tomorrow and see her again.'

I heard the parlour door pushed shut, and tried to shake the feeling that Lizzie was the wise woman, I the foolish one. But I had no choice: Anna had broken the rules and she would have to go. If there was scandal about Isabella leaving, what kind of scandal would there be about me?

I brushed a few crumbs of bread from my robe. Why did Louise bring me food? As if I could eat now. Only days past the village had celebrated the harvest at Lammas, offering thanksgiving with loaves of bread. Anna had made a loaf in the shape of Scat. It had a large circle for a body, a curling tail, and a smaller circle as a head with broad pointy ears and a raised section in the middle for a nose. It had been her way of upsetting Louise, who thought the offering unsuitable, making a jest of Lammas. I had watched their argument, hiding my smile as Anna, her chin stuck out, one hand on her hip, the other holding the odd-shaped loaf of bread, spoke out. Her face had been pale with a red spot in each cheek, her eyes unusually shiny. I had thought her tired and told her to rest. How she must have laughed at my foolishness.

That night, when I could see the pale glimmer of moon between the strut and thatch in the corner above my desk, I walked to my parlour window. Sleep made no sense. I pulled back my curtain and spoke Isabella's name; such a beautiful name for a disobedient woman. If she would come, she would come. I don't know how long I stood looking into the gloom of the parlour, listening to the wind in the oak tree. That scent I had smelled a few times before: dirt, leaves, a touch of moss. The parlour door was closed, but I was sure she was there.

'Isabella?'

She spoke so quietly I wasn't sure what I heard.

'Isabella, you know they call you a sinner. You took vows and broke them.'

I waited, but there was nothing.

'Why come here if you have nothing to say? Did you leave because it was too hard?'

Quietly, quietly, words floated past me. *Do you think these walls …* I leaned forward to hear. *… keep you in?* Her scent brushed my face. *Fly … out that window … you want …*

She was no longer there. Father Simon had said that thinking of Isabella and her sin would unsettle me and he was right. Had she told me to fly out the window? She laughed at me, like Anna. Now there was no one. Only a she-wolf and her shame.

I closed the shutters and dragged a sack from the chest by my desk, loosened its ties, took out the hairshirt, and dropped it onto the floor. It was the first time I had opened the sack since my enclosure. I was nervous; I had never used a hairshirt, but tonight I deserved its mortification.

The smell of the goat's hair was heavy, smothering, and made me cough. I pulled off my robe and shift, lifted the shirt over my head, and pushed through my right arm, then my left. It scratched my elbows. Stiff and heavy, it fell onto my shoulders and around my hips. I hunched my shoulders to try to keep it off my breasts, then made myself straighten and pulled my robe over my head, made my body accept this penance. I bent to pick up the sack. My skin jumped, twisted, leaped beneath the tiny claws. I had been asleep, dead, smothered, but each tear and cut brought sensation back to me. My belly warmed, my nipples hardened against the goat's hair. I knelt before the crucifix and read from one of my books of devotions.

'Jesus, my honeydrop, my lover, your beauty so marred for love of me. Your wounds, the blood running down your arms, down your white chest, onto your legs, streams of life in which I bathe. I come to your chamber, beloved, I run to you, my knight who gave up all for me. Let me join in your suffering, let these small pains help me to join with you. Take me in your arms, embrace me on your cross, pierce me with nails and let me bleed.'

Christ's body twisted as he hung, his head falling to the left, his knees to the right. Lines of pain were carved into the tightened muscles of his arms and legs, into the sharp slashes that ran from the edges of his forehead toward his nose; they were gouged into the curves of his face, his cheeks sunken like those of a corpse. Below his ribs, the skin fell in a hollow, a smooth and shining crescent cut by an almond-shaped tear that oozed blood. He suffered as Emma had, his skin a deep and swollen pink, straining and bleeding out life.

The candle flickered. The shadow of his body lengthened, wavered against the wall. The wick sputtered and the flame dipped low, almost died. His head turned toward me, he looked into my eyes.

Sarah, you suffer. He smiled sadly and I felt a hand on my head. It slipped down my neck and across my back, his skin on my skin. We embraced, his arms around me, his warmth flowing into my flesh, his lips on my cheek, my neck, my mouth. I had never known such warmth in every part. My soul left its sleep and ran toward him, lifting my body. I arched my back so that we touched, skin upon skin in every place, even into the hollows of his stomach. His love was a pain deep in my belly that I had desired for so long, a pain that I could hardly bear, so sweet was it. I would never leave.

My beloved, he whispered as I swooned.

I woke to the bell. Cold sat like iron in every part of me and I could move only slowly. My side where I had lain was rubbed raw and a wiry thread had dug into the side of my left breast; every movement tore the skin a little more. A chill wind pushed its way through the cracks in the thatch. The scratches and tears on my body ached and bled. How had this nagging pain felt like life?

I remembered the previous winter, when I'd been almost unable to move because of the cold that drained all purpose from me. I had learned since then, and prayer had become so much a part of my life that the words carried me; I looked up at the crucifix and began: 'We adore thee, Christ, and bless thee, because through the holy cross thou hast redeemed the world.' I fell into the words like breathing, carried on their rhythm.

In the stillness I remembered, moment by moment, what had happened in the night. My body had felt so open, as if light could pass through it, as if I myself had shone. I'd heard of very holy women becoming one with Christ, but surely it wasn't like that, so much like the act of a man and a woman? That was what Thomas had wanted. The words I read of Christ as lover and spouse: surely they told of his care, pure and chaste, not of the pleasures of the body?

By the grey light of morning my flesh was heavy and leaden as a clod of clay. I thought of St Margaret in her cell, her skin flayed open, red with blood and weeping flesh. Much as I wanted to follow her in her suffering, and longed to hang with Christ on his cross, I had failed. My Rule had warned me, the demon in the story of St Margaret had warned me, but it was too late.

May Day. The danger of eyes. I had opened the curtain to women and Thomas had looked in. I had peeked out at Father Ranaulf. Through the open curtain the demon had shot his arrows. It had turned even my penance with the hairshirt into pleasures of the flesh.

Only paces away, she lay in her bed, my maid, with child.

I stayed kneeling at my squint after Terce, my elbows resting on the curve of the stone. A cough in the parlour. Father Ranaulf's. I stood and moved to my chair near the window.

'Good morning, Father Ranaulf.'

'Sister Sarah. Good morning.'

Silence sat between us.

'Do you wish to make your confession, Sister?'

And so we proceeded as usual. I confessed my impatience with Louise and Anna and my routine failure to take good care of them, as was my duty.

'And I have sinned, Father, in my heart and my body. I have not treated the image of my Lord with a chaste and humble heart.' I hoped those words would be enough.

'What are you saying, Sister?'

'The crucifix in my cell, Father. I … I felt I needed to subdue my body so I put on my hairshirt and prayed. I knelt before the crucifix as I usually do, and I read from my book of devotions the words of suffering with Christ and loving him, but it seemed that his body was … I felt that my Lord held me in his arms and kissed my neck … as if I were his bride, Father.'

That was all I could say. Whether I made sense or not I could not tell. I heard a cart rolling past, one wheel scraping as if it hadn't been properly fixed onto the axle. I imagined the wobble as it turned. The church door banged shut; Martin on his way out.

'Have you prayed since, Sister?'

'Yes, Father, my usual prayers. And I've read to my maids from my Rule, that's all.'

'Your Rule says that Christ is your spouse who loves you, but do not let that inflame the body. Pray the Hours to our Mother Mary. And the hairshirt … you should not wear it. Keep the flesh in need by fasting, but only for today. Nothing else.'

After the absolution and blessing, I heard the scrape of the stool as he prepared to leave.

'And Father, I wanted to thank you for the Life of St Margaret.' I had thought to make some kind of peace after our argument, and I knew I would soon need to confess my failure with Anna.

'It was my duty to copy it for you, that is all, Sister,' he said. 'I've wondered at the choice of some words in the Life, but it has, I think, some helpful teaching on temptation. I trust it will bring you hope, Sister.' The bump of wood as he stood and moved the stool from the window. 'It's unfortunate that Sir Thomas disturbed you as he did. It was not …'

Did he say more? I couldn't hear, until, 'God bless you, Sarah.'

I smiled at his gentle farewell, but when I turned to my cell, all I could see was my shame.

ANNA'S PALE FACE AND the rings of black around her eyes startled me.

'Anna, are you feeling any better?'

'I'm well enough, Sister, thank you.'

'Good. We must speak of what to do now.'

'Yes, Sister. Lizzie's said, 'n' Louise's said, that you say I have to go.'

'It's only proper, Anna. I can't have you here.'

'Course not, Sister, you as is holy.' She looked at me for the first time.

'I told you, Anna, when you came here from the manor, that you were to obey me and to live a chaste life. And you agreed.'

'Even if I were glad to get away from the manor, who says it was me as decided to come here? Despite her words, her voice was low, even. I do as I'm told, Sister, or I starve. That's how it was. And you decided how I should behave.'

'This is an anchorhold, Anna. Do you understand that I vowed to die to the world? That this is a living death, here, in this cell? The village looks to me for counsel and to pray for them. How can I do that now, how can you stay, if you don't obey me?'

'And who says, Sister, that I didn't? Seems to me as it's easier to be holy locked inside four walls.'

'Anna, the bishop—'

'The bishop? What's the bishop to do with this growing in my belly?'

I'd expected at least an admission of wrongdoing. 'It was you who looked out at the world when the Rule warned you not to.' I paused; my words accused me as much as Anna. 'You let some boy look at you, you let him touch you. You decided that much, Anna, and now you're disgraced. And I will not have your disgrace ruin me as well, though it probably has already.'

'Where should I go, Sister?' Her quiet voice unnerved me.

I had no thought of what to answer. 'Lizzie and Louise can help with that. It's not for me to say. Now I must pray.' I closed the shutter, but my legs gave way as I bent to kneel at my altar.

My prayers recited, I refused to think on what I had said to Anna. I tried to sew, the one thing I knew well. I looked at St Christopher's loving face, the space in his left arm where the child should be. No, I refused to think of that; I would work on the fish, their pale outlines waiting to be filled in with scales and fins and big round eyes. I began with split stitch, looping the thread, passing the needle through the cloth, then using it delicately to splice the strands of thread. Another stitch and I caught my finger with the needle. *What's the bishop to do with this growing in my belly?* I shook my head, looked down again. A bump, the bang of pans from the maids' room. Another stitch, but it was too far from the others. I stood up and walked to the maids' window, called for silence. *It's easier to be holy* ... I was enclosed here to pray, wasn't I, a holy woman? ... *locked inside four walls* ... But I had opened my curtain, looked out.

*

Anna was too unwell to work, I had seen that. And she had no family to take her in. For the next weeks — I have little idea of the time — we three in the anchorhold prayed together, but kept our silent distance otherwise. It seemed to me that we all accused one another, merely with our presence. Louise took over Anna's work, and cared for her as well, behaving with such exaggerated humility, such long-suffering, that I felt unreasonable and demanding. The very sight of Anna accused me, and she would have stayed away from prayers and my anger, but while she remained she would obey me in this, I decided, and join with us. Her face was drained of colour, and her eyes, when she had to look at me, stared as if at nothing.

My dreams, night after night, were of Anna dancing and laughing, her mouth opening and closing like a fish. Sometimes grass, sometimes hay, spread beneath her feet, boys pulling her close, tugging at her dress, and when I looked again it was Emma, then Anna once more, calling to me to join in, dancing, spinning, twirling, wrapping herself in ribbons, winding them around my neck, pulling me in to dance and turn.

In the mornings I woke, my face burning, my blankets wrapped tight around me. I knelt at my altar and prayed my Hours, then prayed them again; I would fill the day with prayer, fill every space in my cell with prayer and give the demons no place to creep in.

The scrape of the door, a clatter.

'Sister Sarah, can I look at some letters? And you still haven't told me the story of the dragon.'

'Eleanor, did you ask Louise if you could come in?'

'I crept past. She's too busy to see,' she whispered.

'You must speak to Louise, Eleanor. You can't come in without asking.'

'But I do, all the time.'

'And I pray in here, all the time. It's only sometimes you can talk to me. I'm not here to talk to whenever you feel like it.'

'But God is, and Ma says you're holy like an angel, so you must be too.'

'Eleanor, go away.'

'Are there eggs in the nest, Sister? Can you see them?'

She began to pull back the curtain and I wrenched the cloth from her hands. 'Eleanor!'

'Are you cross 'cause Anna's sick, Sister?'

'Leave me alone. Go.'

I banished everyone I could, even Agnes, so that I could pray. But at night, when they slept, the silence was hollow and I thought of Isabella. They said she'd chosen to leave, a sinner. Or had they made her?

'Isabella?' I tried into the silence. A rustle behind my curtain, moss against my face. She walked into my cell and stood beside me.

'Why did you leave? Were you disgraced?' I could hear my voice gossiping, prattling, but I had to speak. 'The bishop will make me leave, he'll tell me I'm disobedient, the women will shake their heads at me, *foolish woman*, the men will laugh, *whore*. I've told Anna she has to leave. I have no choice. You know what I mean; I'm an anchoress, I have my vows, I've left my old life, shut out the world, vowed to be Christ's alone. My Rule says ...'

A breeze blew past my face, made me pause. *I learned how to love.* I leaned forward to catch her words. *That's why I left.*

A flick of the curtain and she was gone.

The next morning, my Rule was still on my desk, the letters neat, the words straight.

> *Consider no vision that you see, either dreaming or waking, to be anything other than delusion, for it is only the Devil's guile. He has often deceived wise men of holy and high life in just this way, like the one he came to in the likeness of a woman in the wilderness, a wretched thing looking for shelter, or in the likeness of an angel who began by telling the truth, only to deceive him cruelly into sin in the end.*

I had thought the walls were made of stone, that they would seal me from the world. But they fade and crumble. How was I to tell what was delusion?

❧ RANAULF ❧

A THICK LAYER OF cloud had settled over the sun. Ranaulf stopped just after the bridge and looked around, the river and the green to his left, the church and the scattering of houses behind it, fields and more houses to his right, roofs this way and that, smoke from the smithy. He was sweating from the walk, and a sudden autumn wind made him shiver. He folded his arms and kept walking. A figure waved to him from the riverbank; it was that odd little girl, helping a woman to carry rushes. He nodded to her and smiled, though she could probably see neither.

The door to the maids' room was closed and he continued to the parlour door, knocked, and pulled it open. He coughed, his usual signal of arrival.

'Good morning, Sister Sarah.'

Some rustling and her quiet greeting.

'You wish to make your confession?'

'I do, Father, but before that I need to tell you something.'

Her voice made him think of Alain's mead, its amber light.

'Father, as you know, I've tried to obey my Rule. I've prayed my Hours, and read only books suitable for an anchoress. I've prayed for Sir Thomas and for the soul of Sir Geoffrey, and for the people of the village. Some of the women come to see me and I give them counsel and pray for them, and sometimes we chat a little about their work, but no gossip, Father. I've taught my maids and read to them and prayed with them each day. I've kept a cat, but only with Father Peter's permission. Oh, and I've spoken to a young girl, Eleanor, but—'

'Yes, Sister, I know you keep your Rule.' Ranaulf frowned; a tiny worm curled in his belly. Why was she saying this?

'I have to tell you, Father, that even so I have failed in my duty to my maids. One of them, the younger one, Anna, she has … she is with child.'

The worm bit. 'Your maid? With child?'

Silence hung between them.

'How could you let this happen? Sister, she's in your charge.'

'Father, I spoke to her. I—'

'You spoke to her? She's with child and you say you spoke to her?'

'I told her how important it is to live rightly. I warned her not to look at the men in the village, but to do her jobs quickly and come back again.'

'Then you failed.' He paused, let the words do their work. 'If she's the younger one, why did you let her go out into the village? Your Rule says that the younger one must stay inside and the older maid be sent out when needed.'

'Yes, Father, I know what the Rule says. But Father Simon said that Anna was the one to go into the village and that Louise, being too old for such work and a prayerful woman, should stay inside to pray and read. Father, I thought you knew. You come here often and you see the maids: Louise is always here, she is the one who speaks to my visitors, to you.'

Were they tears he could hear, or anger? He would bear neither. He thought back: yes, it was Louise with that strange clucking noise she made with her tongue and her hands making fists across her fat belly. She was the one who watched him arrive or spoke to him, mostly of Father Peter and his health, implying (he could tell by the tone of her voice) that Ranaulf was too young for this duty he'd never asked for. And the other, Anna, he'd seen her once or twice coming up from the river or walking through the village.

A sniff from behind the curtain.

His face was throbbing. 'You've told her to leave, of course.'

'She's unwell, Father, and needs to be tended. There's nowhere in the village she can go. The women must help Avice now that her husband, Sam, has died and —'

'Unwell? The foolish girl got herself into this and she cannot stay. That must be clear to you.'

'It is clear to me, Father, and I've told her she must leave. But have you seen her? How thin her face is? The healer tells me she can't do heavy work and there's nowhere, as I said, so I've agreed that she can stay until—'

'It's not for you to help her. She must leave.' Ranaulf wanted to walk away.

'Why am I not to help?' Her voice was loud. 'Am I too holy, shut away here, to help? I'm part of this village, however thick they've made these walls. Father Ranaulf, when I first came here, a leper took shelter in the church on All Hallows Eve. He was starving, and asked for food or some money, but I told him no, it wasn't for me to help. I was sure then that I was right, that my Rule told me to stay away from the world. But later that night I heard the young boy Martin, Father Simon's assistant, give him his own robe for a blanket … and I wouldn't even give him the food I didn't want. Anna was sent here, she didn't ask to come, and we tell her she must be holy, then we send her away when … when she …' The words broke like a smashed pot. He could hear her choking breath. Her voice came thin through the curtain. 'It was you who told me not to expect God to keep me safe.'

Ranaulf looked at the door, then up to the ceiling, anywhere but the curtain and its accusation.

'I wish to make my confession, Father.' Her voice was quiet and composed now.

Ranaulf breathed out quietly. 'You may begin, Sister.'

He pushed the door shut, wishing he had never said the words. *Don't come to God and ask to be safe.* He had wanted only to defend himself against Sarah's accusations about Sir Thomas's delivery of the book; had plucked them from the past, quoting Abbot Wulfrum. *The love of words is a gift from God, but they can cut you open, too. The work of a scribe is still and quiet, like prayer, but the words you copy are not. Remember that. Don't think that God is safe.* Now she was quoting them back to him and he had to listen.

The door to the maids' room was open and he could see Louise inside, and another woman, probably the healer, bending over a bed. He had seen Anna a few times, the sway of her back, the line of an arm cradling a basket, a twist of black hair. What more was hidden? Places a boy had known, discovered?

A maid with child. He would have to answer to the prior, then to the dean, and then to the bishop, no doubt. The anchoress was devout and intelligent, he knew that; her faith and her mind were strong. But that other, the flesh that St Paul spoke of, the wayward body, how was he to answer for that?

He visited the anchoress, he heard her confession, he absolved her and gave her penance, and he prayed for her. What else could he do? These women had their own lives. As much as they were taught, were given rules for life, books, instruction, there was always something in them that couldn't be touched.

'Father Finnegan, here I am.' The little girl was running up from the houses.

'Ma says I can say hello and not be long about it. It's my job to gather up the old smelly rushes and carry them out to the croft. You been to see the Sister? She's been a bit cross lately. Was she cross with you, Father? She told me to go away. Ma says it's 'cause of Anna having a baby. Ma thinks that's sad, but I like 'em. Mostly.' She jumped side to side as she walked, from the road to the grass and back. 'I told Anna I'd look after her baby so she can pray, but she said she can't stay with Sister. I think that's mean ... Do you like babies, Father Finnegan? Oh, that's Ma yelling now ... Bye, Father.'

Ranaulf raised his hand in farewell. At least the girl didn't expect answers. Ellen, wasn't it?

❦ SARAH ❧

I KNELT AT MY squint, ran my hands across the stone, smooth
and warm. Dust floated in a thin beam of sunlight that cut
across the slice of church floor that I could see: tiny birds,
gold and white, shining and bending. How had it happened?
I wanted Anna gone, away from me. I had been sure that was
right, but Father Ranaulf's anger had made me defend her. Had
I resisted his words for argument's sake or did I truly believe
Anna should stay?

Father Simon's voice at the altar interrupted my thoughts:
Sam's funeral. Whatever happened in the church caught me in
my cell. In the thatch above me, baby birds had begun breaking
through their shells and squawking endlessly for food. I listened,
hoping they would block out the groaning and crying, but
it wound its way through my squint and around my heart,
burrowing deep. My mother and then Emma. The church had
been different but the crying was the same.

Outside in the graveyard there would be more prayers and
tears, the dirt would be shovelled back into the dark hole,
the mound patted down, a scar marking the green for a time.
Though I couldn't be near her, I prayed for Avice, for her

children, asking Mary to bring solace in the emptiness of grief they would carry.

When Louise knocked on the shutters to tell me Maud had come to see me, I startled, felt nervous. What would she say about Anna, and what had others been saying about me?

'Poor Avice. She sat there today, past crying, too tired for more than surviving,' Maud said. I already new her days were long. She fed the children, mixed dough for bread when baby Warin was asleep, tended the vegetables and herbs in the croft behind their house, checked the apples and pears and headed to the fields to help harvest the peas and cut the corn stubble. Christina, her eldest, washed the pots and bowls, fed the chickens and the pig, and looked to the little ones.

'She pays some boys to help her in the fields, but with winter coming on she's to get everything ready, gathering and storing, and then there's the final ploughing of what's to be left fallow. So I said to her as some of us, Winifred and Jocelyn and Madge, oh, and a few others, we'll get some extra bracken for her animals' bedding, nuts from the forest, and the men can get peat and wood, help with the ploughing. My Bill said he'd get some sedge and repair her thatch, though I don't know when.'

I sat behind my curtain, shamed, as I slowly understood that Maud was anxious only for Avice and how she would manage. I had told Father Ranaulf I was part of the village, but as Maud spoke, my concerns seemed still as narrow as my cell.

'And then she has to think about the manor court next week and what the steward'll do about Sam's land now. She's thinking as she'll lease most of it, but first she has to settle inheritance with Gwylim and the court.' She paused, sighed. 'Oh, 'scuse my long story, Sister. I know you'll be praying for Avice, but it does me good to talk to you, even as I don't go in for lots of church. Bless you, Sister.'

She left as she came, pushing quickly through the door. For her, there was no question that she'd help Avice, gathering and digging. The dirt of the fields, of the forest, was the same, I supposed, as the dirt that my Rule told me to dig each day for my grave. I looked at my fingernails; they were speckled with white, but they were clean.

I kept my shutters closed, to both the parlour and the maids' room, and prayed and read.

> *Hold yourself fast within. Not just the body only, but your five senses and above all the heart, and everything where the life of the soul resides. For if the soul is trapped outside, she must be led forth toward the gallows; that is, the punishment tree of hell.*

Father Ranaulf visited as usual, and we spoke as if I had not told him of Anna's baby. The scratch on my left ankle was deep, bleeding, but Agnes said nothing. It was almost a year since I had arrived, and everything I had understood about my time in my cell was shifting, every certainty unravelling, the edge of every rule blurring. From the maids' room came sounds of talking; sometimes I heard Lizzie's voice. They laughed together, even Louise. How easy it was for them, leaving me with the burden and the shame. My mouth was dry with bitterness.

At the end of September, the church was full for the celebration of St Michael the Archangel. The smell that floated through my squint was a mixture of soil and the sweetness of dried bracken and herbs that everyone carried in on their clothing. Father Simon had announced that Michaelmas was a Day of Obligation, and though I could hear some grumbling I knew that most of the congregation would have attended Mass anyway. I was beginning to appreciate how much Michaelmas mattered to everyone: the harvest was all but finished and business would be transacted. Gwylim would come to Hartham to hold a manor court: rents and fines for the year had to be paid to Sir Thomas, servants would be hired and decisions made about village office bearers. And this year there were rumours, fears about Sir Thomas's plans for the common land.

Two days later when the men gathered in the church for manor court the mood was heavy, wary. Words were coloured grey and brown and black, with quick touches of red. Gradually, I recognised the men's voices from what their wives had told me about them. I knew that Avice was there as well, though I thought she wouldn't speak until it was time for her case to be heard.

I heard Jocelyn's Hugh ask, 'Where be Sir Thomas? Won't he come and speak with us? Explain his plans?'

'You mind what you say, Hugh Davidson.' Gwylim's voice was hard. 'You haven't paid that fine for your ox yet, don't think I've forgotten. You know very well Sir Thomas be at Friaston, but he's coming in a day or two to inspect his land. See then if you'll be making demands of him. Be so brave as to challenge him then, will you?'

I eventually stopped listening to the detail of names and fines, the arguments about customs of the manor dating back before

Sir Geoffrey's time. But I could hear Winifred's Roger, almost as loud as his wife; Ellie's father, Osbert, easily angered; Maud's Bill trying to calm him down; and, above it all, Gwylim's voice, heavy like a club, but quick with threat when he was questioned.

I remembered him from the edges of my old life, the few times I had visited Friaston Manor: brown-red hair and big hands, abrupt, busy with his work, taking no notice of me. Why should he? He knew Thomas's interest in me would come to nothing; Sir Geoffrey was too good a man of business to allow otherwise. His loan to my father was already a risk, one ship at the bottom of the sea, and no doubt Gwylim would have pointed that out, but the lord had loved fine clothes and for once he had let his vanity overrule his hard head. But as for his son marrying a cloth merchant's daughter? I imagined Sir Geoffrey and Gwylim would have laughed over the account books at that idea. And perhaps I would have laughed with them, if I'd been asked what I thought.

In the church, Gwylim was shouting above the angry muttering. '... if you'll listen to me I'll say't again, more slowly if you be so dim-witted. Income from this estate is down this year. Especially from the mill. I know there are handmills in your houses that you use for grinding wheat. If you've forgotten the law, let me remind you.' He spoke slowly, as if to dullards. 'All grinding must be done at Sir Thomas's mill and nowhere else. Those fees for grinding are due to him as lord. Not difficult to remember, is it? And because you seem to forget your dues, Sir Thomas has decided that all handmills will be collected and taken to the manor. Tell your women when you get home. Be sure I'll check every house and find every handmill.'

'How's a man to feed his family and pay them fees, Reeve? When Sir Thomas's crops are down, so are ours.' It was Roger, indignant.

'Work the land better. You need me to teach you how to farm, boys?' Gwylim's voice was thick with scorn.

The uproar was frightening, even muffled by the stone wall in front of me.

Eventually Gwylim cut in, roaring over them all. 'And I'll be pacing out the new border of the common land. Sir Thomas will add to his flock next market and he needs more pasture for the sheep. You know the fines for trespass so mind your animals and keep them outside the new border.'

This was what Maud had told me about. Many of the villagers relied on the strong price of wool to add to their income, but their stock needed land for grazing. My face was hot; I wasn't the only one that Thomas forced to his will.

'You can't do that. It ain't lawful,' Hugh yelled.

'Not for you to say what Sir Thomas can do, Davidson. You should be grateful you have a place at all.'

I winced; had I not wanted to say the same thing to Anna?

Three days later, Sir Thomas came to inspect his property.

'Sister Sarah.' His voice came in my window and flew out, then back in again.

My skin prickled and I could feel a flush in my neck. The door being dragged shut, the stool thrown aside, the fruity smell of wine. As I stood, I knocked my Rule from my desk. Should I try to close my shutters? But he was there, at the window.

'I want to see you. Don't be angry with that old cow outside. I sent her away.' Then, in a whisper: 'No, I'll tell you a secret. Father Simon asked her to visit him because I told him I wanted to see you … good Father Simon. And the young girl won't disturb us. I've been reading the accounts with Gwylim, but he's so dull, I came to visit you, my lovely Sarah. But you sit here in the dark, just your crucifix 'n' candle, like always.' His voice was slurred.

I looked toward Christ, his arms stretched out above my altar, only eight paces away, and whispered a prayer for protection — though nothing had protected me the last time. My cell lengthened, the walls shifted away from me, farther than the road to the bridge, the road to Leeton. Christ flew from me, so far that I could barely see the shape of the cross.

'You know there are flowers outside your parlour, Sarah? No, you can't see them, won't see them ever again. Did your maid plant them for you? The sweet one, I mean. *Anna.*' I turned to the window. 'How is she, Sarah? She won't come out of her room to talk to me. Ravishing. The flowers, I mean …' A snigger. 'I told her she should be more friendly, women should be more …'

A chill crept into my chest. I moved back to my fireplace, away from the swaying curtains, away from the words. What had this man to do with Anna? No noise from the parlour; I wondered if he had fallen in a drunken stupor. Arms by my side, palms flat, I moved my hands against the stone until my grazed skin told me the wall was really there. I licked the blood from my right hand, tasted metal, felt grit grind between my teeth.

A mumble and some stumbling. 'Sarah, you know my wife, the lovely Lady Cecilia. She should be more friendly … but no, hard earth, she is. Night after night I plough in my seed, but

nothing'll grow in that ground. My lady's like this village. Good
only for pasture ...

'Sarah, are you there? Has my little holy bird flown the coop?
You don't say much, Sarah, and I need you to talk to me. I do.
I need ...'

A grunt and then silence. I sank to the floor and pulled my
knees up to my chest. *The sweet one, Anna.* I could bear him
breaking the seal of my walls, but not this. I don't know how long
we stayed like that: Thomas asleep in the parlour, me huddled
in the dead fireplace, before Louise returned. She clucked and
tutted, then called for some men to carry Thomas back to the
manor; I could hear their muffled laughter and whisperings as
they bore him, insensible, away.

❧ RANAULF ❧

FATHER PETER LOOKED LIKE he was sinking into the bed, as if his body were slowly becoming part of the pallet; his voice was thinner, though it was still quick.

'Ah, my brother scribe, so good to see you. You've brought something for me to read?'

'Father, no, forgive me. I come to ask your counsel.'

Ranaulf had resolved to be frank about the maid being with child, but Peter's questions, seemingly innocent, searched out the things he had hoped to step around: his failure to notice that the young girl was the one who went out into the village and his failure to provide guidance to the anchoress on the duties and habits of her maids. He felt his face becoming warm.

'I was uneasy when the young girl arrived, the arrangements the manor made,' Peter said. 'I spoke to Sister Sarah, but I should have talked with you as well, Father. We all bear some of the burden of this. And where is the maid now?'

'She's ill, and no one to care for her but Louise, so she remains in the anchorhold.'

Peter was still for some moments. 'I've never heard of it, a woman with child in the cell of an anchoress. She can't remain, but we must care for her until she finds a suitable place. Yes, I think that's right. Our Lord was born in a cave, they say, when no one would take in his mother. Do you think, brother scribe, that Bishop Michael will see the connection?'

Ranaulf's face flamed. The stool by the bed was so low that his knees were near his chin; he felt like a chastened novice. 'No, I'm sure he won't.' He knew he would have to answer again and again: how it happened, how he had allowed it to happen.

'And her patron, Sir Thomas ... I can't remember whether the corrody mentioned appropriate behaviour as a condition, but after Isabella, I imagine it—'

'Isabella? You mentioned her once before. You said she left the anchorhold.' Ranaulf leaned forward.

'Yes, her name lingers around the village like some spirit. Sister Isabella was a widow — young, no children. She professed as a Carmelite at Challingford, then became an anchoress. Nothing strange in that, all approved by the bishop. Father Simon was her confessor, Sir Geoffrey her patron. I was at Westmore at the time, but I've heard a few words spoken of her here and there. She had been enclosed a few years, five it may be, and then asked to be released from her vows. She spoke to Father Simon then the bishop and they finally agreed, with warnings, of course. Well, condemnations, really — about her inconstancy and causing grief to God and the Church.'

Ranaulf had been staring at an undarned hole in Peter's blanket and looked up as a silence descended; perhaps the old man had fallen asleep.

But Peter was looking at him, his eyes watery. 'It's an extreme life, brother scribe, isn't it? Harder than I could endure. At the time I was inclined to agree with the bishop's displeasure with Isabella, but now I'm more sympathetic to her decision to leave.' Peter coughed, lapsed into contemplation.

Ranaulf thought of the voice behind the curtain: tears, anger, contrition, the sharp prickle of her questioning mind, the despair he turned away from. 'Why would Sir Geoffrey agree to another recluse, after such a failure?'

Peter turned his head again. 'I wondered that myself when I heard the story. But it's Prior Walter's duty to obey Abbot Wulfrum and to be a steward of God's provisions; to build the priory to God's glory, as he says. So we need an income, and the prior, as you know, can be persuasive. Death hovers around us all, but especially those of us who are old: me, Sir Geoffrey ... he knew he wasn't well. Perhaps the urgency to prepare for death, to think of his soul, to have someone to pray for him each day was compelling.' He began to wheeze.

'I should leave you,' Ranaulf said, but stayed on his stool, the early morning light kneading some softness into the cold air, the only sounds Peter's straining breath and a shout or two from the men working outside. Ranaulf had heard of Sir Geoffrey's stern ways when it came to money and land, but even powerful, wealthy men — perhaps those men more than others — worried about what they couldn't see or touch, especially when death began to stalk them. They wouldn't hesitate to lavish money on a patronage if it bought them a little reassurance in matters of the soul. A holy woman to pray for them, before and after death, would be a comfort, and some no doubt even thought of it as insurance.

'Besides,' Peter spoke again, 'this time Sir Geoffrey had less involvement. You know all this, of course. The corrody makes the anchoress entirely our responsibility: food, wood, spiritual care. Sir Geoffrey was still Sister Sarah's patron, but from a distance. And now, of course, Sir Thomas. If anything goes wrong, the land the priory received reverts to him. Sir Geoffrey no doubt felt it was worth it, for the sake of his soul. And maybe, who can say, he saw the patronage of a new anchoress as penance for the manner of Sister Isabella's departure.'

'But wasn't it her decision to leave? No cause to blame the lord?'

'Her decision was her own. I hear that she decided she was unsuited to the life. It was the manner of the unsealing of her cell that caused concern. There are stories.' Peter hesitated. 'The village loved her, but there's talk of anger, even violence as she left. Who knows what happened.'

Ranaulf straightened on the tiny stool and peered at Peter. 'Violence? Towards an anchoress?'

'Apparently. Talk of what had happened was whispered widely in the village until the bishop came and threatened. Not exactly threatened, of course: he mentioned the shame such gossip would bring to Isabella and to the village. Words can bind us just as much as they can free us. They won't talk now, in the village.'

'Violence?' Ranaulf repeated. 'But who?'

'Not Sir Geoffrey, I'm sure.' He looked intently at Ranaulf. 'Our Mother Church protects us and her bishops keep order, but her anger is severe. You must be wise in this, Father Ranaulf. Walk carefully for the sake of our sister ... and the young maid.'

The sun had reached the cloister garden, a bright block at one end. Brother Ambrose was on his knees in the shade, tending to some herb or another, his nose almost touching the ground. Ranaulf stepped past him and pushed open the door to the scriptorium.

'Father Ranaulf.' Cuthbert greeted him but didn't look up, brush in hand, peering at whatever he was painting.

'Mmm,' Ranaulf responded. He moved to the shelves lining the long wall opposite the windows and lifted down a bundle wrapped in parchment. Not many pages yet, this chronicle of the priory: the Life of St Christopher, the dates of the first buildings, the charters of acquisition. The corrody between the prior and Sir Geoffrey for the spiritual support of the Hartham anchoress was there, he had copied it himself. He scanned the lines:

> ... to appoint a monk chaplain of a chaste way of life from the said Priory of Cramford, who will provide spiritual sustenance for said recluse, Sarah of Hartham, and her successor recluses. The said chaplain will likewise ensure that Mass is sung in the church of St Juliana, Hartham, to which the anchorhold is adjoined, for Sir Geoffrey of Friaston, his ancestors and his heirs for ever in perpetuity, to wit, in the absence of the vicar of Hartham, the said chaplain will sing Mass in the church of St Juliana ...

Here it was, farther down:

> ... and will ensure by such godly support and discipline that the said recluse will live a godly and constant life ...

Ranaulf let the pages fall closed. Who would be held accountable before the bishop for the maid's sin? He ran through the arguments: that a confessor's responsibility was to the recluse alone, that he could not be held responsible for the actions of a maid in the service of the anchoress. That seemed clear to him. But the other case was insistent: it argued that the confessor had failed in his duty to ensure the anchoress was sufficiently well taught so that she would be able to guide her maids in a holy way of life, one of her most sacred responsibilities.

He refolded the bundle and turned to his desk. On and on the two sides argued: one to his left, one to his right, hands clasped, fingers pointing, eyes to heaven, eyes sharp and accusing, legal and godly language intertwined. He was responsible, and guilty; no, he wasn't; yes, he was; but no … They followed him to Mass, and it was only when he closed his eyes that they sank into silence and he could think beyond them: what would happen to Sister Sarah? And the maid?

Prior Walter had almost no eyebrows, Ranaulf noticed. Were they very pale or simply not there at all? Strange that he hadn't seen it before. Perhaps it was simply that the wispy crescents above his eyes could be raised no higher.

'Did you think that the baby could stay in the anchorhold? A happy family?'

It would be foolish to answer, but it seemed that the prior expected something. Ranaulf willed away the flush creeping up his neck.

'Do you comprehend, Father, what this means for the priory? Our lands? If the anchoress leaves, we lose land — not only farmland, but the pasture. Where would we graze the sheep? And the woodland, we would lose all that we need for building here. Then there's the rent from the farms, the produce. And the bishop. You know how he values recluses in his diocese, how the king encourages them, the status it gives us … or gave us.'

Ranaulf had anticipated everything the prior would say, had rehearsed some responses, but knew that they would only fuel the prior's indignation. He focused on the prior's mouth, the quiver of its anger. He let the throbbing redness of his face answer for him.

'Books are all very well, and the scriptorium is what the abbot wants, but you must attend to other matters, Father. That maid, she has to go. Make sure it happens. Tell the villagers, or ask Father Simon to tell the villagers they must not speak of this. What good that will do I don't know. Use some words of scripture, something about gossip, and tell them they must defend the honour of the anchoress and, above all, of Mother Church.' The prior concluded with a sigh and walked out.

'What was that about?' Cuthbert looked up from where he had been dabbing for some time at one fold in the blue robe of the Virgin Mary, his brush dry of paint.

'The anchoress of Hartham. You must know by now. Her maid is to have a baby.'

'Oh, that, yes, a matter important enough to upset the king, the way the prior was talking.'

'The anchoress has failed to teach her maid, but she's a faithful woman. I would help her, if I could.'

'No doubt. The villagers say she's holy and they're glad to have an anchoress again, after Sister Isabella left the way she did.'

'Isabella? Have you been talking to the villagers about her? What do they say?' Ranaulf took a step towards him.

'Not much. Only Aylwyn, one day when he'd been at the tavern too long, started to tell a tale about Isabella and the bishop, said he heard something in the anchorhold.'

'Aylwyn? Who's Aylwyn? What did he hear?' Ranaulf moved closer to Cuthbert.

'Aylwyn, the stonemason from Hartham. You must know him, Father. He's here most days working. He said that the bishop told the villagers it would be a sin and would bring shame to the village to talk about it, but then Aylwyn had laughed, an angry laugh, and said that Sir Geoffrey had cut closer to the bone. He warned them to forget it all, if they wanted to keep their land. But it was some years ago now, and you a priest and able to absolve him, Aylwyn might speak.' He paused, looked down at his work. 'Nearly done. What do you think?'

Ranaulf looked closely at the page and gasped. In the top left corner was a painting of the Virgin Mary set inside the curve of a large capital *T*, her hand raised in blessing, her face gentle. Ranaulf wondered how, with only a few marks, Cuthbert had shown mercy and compassion.

'This is truly beautiful, Brother Cuthbert.' Ranaulf sighed.

And there, in the bottom right corner, sitting inside the curl of a leaf, was a creature with a human head, tonsured, but no body, only two legs and two arms sprouting from where his neck should be. He was reading a manuscript.

Ranaulf smiled. 'Couldn't resist, Brother?'

'Well … just think of it as Prior Walter,' Cuthbert whispered.

～ SARAH ～

'I CAN FEEL IT moving. Just here, Louise. Look, you can even see it, that bump there, like a small turnip; that must be a foot, or maybe a knee.'

'Yes, girl, I see it there. I remember how my skin was stretched with Wymer, he was such a big baby, always kicking, he was. And a long birth. So long. Oh, but that baby ain't big, she'll be born just like that. You'll see.'

'A girl? Do you think so?'

'If ever I saw one, that's a girl there. Look how your belly sits so neat.'

I looked toward the maids' window. I wanted to be able to join in. Anna was excited now, but I could feel only dread. It seemed that the past was gathering. Thomas had returned to Friaston, but his words clung to the stones. *The sweet one, Anna.*

Threat hung in the air, dark words and angry muttering about the changes Gwylim had announced. Maud told me that before his departure Thomas had stepped out the land with Gwylim, pointing to virgates and houses near the pastures. And Father Simon added to the mood. He rarely gave any kind of sermon, except on days of celebration, but the previous Sunday he had preached long and loudly on the sin of lust and the punishment to be paid for a few moments of sinful pleasure. There was general coughing and murmuring and Winifred even laughed out loud, setting others tittering in spite of their anger. Everyone knew how much Martha visited the rectory; Father Simon was not his own exemplum. The week before, his sermon had railed against the sin of gossip.

'We in this parish have been blessed by God. We have a holy history. Sister Agnes and her venerable bones continue to guide us. If at times we fall from our high calling, that is not a matter for gossip. You have been warned once before about the dangers of idle talk and slander, the Devil's tools, and you have mostly obeyed our lord bishop's exhortation to silence. Be sure that now, also, you mind his words.'

Anna remained. My anger was so caught around with the quiet challenges from Maud and the other women, I'd said nothing more about her leaving, though I hadn't decided she could stay. When she was strong enough she did some of the cooking, or told Louise which herbs to add to the meals, though she ate little herself.

'Louise, thyme is good for pottage. You have to try it. And if you let it be, as is growing outside the door, there be plenty.'

'It smells so strong, though,' Louise argued.

'That's why it's good for dull vegetables, or for meat as is old and rancid. And some rosemary, too.'

Lizzie visited her often and brought herbs for her tea. I kept the shutters closed but I could tell that Anna was asking questions.

'That girl learns quickly, she does.' Lizzie had asked to see me. 'She could make a healer herself when she's able. Each time

I come she asks more, and she remembers what I've told her. She thinks ahead to her next question, and that's what makes a good healer. Always asking questions.'

I said nothing.

Lizzie sighed loudly. 'So, to my way of thinking, Sister, Anna's still sickly. I've given her marshmallow to make tea with, to help her digestion, and she must be eating egg yolk, and only the innards of young fowl or fish.'

'Lizzie, you must tell Louise, not me.'

'Yes, Sister, but you look to her care, so you must know too. If she can't digest her food, her blood to feed the baby will be too rough. You know Ellie, poor child, the one that likes to talk to the Father who visits you. She has, if you look on her face, and all the way across her chest, the marks of blood on her. 'Twas her mother, Madge, took scant care when she was with child and that's what happened to the mite: stained with Madge's blood, the blood of her flowers like, that feeds the baby when it's inside the mother. Marjory from Friaston, she's a healer there, said a monk told her that's what happens, and he'd read it in a book. And I told Madge not to eat spices or salt, and to rest some more so her blood would be warm and pure, but she had others to look to, didn't she, one still not walking, and Osbert as was always out in the fields or looking to his sheep. Not much chance to rest.'

'Yes, Lizzie. I know Anna must take care.' I shouldn't have allowed these conversations, but somehow she talked on and on, determined to give me all her learning and advice. I studied the weave in my curtain, retreated into memory. Emma had been more than well, happy and even livelier than usual, so glad to be with child, though she rested because she knew she must. *That there's a boy*, women had said to her. *Look at that colour in your face and that shape in your belly; bound to be a boy.*

Lizzie was still talking. 'Now Sister, we can get a man I know of in Friaston to write out some words as I can put into an amulet. Though it will need to be paid for; it's not as if he'll make the charm for free.'

'Amulet, Lizzie? What are you saying? What amulet?'

'Just some words, Sister, as I say, special ones, written on parchment and then folded up, so that Anna could wear it and it would help make her and the baby well.'

'I know what an amulet is, Lizzie. But why are you talking about getting one? It's not your place to be using magic.'

'It's not bad magic, Sister. Course not. But there's words that can change a body, just like some other things can, stones and herbs and such, even doctors say that. They're special words, not just any, like I said. That's good magic, it is. I've used it before, just like I use herbs and ointments. That's my trade, Sister.' Her words were tapping their feet.

'Yes, herbs and ointments, Lizzie. That's medicine. But if you don't know what this man is writing, how do you know he's not calling down demons?'

'Well, Sister, Reggie — that's the man who writes them — he knows about writing special words same way as I know about herbs. You don't always know what I put in the teas I give you, but you drink them, and you get better, don't you? It's the same with Reggie. Just 'cause I don't know what the words say, doesn't mean they're bad. Same as the things Father Simon says in church. I don't know those words, but he does, and he says they're words to talk to God with. Same, it is.'

I looked at my desk, my Rule open, its lines of words that made sense to me, but how would Lizzie know one word from another?

'I won't pay for an amulet. But I'll pay you to make up some herbs for Anna to wear by her skin. There are some, you've said, that could help if she wears them.'

'There may be, but as I said to you, the girl's been taking rue to see if she could be rid of the baby, that's why she was so sick at the start. And she stopped, she said, as it didn't work, but I think, as you said she had to go, she started taking it again.'

I tried to ignore the stab of coldness in my chest. 'Lizzie, I know you want to help Anna. Give her the herbs and teas that you know will be good for her.'

'Well, Sister, it's you that has to pay, so I must do as you say. Anna needs to rest more and eat no salt nor spices. But you see, what she really needs is a charm.' Anger flickered in her voice. 'But I'll do what I can for the poor girl.'

I stood and walked away from my window, not waiting to hear the door close. Had Lizzie told me about Anna taking rue again to make me agree to an amulet? Did she think I was responsible for that? Anna made her own decisions. I knelt to pray, but all I could see was Anna's pale face and dark-rimmed eyes.

'Sister Sarah, 'tis the child Eleanor wants to speak with you. She says you've told her to always ask me first.'

'Tell her yes, Louise, I'll see her.' I needed a visitor who would make me smile.

I stepped across to my parlour window and pulled back the curtain. Eleanor tugged at the door and slipped through the small gap she had made, then climbed to kneel on the stool and leaned her elbows on the ledge.

'Sister, you not cross anymore?'

'A little, but not at you, Ellie. How are you?'

'Everyone's sad about Sam and there's lots of work still.' She ran her fingers down the weave of the curtain as always, then poked at it, watching it billow and fall back. 'Are the baby birds still here?'

'They're very big now. I don't know how they all fit in the nest, so I think the mother bird will push them out soon.'

'Push them out? That's mean.' Eleanor frowned.

'Only so they can learn to fly. Otherwise they'd stay there, waiting for her to feed them.'

'Oh, that's good then. But Sister, my letters. I remember *s*, like this, and I remember *e* like this — that one's at the start of my name.' She drew the letters on her palm as she spoke. 'But can you tell me more?'

I showed her *l* — 'that's just like a stick' she said — and drew another *e*. She said *a* looked like a lady with a cap, and I was sure she would remember *o*, but the other letters of her name were more difficult.

'When no one's looking, try drawing them in the dirt with a stick. But make sure no one sees,' I said.

'I won't tell. I like this secret. And then can I learn your name?'

'You already know some of it — the *s*, and the *a* and the *r* and then another *a*.'

'So you use some of my letters then?'

I smiled. 'Yes, I do.'

'Good. And next time, could you tell me the whole dragon story? Bye, Sister.'

She squeezed out the door again.

The story of St Margaret. I had left it unfinished for weeks. It was my duty to read it to Louise and Anna, to finish what I had begun with them. I knew why I had hesitated, holding back from Anna some of the comfort she would want, as if to punish her. For so long we had spoken only necessary words, prowled around each other, dogs with hackles raised. I was weary in my heart. And the one thing I refused to listen to, the words I would not focus on, were Thomas's drunken ramblings; I pushed them into a dark corner of the cell and turned my back, willing them to stay.

Determined to finish the story, I carried my chair to the maids' window, opened the book that Thomas had delivered and began to read.

'The next morning, from all around the city, from every street and alleyway, the whisper flies: Olibrius has ordered Margaret brought before him. They all crowd into the town square to see what tortures and pain will be inflicted on her beautiful body. Olibrius uses the same temptation as the demon: worship our idols and you will be blessed, he says. But Margaret rejects such pagan ways, and tells them, foolish people, that they should seek God's blessing instead of bowing down before idols made of stone and wood, bloodless and boneless, filled only with invisible demons.

'Olibrius becomes even more angry then, and commands that she be stripped naked and hung up high, her body burned with blazing candles. The cowardly soldiers do as they are told. Her snow-white skin crackles and bursts into blisters in the flames. Margaret cries out, asking that God will set her heart on fire with the flame of the Holy Spirit, that his love will blaze in her loins.'

I remembered that night, the pricking and tearing of the hairshirt, then the warmth of Christ's body against my skin, the way he wrapped a hand around my neck, the touch of his lips, my body melting into his. Flames. I had thought they were sin, had confessed them, repented them. Perhaps not. Was it the blaze of Christ's love in my body? A cough and a shuffle; Louise wanted the rest of the story. My face was throbbing with heat and I bent lower to read.

'"Why wear yourself out like this?" Margaret says to Olibrius. "Christ has sealed my limbs. I've given him willingly the jewel of my virginity and in return he has granted me the crown of a champion."

'Olibrius is like a madman, furious with impotence. He orders a huge vat of water be brought, and that Margaret be bound hand and foot and thrown into its depths. Margaret prays that the water be a baptism, the water of cleansing, so that she might enter the bright chamber of her beloved. At that, the earth begins to quake; a dove, as bright as fire itself, sets a crown on Margaret's head and calls her to heaven. Her bonds broken, Margaret comes up from the deep water singing praises to God.

'The crowds that have come to see blood spilled see miracles instead, and five thousand are converted. And some women and children as well, though they aren't counted. Enraged, Olibrius has them immediately beheaded, every one of them, and they ascend to heaven as martyrs. By now the sheriff is red and boiling with anger; his tortures are useless, so he orders that Margaret's head be struck from her body. Margaret asks the executioner, the sword already in his hands, that he wait while she prays.

'"Almighty God, I ask that you give your blessings to anyone who writes the book of my life, or acquires a copy, or eagerly asks a reader for it. Let all their sins be forgiven at once. Whoever makes a chapel, or endows one with light or lamp, grant them the light of heaven. In the house where a woman is suffering labour pains, as soon as she calls to mind your name and my pain, Lord, quickly help her and hear her prayer; and in that house let no malformed child be born, neither lame nor humpbacked, neither deaf nor mute, nor afflicted with devils."'

I paused a moment; the air prickled.

'As Margaret prays, a blazing dove comes from heaven carrying a burning cross and speaks sweetly to the blessed woman. "I swear that your prayers will be heard and granted to all who do what you have asked. Wherever your body is, or any of your bones, or the book of your passion, if the sinful come and lay their mouths on them, I will heal them of their sins. No demon shall dwell in the house where the story of your life is written. Now come to your bridegroom, beloved lady, for I await you."

'With one strike of Malchus's weapon, Margaret's body sinks to earth while her spirit rises up to the starry chamber of heaven. And Theochimus, who has witnessed it all and vows to write down the story, carries her body to the house of her grandmother, Clete. St Margaret shines now in heaven, seven times more brightly than the sun, and sings in the host of angels forever unsoiled. Amen.'

I closed the book. Louise was quiet, no doubt imagining how Clete had organised the washing of Margaret's body, supervised the servants, given orders for the burial and preparation of the tomb. Anna pulled her stool closer to the window, her head bent but eagerness in her shoulders.

'Is that true, Sister? All those things that St Margaret said? Would it be for anyone, like, even those as ... even for those like me?'

'St Margaret promised to answer prayers, that's what she said. To help women in labour.' We both knew what I was admitting, though Anna said nothing. 'You need to confess your sins, then we'll pray to St Margaret. Now it's time for Compline.'

The next morning, Eleanor pushed through my door before I had opened my shutters, and called and knocked loudly enough to bring Louise bustling into the parlour.

'What are you doing, girl? Get out! Pushing in like this!'

By then I had opened my shutters and my curtain. Eleanor was standing on the stool, something in her hand, tears making tracks in her dirty face. I told Louise to leave us, though she left the door open as she went, clucking her tongue.

'They don't all fly, Sister. They don't.' Eleanor held out her hand, and in it, a tiny dead bird, its feathers dull and flat. 'This one was in the grass, just out there.'

'Oh, Eleanor. Perhaps he was sick, or too small.'

'You said the mother pushed them out so they would fly. You said.'

There was nothing to do but to pray with her, and ask her to bury the bird nearby.

ANNA'S FACE AND ARMS were thin and her stomach big, as if the baby were taking everything from her. There was still a good time to go, but Lizzie was afraid the baby would be born too soon. I stayed on my knees between Terce and Mass, read from my Rule, then returned to my altar. In every word I saw Anna's name, in every psalm of lament my own failure and fear. I pleaded with the Blessed Virgin for mercy, but I called on St Margaret to give determination to Anna. She needed the power of bursting the dragon's back, stamping on the demon's neck, more than Mary's motherly embrace. Some prayers, though few, I said for the baby. I confessed my sins to Father Ranaulf, I prayed to banish demons, but I stepped each day around the rock that had bruised my shins, the truth I would not face. It was not Fulke or some other village lad in the dark, behind the dovecote or under a tree in the forest, the two of them laughing and moaning.

My Rule understood my sin.

If a man sees and falls into sin because a woman is uncovered, she must pay the price of his sins. Dread this judgement very much. If a man is tempted so that he commits sin in any way, though it is not with you but with desire for you, or if he seeks to fulfil with some other the temptation which was aroused by an act

of yours, be assured of the judgement: you must pay, and unless
you confess it, you must be punished for his sins.

I could not ignore it anymore; I had to finish my own story, see
it all.

The stable is warm and dangerous. Outside the wind is strong,
but in here the straw muffles sound. Harnesses, saddles, tools of
all kinds hang from the walls, metal hammered and bent into
curves and points and shafts.

I walk ahead, trying to find words to explain, to stop him
telling me what he wants. I pause, reach up to pat Thomas's
favourite black horse, but it pulls its head away sharply and I step
back.

'Don't worry,' Thomas says. 'He's a fine horse, but not friendly.
He loves to gallop best of all and won't bear anyone stroking him.'
He steps in front of me, touches my cheek. I try not to look at his
eyes, the tiny speckles of yellow among the brown. I know what
he wants to say and speak quickly, to prevent him.

'Since I was a little girl I've thought I would take the veil.
I've been to St Catherine's at Compton ...'

'But you need not, Sarah.' He slips his hand behind my neck,
the roughness of his skin scratches mine, stirs it. I close my eyes
so that I won't see his, so that I won't think about this. His lips
on my neck, my mouth, his breath against my cheek, his hands
sliding down my back. I move closer, my arms around him, arch
my body against his. Heat loosening my belly, my body light;
I let go, forget.

A bang, the clatter of wood, and I flinch, pull away, look
around.

'It's just the horse,' Thomas says, and takes my hand.

I see myself; I stand next to the woman holding that man's hand, the woman with swollen lips, her cheeks and neck flushed red as if scorched, her eyes glassy, her legs weak, hardly able to stand alone.

I step back, away from that woman, touch the wood of a pillar, cross my arms. I look at his boots as I speak. 'I wanted to say, before, I wanted to tell you I've decided, the bishop has agreed, if there's a patron to support me, that I can become an anchoress. When Emma died I realised it's what I want.' I run out of words, look up.

The light is behind him, his face dark. 'Anchoress? Sarah!' His voice is puckered, ugly.

A crack, wood on brick, and Thomas turns around. The stable boy is at the door, his barrow tipped, the load of hay fallen at his feet. Thomas mutters, walks away and I move toward a pony, grey and fine-boned, at the back of the stables. The slap is loud, sharp, even though the straw dulls the sound. The pony's startled eyes, the cold stab in my chest.

As Thomas comes toward me I speak too fast of breeds and saddles, something about bridles, the little I know. He says nothing. Behind us, the stable boy scrambles to his feet, his cheek red from Thomas's hand, and runs out the door. I say I need to leave, my father will be waiting. His silence is heavy.

I try to walk past him, but he steps in my way, reaches out and holds my shoulders, forces me back toward the wall. I feel the tension in him. I duck, pull sideways. 'Thomas, I need to—'

He pushes me hard, my head banging on stone, ringing like a struck pot.

'You tell me what you need, Sarah. Just like that. You think you can tell me what you want, what you've decided. Who do you think you are? Holy Sarah.' He thrusts himself against me, his breath sharp in my ear, his shoulder digging into my throat.

'Thomas, no.' I struggle, try to step away, but he locks my feet between his boots and I can't move. 'Thomas, please!' but he presses a hand hard across my mouth. The stone behind me grinds against my head. For a moment, a lull in the storm, it is quiet. I hear a voice. *Give in, Sarah. This is the price of your weakness.*

Perhaps he notices my stillness, I don't know, but he looks into my face. 'I've told you what I want. Now, before you seal yourself away, I will have it.'

I close my eyes. I smell the sweat and spice and dirt on his hand, traces of meat on his breath. He drags at my face as he pulls at my skirts. The edges of my teeth cut into my cheeks, blood sharp on my tongue. He pushes my legs apart.

'Sir Thomas, you there? Did you see the new pony's just arrived?' It's Gwylim calling; he opens the door to the stables.

Thomas is still, his nails digging into my cheek.

'Sorry sir, I didn't know. Just checking about the pony.'

I pray Gwylim will stay, but I know it makes no difference to Thomas. He flings me away. For now I am discarded.

'Holy Sarah. I *will* make you.' And he is gone.

I lie in the dirty tangle of straw, the smell of horse shit strong and earthy, feeling nothing but the ragged stinging in my cheek. Beyond my words and decisions, Thomas had seen my desire.

I was on the floor by my altar. The smell of the stables hung around me, the scratch of straw on my skin. The story had been mine alone, like a scroll rolled up and bound, hidden behind the hearth, but it refused to stay concealed, unwound itself, spilled its words. Something sat hot and dark in my belly; shame, I thought.

I was too restless to sit still and I paced the length of my cell and back, again and again. Me, and now Anna. Had he talked softly, held her hand, touched her cheek, then pushed her against a wall? The wall of my cell, perhaps. Had he covered her mouth too as he whispered in her ear, his words thin and silver like a knife? Did she cry afterwards, blood in her mouth?

I walked faster, but there was so little space. I thought it was anger that I felt — the familiar old anger at my father and his demands that I must marry and help save his business. But I tasted salt on my tongue; I hadn't been aware that I was crying. This — Thomas and Anna — I had to pay.

Isabella. She would understand disgrace. I spoke her name, low and slow, again and again, a litany.

'Isabella, it's my fault,' I whispered. 'Anna, I need to save her. I watched Emma die, her life draining away, and now Anna is weaker; it's the rue she took to be rid of the baby. It began that day in the stables, then May Day.' I opened the curtain. The door was closed, but a breeze gusted through the opening, the dampness of the forest. It was so dark, but I thought I saw a movement. I shuddered. Isabella was there, I was sure.

I wanted to explain, to tell her everything. 'I know he made Anna, forced her because he can't get to me. My Rule tells me I must pay for his sins. Anna mustn't die.' Admitting it, speaking the words, was letting out a breath I had held since I first knew Anna was with child, even before Thomas's last visit. Silence for a time, only the murmurs of night.

Sarah. Her voice was low, the soughing of the wind, and I strained to hear her. *You want to save her? Because of Thomas?*

Yes, I thought. 'It's my fault,' I said.

Only a sigh of air. The curtain wavered. I knew that she was gone.

⚜ RANAULF ⚜

THE TWINGE IN HIS shoulder was tightening into a cramp.
Composing. He had always wanted to write down his ideas, but
this was a slippery beast — not theology or a record of history,
not even a saint's Life. He had a few dates, and although Father
Simon hadn't been precise, Louise had been certain enough for
him to commit the details to ink and paper. And so he had begun.

In the thirty-sixth year of the reign of King Henry the Third,
and after due consideration and agreement of Bishop Michael,
Isabella of Crowsham was enclosed as anchoress at the church
of St Juliana, Hartham. Sir Geoffrey Maunsell of Friaston
undertook to support said anchoress in all her earthly needs in
exchange for a Mass to be said daily for the soul of Sir Geoffrey,
his heirs and his ancestors, as long as she was to remain in the
anchorhold. Father Simon, vicar of the church of St Juliana,
agreed and undertook to celebrate Mass each day in exchange for
a yearly sum to be paid to said church.

Ranaulf paused and chewed at his lip. He wondered if this was
all foolishness; that was why he hadn't yet told Peter about it. He

shook his head, focused on the words. It had taken him weeks to gather even this much information. Wherever the charter of Isabella's enclosure and release was hidden, it was nowhere that he could touch it. But people remembered; Aylwyn the stonemason remembered her enclosure clearly.

'We were blessed to have a woman to follow in the footsteps of Sister Agnes and her holiness. And Sister Isabella was so pretty. Day before she was to have the churching, or whatever you call it, I went ... I was a boy then, Father, and curious, that was all.'

'You were a child, Aylwyn, yes. Go on.'

'Well, I sneaked into the church when she was praying. I thought she was an angel, me being so young like, and then, Father, her hood slipped down and I was sure she was an angel. Hair like a fire, I thought, on her head. It was cut short, but like a fire. Only for a little time I saw it, before she looked around and pulled up her hood again. I ran then, as I knew I shouldn't be there.'

Ranaulf had wanted dates, precise information: enough to make a record, even if it was only from the memories of villagers, but as he listened to Aylwyn he discerned that what he needed was a story, or at least a mixture of history and events. That was a chronicle, surely, but had anyone ever written of an anchoress in this way?

'And her leaving, do you remember that?'

Aylwyn looked down, brushed the dust off the stone he had been cutting, gently set his mallet on top. 'Her leaving, Father?'

'This is for a chronicle, an official document. It's not wrong to tell me.'

'Well, Father, an' you say so ... But the bishop gave orders we weren't to speak, and Sir Geoffrey said we'd pay if we talked about it.' Aylwyn stirred the dirt with his foot.

'Sir Geoffrey can't harm you now, Aylwyn, and I'll absolve you if there's any sin.'

'Well then, Father.' He picked up the mallet and cupped the head in his palm. 'This was years later, don't know how many. Never heard much of Sister Isabella, course, as she were shut away, but my ma visited her sometimes, an' there were times I looked across at her squint when I was in church and I thought of that hair in the dark, just there, all the time. Then one day she was leaving; don't know how we found out. May be Father Simon told us, may be it was just the talk, but they said the sister was leaving and the bishop had to come and say some things.'

'Bishop Michael, it was?'

'Ay, Bishop Michael. Come to make it proper, like. But Father Simon said we were to stay away, as it wasn't ours to be watching. He said it was very grave and serious for an anchoress to leave and Bishop Michael was disappointed and angry at her ... her inconstancy, that was it. But Fulke, a bit like I was, curious, you know, you'd best talk to him, he saw it all, or heard it more like, 'cause he hid in the tree in the graveyard.'

'What did he hear? The bishop giving permission for Sister Isabella to leave?'

'Ay, that and more. Shouts. A man's voice and then a woman's, Fulke said. But, Father, you should talk to him.'

Fulke was out in the fields cutting and gathering the corn stubble, so Ranaulf trudged across the stretches of dull yellow and waited until the workers took a break. Eleanor saw him arriving and ran to take his hand. The villagers were familiar enough with the sight of him, but Ranaulf rarely did more than nod at them and they turned to stare at him, openly curious.

Because he'd been forbidden to go near the anchorhold, and because what he'd heard had scared him, Fulke was even more reluctant than Aylwyn to speak. Slowly, with promises that he was doing the work of the Church, Ranaulf learned a little more.

There'd been a short prayer and pronouncement at the door of the anchorhold, at which Father Simon and Bishop Michael were present. Fulke had waited, tucked in the fork of two huge branches in the oak tree, to see the anchoress come out.

'Curiosity, was all, Father. Nothing more. Just curious 'bout what she'd look like.'

The bishop had spoken loudly, his voice deep, like he was in court, Fulke said. 'I remember he talked a lot about sin, and how to leave was a … the word will come to my remembrance, Father, because I asked a friar that came travelling through our village preaching, I asked him what it meant. Couldn't ask Father Simon, could I, or he would've known I was listening. It was … it was … *nefarious*, that was the word he used. Nefarious sin.' Fulke looked up, smiling that he'd remembered, until he noticed the scribe's frown. 'And he talked about her running about in the world, and the Devil chasing her. Then it went quiet for a bit. I looked across to Crows' Acres, where they were ploughing, as I'd be missed soon if I didn't go. Then, it was just a movement in the door, and a shout, but cut off like. I climbed down to see, and crept around the side of the cell, just near the corner. The bishop was saying something strange about Israel and adultery and the desert. I think it must've been from the Bible.' Fulke looked up briefly, then down again to the shredded pieces of corn leaf in his hand.

Ranaulf took a deep breath. Those words were familiar, from the Old Testament; it made sense. God had given Israel grain and wine, but she had left him and gone with other gods, so God condemned her as an adulterer.

'And then sounds like slaps. I've heard that enough in my time, Father, but a bishop doing that? I forgot where I was and looked in the door then.' Fulke bent to pick up a stone, rolled it in his hand.

Ranaulf waited.

'He was holding her robe with one hand, and slapping her face. Then her robe started to tear. She was so pale, a kind of yellow colour, and the bones in her shoulder stuck out, sharp like. Around her mouth were sores, dark red with dried blood.' Fulke grimaced. 'Her hair was orange like Aylwyn had told me. She made no noise, Father. Nothing. That was so strange. But her eyes, I always remember her eyes. All around them the skin was dark, but she looked at the bishop with those fierce eyes, on and on. I've never seen such a look. And one time, his hand in the air, he stopped like, just let his arm drop, as if she'd made him.' Fulke threw away the stone as if it were hot in his hand. 'I ran then, afore he saw me, ran then to get my ma, and some other women came too. I went off to the fields after that, Father. I wish I'd never seen it; I felt so bad that I had. She was a holy woman living in there, and though we never saw her, we knew she prayed for us. Might not have thought about it if she was a village woman, him being a bishop and all … but an anchoress, a holy woman …' Having said so much, the lad ran out of words.

Later, Ranaulf looked through the Old Testament, eventually found the verses in Hosea.

*Let her remove the adulterous look from her face and the
unfaithfulness from between her breasts. Otherwise I will strip
her naked and make her as bare as on the day she was born; I
will make her like a desert, turn her into a parched land, and
slay her with thirst.*

Ranaulf sat back and set down his quill. The pain in his shoulders
had spread into the base of his skull. She had sinned, no doubt,
asking to leave after making vows. The bishop had a right to
be angry with her inconstancy. Penance was appropriate,
certainly, but violence? And they were villagers' words only, the
accusations against the bishop. What was he doing, talking to the
villagers who'd been sworn to silence, writing this down: it was
the worst disobedience. He would stop. No, he had come too
far to stop.

The women had been less reluctant to tell him the story.
Maud in particular had scant fear of hell or the bishop and had
barely listened to Ranaulf's reassurance that she would not be
sinning by speaking out, and Winifred and Madge had confirmed
her story.

'Isabella didn't say much,' Maud had told him as she dug
under the dead pea plants in her garden. She straightened then
and wiped her hands on her skirt. 'She'd wrapped a blanket
round herself, but I could see the marks of his hands on her
shoulders, the bruises already coming. And her mouth was cut
and bleeding. I brought her to my house. Her robe was torn
so I gave her something of mine to wear. She never did say
what happened. If y'ask me, Father, the bishop couldn't get it up
anyway, to do more to her. That's why they shout and hit, men
like that; can't get it up.'

Ranaulf couldn't keep down the flush.

'Forgive me, Father, making you uncomfortable, but I've waited years to say this. This means you'll do something?'

'But Isabella, what happened to her?'

'Wouldn't stay more'n one night, said she was getting away. Wouldn't say where and I don't know that she had a place to go, coming from the convent like she had, and shamed, or so the bishop said, for leaving her cell. Some say that was her body they found in Black Pond a while after, though it were too rotted to tell. Father Simon said she drowned herself for shame.'

'But the convent would have taken her back, I'm sure.'

'May be so, Father, and may be she lives there now. Young Fulke said he thought he saw her not long ago on the mill track near the road to Leeton, but the lad is fanciful. And may be she's dead, but whatever Father Simon or the bishop say, I know she didn't drown herself. She were angry, Father, not shamed.'

Ranaulf folded the pages together and slipped them under the priory's Book of Hours. This account, this cobbling together of memory, was risky, he knew. He smiled grimly at his own mild word. Risky? It was much more than that. But it was the only thing he could think to do. A copy sent to Abbot Wulfrum, perhaps to another bishop … enough to ensure that Bishop Michael's behaviour was known by those with some power in the Church. If he, her confessor, told of Sister Sarah's devotion and obedience the bishop might be shamed into letting her stay. It was all so tangled, so ugly; he wanted none of it.

He picked up a piece of pumice stone and rubbed it gently over a new piece of parchment. It was a mercy the pages of the chronicle weren't bound, so he could keep the account separate;

he could add the dates of Isabella's enclosure to the main document — that would be suitable — but he would include the full story of her departure only if he decided it was necessary.

He looked up toward the window. An anchoress with a pregnant maid. How could he speak of her devotion? She had shamed herself and him. He put the pumice stone down on his desk without looking and it slipped, fell to the floor and shattered quietly. A thousand tiny grey shards, a pile of dust. Shame. He thought of Maud's words: *She were angry, Father, not shamed.*

⊰ SARAH ⊱

OUTSIDE, THE SOUNDS OF carts, beasts grunting and straining, the men shouting and calling, as the wood was carried in for the All Hallows fires. The previous year on this day my cell had been so new to me, my desire to obey my Rule and please God so fresh. Harry the leper had asked me for food. So much had changed.

I tried not to notice the swell under Anna's robe and the sway in her walk, and even though her face was thin and grey there was something in her countenance, the unspoken secret that Emma had carried as well. She had turned inwards, not because I was angry with her, or for shame, but because she had another life inside that called to her. I thanked God that he had saved me from this, but still I watched the soft lids of Anna's eyes, the tiny curl at the edge of her mouth, that I had seen in Emma. That knowledge none of us could touch. Was it like prayer? I wondered.

I could feel tiny ripples in the paint, traces of the brushstrokes: here they followed the curve of the dragon's green tail, here the whorls of its large black eyes, and here, on Margaret's face, I could feel scarcely any, the artist's touch so delicate. Who had painted this, its intricate detail? The dragon's back was split neatly like the pod of a pea, the saint's legs still swallowed in its body, the hem of her robe hanging from its mouth like a tongue. She stood tall, gazing up at the dove. It was black inside that prison cell, and even darker deep inside that monster's belly, that hell and death. The whole story in one small painting: suffering, death, resurrection, prayer and blessing. And so for me: inside my cramped cell, there was another, even smaller, blacker place; I could see its open mouth, waiting.

I wanted the last page, but I started at the beginning and turned them all, one by one, listened to the rustle. Here, Margaret's prayer. I read aloud.

'Whoever makes a chapel, or endows one with light or lamp, grant them the light of heaven. In the house where a woman is suffering labour pains, as soon as she calls to mind your name and my pain, Lord, quickly help her and hear her prayer; and in that house let no malformed child be born, neither lame nor humpbacked, neither deaf nor mute, nor afflicted with devils.'

There was the promise; it was enough, surely, that Anna should call on the name of the blessed Margaret. I read on.

'As Margaret prays, a blazing dove comes from heaven, carrying a burning cross, and speaks sweetly to the blessed woman.

'"I swear that your prayers will be heard and granted to all who do what you have asked, and much more. Wherever your body is, or any of your bones, or the book of your passion, if the sinful come and lay their mouths on them, I will heal them of their sins. No demon shall dwell in the house where the story of your life is written."'

The bells were ringing, though I hadn't heard them begin: All Hallows, the day of the dead. On and on, tolling the beginning of winter. I lifted the book gently and kissed the page.

I was praying the next morning when Louise knocked on the shutters. A sharp hum ran through my arms and legs as if I had been struck; I knew it would be Anna. She had been bleeding in the night, Louise said, and was curled up in pain.

'I've asked Lizzie to come and she'll be here as soon as she can. We're to leave her to rest until then. Little scrap, she's so white. I've given her some ale, though she will only take a sip.'

'And the baby? Do you know?'

'Well, as I'm not Lizzie, Sister, hard to say.'

I closed the shutters, turned back to my altar and began to read. *O come, let us exult in the Lord, let us rejoice.* The wood of my kneeler was hard, pushing its way into my skin, refusing me. *Let us come into his presence with thanksgiving.* I moved my knees, searched for the curve worn into it over the years of Agnes's and Isabella's enclosure. *For the Lord is a great God.* I shifted my shoulders. *The Lord will not cast off his people.* A murmuring from the maids' room, some bumping and clattering, then the smell of herbs. *For in his hands are all the ends of the earth.* Anna lying pale on her bed, blood on her legs, Louise and Lizzie leaning over her. *And he beholds the heights of the mountains.* I closed my eyes, looked for black.

'Father, the time is coming closer now for Anna's child to be born, and she's still sickly and weak. I've told her to rest and Lizzie is giving her decoctions, and some oils for massage, but—'

'Is she still here? I thought it was clear that the maid could stay only until she was well enough to move. I'll pray for her, but the detail's a matter for you women, surely.'

'It is, Father Ranaulf. But in the story of St Margaret you gave me the saint says that if anyone reads her story, or writes down her story, she promises to help them and to carry them safe through childbirth. And Lizzie tells me of women who have parts of her story copied and folded up so that they can be carried in an amulet. And then, when the woman's time comes, the parchment is laid across her body and brings special help. Perhaps, Father, if you were to write down some of St Margaret's story it would be a blessing for the poor child.'

The silence felt thick. I rubbed some loose grains from the stone in front of me and waited.

'You have the story of St Margaret that I copied. You can read that to her.'

I had expected Father Ranaulf would object. 'But it's not the same as an amulet, something that she can wear close to her body.'

'Sister, this is a serious matter. I know St Margaret promises to help women in childbirth, but this business of placing the parchment on her body, and even more so the amulet — it's magic surely. *Sortilegium*, that's what it is, magic and superstition. The work of the Devil. Prayer is enough.'

'Lizzie has seen over many women in this village, and she has—'

'Well, Lizzie, yes, and her magic ideas. But Anna is in your charge, and you are in mine. And I say there will be no magic.'

My chest flamed at his absolute refusal, but I knew I mustn't argue. 'But Father John, in Leeton, told us that there's special power in some objects, like stones and plants. My pa suffered from nosebleed and he used to wear a bunch of shepherd's-purse around his neck and recite the Pater Noster to heal himself; Father John told him to do that. And words, like prayers, have power—'

'That's why we must be careful. The Devil uses words too, Sister. Words to deceive us.'

'Then, Father, why does St Margaret make such a promise?' I could hear my voice rising.

'St Margaret promises to help those who keep her story, or read it. She doesn't tell us to make an amulet. You have the story, you can read it. You ask for more?'

'For a woman in your charge, Father, as you said. She's in my charge and I'm in your charge, so Anna must be in your charge too, at least in part.'

'They're slippery words, Sister. Sophistry.'

That word was new to me, but I understood what he meant.

'I'm a scribe, a monk, and your confessor. That is all.' His words might have cut the curtain hanging between us. 'Anna has sinned, not only against God, but against you, and brought shame to your calling.'

'Yes, Father, so you've told me. I've spoken to Anna. And now we have to show forgiveness and mercy. Surely. Anna and the baby are just as much my care and duty as before.'

'I agreed when you said the maid was too sick to be moved, but I thought that was for a short time only. Now you say she still cannot leave. The sinner must pay for her sin.'

I stood up suddenly and moved my face closer to the curtain. 'You're not saying, are you, that we should leave her to sicken and likely die, Father?'

'If God decrees that is the price of her sin, then—'

I tore the curtain across. 'God does not punish those he loves with death! Even if his ministers have no mercy, God does.'

His face was a little lower than mine. He flinched and pulled back as if I'd hit him, then looked at me with his head slightly turned away as if the blow might still come.

'God is merciful,' I said quietly, and drew the curtain again, the top of the white cross just in front of my eyes. I stood still, unable to move.

'Sister Sarah, we will both pray forgiveness for what has happened here today. And we will both pray for humility ... In the name of the Father and of the Son and of the Holy Spirit. Amen.' I heard him close the door behind him.

The bell rang for Nones so I walked to my altar and knelt as if nothing had happened. My head had quietened somewhat, but I felt almost too tired to hold myself up. When I closed my eyes and crossed myself his face was before me, and for the first time, it seemed, I saw it; when I had pulled back the curtain, my anger had filled my sight. His skin was pale, as I had expected, his nose long with a bump just beneath his eyes, and I was surprised that I had noticed the slight ridge in his bottom lip. His eyes, wide in shock then almost closed in fear, were clear nonetheless, and my body flushed with shame — not because he was my confessor, and not even because I had broken my Rule, but because I had done to him what Thomas had done to me.

~ RANAULF ~

HEAD BENT, HANDS PUSHED into his sleeves, feet shuffling, he was still half asleep.

The sky was black, but already a bird had begun to sing: one note, tentative, and another, a little stronger. He stretched his neck from side to side, tried to loosen the cramp. The chapel was even colder than outside; it would keep him awake, at least.

Christoph began, '*Miserere mei deus*,' and the gathered monks joined in, a deep rumble, voices still buried, a few coughs, a throat cleared. Next to him, Ambrose yawned, his shoulder touching Ranaulf's, cushioned and warm.

She would be kneeling as well, on the other side of Cram Hill, in her dark cell tucked in the shadow of the church. Her head bent, her words the same, without this mumble or the sharp smell of sweat. That pale face, thin and hidden from the sun — for how long? Over a year now. How did she continue in that dark solitude? Her mouth with a tinge of blue, her eyes small but bright; he had ducked away from them like a little boy. Her demand for mercy a slap.

He had almost finished writing the account of Isabella, and at night, with darkness around him, the details of what had happened began to take shape before him. The cell door, the bishop's open hand, the anchoress's eyes. He was writing it down to protect Sarah from the bishop's anger, and yet he needed her to remind him, beyond his own fears, of what mercy looked like.

The abbot's visit, delayed twice, was upon them. Prior Walter was anxious, angry, giving orders that were impossible to follow and behaving a little, well, a little like a woman, Ranaulf thought. He demanded that the scriptorium be tidied, looked through the manuscripts on the desks, examined the chronicle, such as it was, read again the details of land acquisitions, the pieces of the priory's history that Ranaulf had composed so far. Not very much to tell, apart from the few pages about Isabella tucked inside the scribe's robe.

'Some more, Father Ranaulf, on our blessed St Christopher, I think,' Prior Walter said. 'I'm surprised it isn't finished yet: the torture, the witness, the beheading. Most important! Have it complete before our abbot arrives.'

Ranaulf opened his mouth to speak, then closed it; no point, he thought. He was more worried about what the abbot would say about Sarah.

Ranaulf thanked God, for the first time, that the scriptorium was so small; there was not enough space for Prior Walter to squeeze into the room with Abbot Wulfrum, and he walked away, muttering.

The abbot spoke the words he needed to say: 'This business in the anchorhold and the foolish girl, Father. Unfortunate, worrisome, though it concerns the dean more than me, and Prior Walter, as you well know, is very anxious. Have the maid away, beyond notice. Out of the village. And do it quickly, Father. This has continued too long. Now, let me see your work.'

He was impressed with progress in the scriptorium, congratulated Cuthbert on his illuminations, admired the consistency of Ranaulf's script, nodded over the entries in the chronicle. It was then, discussing the priory's small library, that Ranaulf shifted the conversation to pastoral manuals; he knew the abbot's love of books and ideas.

'What is your opinion, Abbot Wulfrum, of Raymond of Penafort's *Summa on Penance*? More precisely, his teaching on magic?'

'Ah, Penafort. We have the commentary now. William of Rennes' glosses. He makes Penafort clearer. Good pastoral teaching for clergy. Sensible. His teaching on magic — why do you ask?'

'A question from a villager. The issue arose of prayers written on parchment and worn as amulets.' Ranaulf could feel his neck colouring; he rarely spoke other than the truth. 'I've read Augustine, he writes of incantations as magic, but as for amulets, I'm not sure. His words aren't clear.'

'Amulets. Delicate issue. Delicate for the laity. William is clearer than Augustine. He agrees that writing holy words and prayers is of no fault. But he says it's superstition to believe there's power if they're written at a particular time. And I agree. Prayers written down, that alone is permissible. A villager might hang a paper around their neck or such. But familiar words only, none of these characters, unfamiliar names. And the words must be spelled correctly, of course; God bears no witness to falsehood.' Wulfrum stood suddenly taller. 'That's why a cleric, someone who knows, must write them.'

'Indeed.'

'Wisest, I think, to tell your villager to pray. And not, mind you, this dangerous business of praying over an apple or a pear with markings on it. William makes a point of that. And no old wives with their meddling and superstitious ways. Lay hands on the sick person, pray.' The abbot walked to the door. 'Always stimulating, Father Ranaulf, a talk with you. Brother Cuthbert.' He nodded and was gone.

'Magic? What was that about?' Cuthbert asked. 'You don't talk to the villagers, so you say.'

'It's the anchoress. She asked.'

'What might she be getting up to in that cell of hers? Can't tell, can you, a woman locked away. What will you say to her?'

'She's a godly woman, Brother; she prays in that cell. She's concerned for her maid. But I'll tell her no, there is to be no charm, no amulet, no words on parchment or pears or the like. Prayers only. That's clear.'

'The maid is still there, in the anchorhold?'

'It's irregular, and more. It seems wrong, I know, but we also need to consider our Lord's care for the outcast, the sinner. Even the woman taken in adultery. We're none of us without sin.'

'Well, not you, perhaps,' Cuthbert said, but his laugh was cut short by the scribe's frown. 'Aylwyn mentioned something, said she's quite sick, poor girl. Has his theories about the father, too.'

'Oh no, Brother, you know gossip is a sin.'

'Yes, yes, I know. Don't lecture me, Father. But you might be interested. The villagers are angry. There's unhappiness enough about Sir Thomas taking over part of the common land, but this as well ... Don't underestimate them.'

⊰ SARAH ⊱

FATHER RANAULF'S VOICE SOUNDS like stone that will not crumble. I have resented it, wanted to shout and scream at it, shake his dry words until they lose their order and their certainty. But that day, the day he brought the pages, his voice had tiny grains in it, specks of sand that shifted as he spoke, as if uncertain where to settle.

I took the bundle that he handed through the curtain, my finger grazing his hand, the parchment rustling. It was only a few unbound pages wrapped in a scrap of leather. They sat quietly on my knee while he apologised.

'I know that your Rule forbids you to take anything in safekeeping for others — papers or money, even church vestments or chalices — but it seems that things are not as we hoped. The prior says the scriptorium is a waste, but still he comes, often, to read the charters, to look through the scrolls, to make sure that our work is sound. Whatever his reason, I cannot leave these pages for him to find. You may read them if you wish, but I warn you that they may prove as difficult to read as they were to write. Even though I've written but a simple account, it has stayed in my mind. And in my dreams.'

I was too surprised at his words to say anything. What was this account that made him so uncertain, that made him dream?

'The dean has written to the prior. The bishop is considering events here, he says, and will make his decision soon. I hope these pages, if needed, might help to protect you from his judgement. They might be no help at all. I would use them only if needed. If not, I will take them and burn them.'

When he left I looked at the creamy pages. The writing was slanted to the right, the letters small, curved and flowing: instead of straight lines, letters like 'l' and 'b' had hooks that lifted and curved like a bird's wing; the tails of other letters fell beneath the line. It was beautiful, not as serious as the square, solid letters of my Rule.

It took only a short time to read, though I read it over and over. What I thought, I do not know. My skin was hot, so much so that I pulled up the sleeves of my robe, touched my wrists to the cool stone. But as I read again and again, cold spread from some place in my belly, a chill that travelled through my arms and legs, turning them to stone, stopping my thoughts. Five steps away, may be fewer: Isabella. Two men, the open door gaping, light penetrating like a knife. Isabella against the wall near her altar, her face throbbing purple. She left, she sinned; was this the price she had to pay?

It was not until the blackness of night, lying in my bed, that I began to grasp what Father Ranaulf had said to me; he was trying — feebly though it may be — to protect me, and most likely himself, from the bishop's rage. But at the same time, he risked the anger of the Church for revealing the secrets of one of its own.

THE VILLAGE THAT LIVED its life around my cell, all the
noise and smell, worry and dancing, anger and laughter that
had spilled through the cracks in the stone, all fell away into
silence. It narrowed down to this.

Louise brought the apple and offered to cook it, or at least
slice it up for me; she knew my teeth were no longer strong
enough to bite into it. No, I wanted only an apple and a knife, I
said, and told her to pray in the church while I spoke with Anna.
I had barely slept all night, thinking on this, but now I was calm.
Perhaps I was practised in disobedience.

I had told Lizzie that she could take my copy of the Life of
St Margaret to lay across Anna's belly when the time came, or
to have nearby: 'St Margaret promises to hear her prayer, so that
should be enough,' I'd said, but Lizzie had heard the doubt in
my voice.

'Marjory from Friaston, she tells me of women who call on
St Margaret by eating a piece of apple or pear with her story
marked on it,' she had said, and paused. 'Or may be butter.
Something as can be marked with some words, then eaten. It's
a kind of charm. I'm thinking that reading and writing isn't the
only way ...'

'Yes, I've heard of that. And the story of St Margaret, or perhaps her prayer, couldn't be from the Devil,' I'd agreed.

'Marjory didn't say that much about what's to be marked, but I suppose it's a word or two. You can write down words, Sister?'

'I read though I don't write, but I can copy some letters ... if I decide it's the right thing to do.'

The apple sat roundly in the dimness. I could hear Father Ranaulf's words as he left Isabella's story with me: he had read some more about charms — St Augustine, someone called William, even his abbot, and they all said no to charms, to words written at a special time, to apples and pears inscribed with words. 'It's not simple, Sister, but the abbot was clear: no amulet, but tell her to pray.' I opened my book, read again St Margaret's promise to protect women who had a copy of her story or called it to mind, and to give light to those who provided a chapel or even a lamp in her name. Words, parchment, stone, light, memory. Father Ranaulf had said I must use only words, and only the ones that he had written, but St Margaret promised to hear more than words. She would notice things that could be touched that called on her help. I wouldn't trust to words written by someone such as Reggie, but St Margaret offered another way I could help Anna.

The light from my candle flickered. It lit up one side of the apple where it curved, red. I picked up the apple, cupped it in my hands, felt it lying heavy against my palm, ran my fingers across its smooth skin. I had confessed to Father Simon my sin against my confessor, pulling back the curtain and presuming to know better than him. But if I wrote on this apple, took it and gave it to Anna to eat, I would disobey him further. I understood that, but I had vowed to do everything I could for Anna, to pay the price for Thomas's sin.

I pulled the candle close and picked up the knife. The wood of the handle sat smooth and neat in my right palm. I knew little of what to do next. Written prayers started mostly with the mark of the cross, so I began with the downward stroke. The skin resisted and I pressed harder, but I was clumsy; the knife slipped, made a long, thin cut, longer than I'd wanted. I would need to use the tip of the knife as a quill to cut out thin pieces of the apple's flesh. I adjusted my grip, holding the knife by the base of the blade, trying to keep my fingers from its sharpness. Another long stroke, like the first and a tiny distance away. This time I cut more slowly, a finger on the apple to steady my hand, working at an angle to pare away a small piece of the fruit. Skin and flesh sat loosely; I pulled it free, put it in my mouth, tasted a slight tang, felt the tough skin. A thin white wound sat in the redness. The horizontal bar of the cross came more easily, and I realised it was better to pierce the skin with the tip of the knife, over and over, rather than attempt to cut it with sweeping strokes.

I began the S. When I'd shown Eleanor the letters of our names, I had traced curves easily on her palm, but the top curve of the S — how was I to mark that on an apple? As I looked closely at St Margaret's story, I saw that most of Father Ranaulf's letters, even the ones that looked like curves, were formed of tiny straight lines with other straight lines added at an angle. I tried to copy what I thought he must have done, even though my lines were jagged and awkward. I continued, making letters with straight lines and no curves, moving slowly around the apple. Juice dripped onto my hand, my fingers were sticky and

I sucked them one by one, then licked the skin between them, both sweet and tart.

I had such a small space to write on that I decided to use only the first letter of the saint's name — *St M* — then 'mercy. Amen', followed by another cross. I looked up the words in the story to be sure I spelt them correctly.

Cutting the *A* for 'Amen', I moved my fingers onto the blade, gripped it too tightly and felt a sudden burn, long and thin. The cut was not bad — a thin stripe on the inside of three fingers — but it stung. I squeezed my hand shut, pressed my fingers to my robe then up to my mouth, the taste metallic. Blood welled slowly, dripped, and gradually stopped. I used the hem of my robe to wipe it away and continued to write.

At first the letters were white, stark against the red, but by the time I had finished, the early ones had begun to brown and the edges of the peel were curling inward. My jagged prayer looked like decay. I walked to the maids' window and called to Anna to come quickly. She stood a few steps from the window, leaning backwards against the weight of her belly, her eyes wary.

'Sit down, Anna.' Now the time had come, I was nervous. I explained that I had made a prayer for her, a way of calling on St Margaret's help. I held up the apple, sad and browning.

'You did this?' she asked.

'Yes, I did. Father Ranaulf is uneasy about anything that's not a spoken prayer, or one written by him, but St Margaret says that if someone lights a lamp or builds a chapel —'

'All those letters? You did that? And for me?'

I became still for a moment. My anger at her, my sense of shame and failure; she had not expected my concern as well. I sank slowly onto the bed. I wondered then if I should tell her that I knew about Thomas, and I began to shape the words in my mind. But I stopped; I wanted her to know that I would do this for her because I loved her, as I'd loved Emma, not simply to pay for a man's sin. Or my own.

The candle flame guttered and went out. I looked up into the dimness. Anna was sniffing, and in the soft light I could see her eyes were red from crying.

'You need to eat this now, before it turns even browner, and I'll ask St Margaret to accept our prayer.'

I read out the short prayer, pointing to each letter as I turned the apple around and picked up the knife. The outer skin was dry and the flesh becoming pulpy, but the centre was crisp and I had to press hard; my fingers flared with pain for a moment. The apple fell in two, then I cut into it until thin slices lay scattered, white crescents with dark seeds tucked inside.

'These are like tiny pieces of the moon,' Anna said, and smiled. She ate slowly, piece by piece, then leaned through the window and touched my hand, her fingers wrapping around mine. 'Sister, you eat some. With this baby, there's nowhere left inside me for more. And if it's prayer, you should have some, too.'

I picked up a slice and touched the wrinkled slash, part of a letter, though I couldn't tell which one. And there, on the flesh, a smudge of red. Was it enough?

THE NIGHT WAS LIKE any other. Why should it be different? Advent had begun, the time of preparing to celebrate Christ's birth, and I thought of all that I'd read about Mary's quiet acceptance of God's will. Nowhere had it spoken of fear and the labour of a woman's body.

Louise knocked on my shutters after Compline to say that Anna had her pains. It was early yet for the baby to be born, but not too early, Lizzie said. They had taken Anna to Lizzie's house; Maud would go to help, and Jocelyn and Avice.

'I thought to go now, Sister,' Louise told me. 'Might be as I can be some use. Poor little scrap.'

I gave her the Life of St Margaret — it seemed a small thing now — and went to kneel at my altar. I knew the psalms to pray; so many of them, even psalms written by a king, were cries from the depths of pain. Prayers spent, I dropped my head onto my Breviary, but I could not sleep. I walked to the maids' window. Louise had left the door open and I could see only to a thin slice of the night, clear and cold, one bright star high above Cram Hill. Only a few sounds: an owl, a blackbird looking for dawn, a door creaking, the faint hiss of pissing.

I pictured the women gathered around: Jocelyn waiting to be told what to do; Maud rubbing Anna's legs, taming the pain; Avice cradling her head; Louise with the book near her shoulder, holding its pages open, praying. At a table nearby, Lizzie frowning, deciding on decoctions, mixing ale and honey and milk with herbs. Anna's face I could not see.

Doors and windows thrown wide, cupboards and drawers pulled open, a ribbon tied around her belly and then loosened. Unbind, release, call the baby into this world.

Lizzie had taught me a charm to command the baby to come forth and I recited it, over and over. I remembered Maggie the midwife chanting the same one to Emma, for what worth it was. *Maria virgo peperit Christum, Elisabet sterilis peperit Iohannem baptistam. Adiuro te infans, si es masculus an femina, per Patrem et Filium et Spiritum sanctum, ut exeas et recedas, et ultra ei non noceas.* I knew enough Latin, along with Lizzie's vague comprehension of the charm's meaning, to understand what I was asking: Mary, though a virgin, gave birth to Christ; Elizabeth, barren, gave birth to John the Baptist. I adjure you, child, boy or girl, by the Father and the Son and the Holy Spirit, come forth and move away, and cause her no more harm.

Cause her no more harm, child.

The night shifted, memories circled. Emma's moans, my sister in such pain, the sound that came from deep within, ground struggling to break open. Rocks shifting, roots twisting and lifting through soil. I could feel her body tighten inside my arms. And her quietness. Where was her anger, her refusal? Another pain, the strain drawn into her face. A quiet moment, her eyes closed, I ran outside, my body turned to liquid.

The cold night, my cell, the faint sound of moaning across the still darkness, then nothing. A door opening, women's voices — that was Maud, I knew — more groaning. Lizzie's quick commands.

The night lost all shape. I ran for cloths, water, basins, heated an infusion over the fire, lifted Emma to sit and rest against me, cradled her, wiped her forehead, whispered in her ear, tried to take the pain into myself. Worthless. Every single thing we did. Finally Emma was too exhausted to sit up and I watched the blood seep into another bundle of white.

Somewhere in that bloodstained circle, I had told Godric to get Father John. Maggie was calling to Emma, telling her to stay, to breathe, but she knew it was hopeless. Father John baptised the baby still inside her. Life and death closer than a single breath. I walked outside. Godric was standing at the door, white and silent like his wife.

A wail circled and fell. I stood up but I was alone: my altar, my squint, my stone walls. The crunch of feet on gravel, a door banging. Perhaps it was mine. No, not my door; no way out, no way in. What use would I have been anyway? That bang, I knew, was the door to Father Simon's house: Anna or the baby, or both, were dying.

WHAT DO I DO inside these four stone walls? I shout and the walls swallow my voice, tear the skin from my fists. Christ hangs as he always has, head bent, as if nothing has happened. Look, look at me. Condemn me. Mary's dear arms have nothing to do with me. Stay away, stay away all you that pretend comfort.

See this trail of blood that never stops. Broken bodies, life poured out. All I have are grazes on my knuckles, three cuts on three fingers, my useless virgin purity. This delicate blossom that grows neither fruit nor beauty. St Margaret tore the dragon in two and sang her song of victory. What was her triumph? A bloodless birth, like a beanpod breaking open; no pain, no tearing. And no use to Anna. How could she call herself the protector of women in childbirth? She made her promises and looked the other way.

They bring me flowers, or a prayer, soft words. Leave your comfort. Flay my skin, watch it bleed. Nothing will change my shame.

I told them to leave me to wash Emma's body. The water rippled and swirled pink then darker pink then the red of blood and water. They say that came from Christ's side on the cross when he was pierced with a spear. His swollen wounds faded from red to pink then to white as death took hold. That damaged place between Emma's legs, her thighs smeared in blood, her belly still rounded. And her face? I want to say it was peaceful, that the Virgin Mary spoke comfort in her ear, or that Christ took her into his arms and so she saw heaven as she died. But there was no look of peace, or of pain; it wasn't Emma at all, just a body we washed and buried. I prayed, spoke some words, but they made no sense to me, just echoed around the walls looking for a place to go.

The villagers worry. I can hear them; they sound like a swarm of bees, anxious for the recluse and her grief. Their worry hovers at my window, flutters against the stones, nests in the rafters. Buzzing, always buzzing. This woman who talks to spirits, this holy, shameful woman, how will she bear it? I shout to them that I am content and quiet inside my cell. I need nothing more. I walk from one end to the other and back again; that keeps the buzzing away for a time. Back and forward, back and forward, from my window to my altar. Sometimes I look at my door, that strange block of wood that keeps everything inside. If I opened it, I would blow out like leaves.

Lizzie comes to tell me the baby is well, Gillie is nursing her. What baby? I say. They buried them outside. The baby was blue, the mother was white. Lizzie frowns; I can hear it, that frown. The dirt of the grave is ugly. I heard the scraping of their spades, Father Simon's mumbles. Everyone pretended God was listening. I shouted to them, told them St Margaret was looking the other way.

I could not see Thomas, but he would touch Father Simon's hand, look toward my cell, and shake his head; he had done all he could for the anchoress, poor woman, gone mad with grief. I knelt at my squint and whispered to them all, told them the truth about Sir Thomas — Maud, Avice, Jocelyn, Winifred. Lizzie knows, she had always known, had tried to tell me that first day, but I wouldn't listen. Now they all know.

I'm so tired. The walls and I sit together. I listen to the stone's quiet breath, its steady heart. The stone whispers to me, *Drink some ale and wait, Sarah.* Sup a little and tell me stories. The bread is dry now, but I dip it in the ale and try a piece; it tastes good. I collect the crumbs from my robe. One by one. Perhaps the birds in the roof would eat them. I look at my hands, the lines of dirt in my palms and between my fingers, my nails chipped and rough. Days and nights pass, we are quiet together. Tell me stories, the stone says.

Someone has left her embroidery on my desk, a picture of a man with a warm smile and gentle eyes, looking toward one shoulder, at nothing but an emptiness he carries in his arms. He is standing in water, curls of blue and green lapping around his feet, long strands of yellow and orange and purple, waves wrapping around his legs. I run my fingers across the stitches; they feel familiar. Who has sewn this, I wonder.

'There was a man once,' I tell the stone. 'He is tall, so tall. He lives by a deep river and carries people to the other side, wading through the deep water, fish swimming around his legs. One day a child asks him to take him to the other side and the tall man carries the child on his shoulder, step by step into the cold flowing water. The water is deeper this day ...' But no, I stop and think. 'It's a woman, not a man, I was confused ... The river flows faster and the child is heavy, so heavy that the woman thinks she must sink under the weight. Down into the depths, down to swim among the fish. She struggles at first, the child as heavy as the world on her shoulders, tries to keep her head in the air where she can breathe. But she cannot, and she goes down under the waves. And as she sinks she sees silk weaving and waving, red and yellow and purple monsters of the deep. And the child sinks as well, the two of them wound around with silken shrouds.'

The stone listens and suddenly I remember.

'Anna. Anna's gone,' I say. 'She gave me an apple to eat on May Day, warm with honey and currants, then she ran outside, laughing. And I gave her an apple, wrote words on it that we could pray with. We sat here and ate it together one night, slice by slice, Anna and me.' My eyes prickled; I would not cry. 'But she left. I heard a door bang and then Louise said she was gone.'

We sit in the quiet.

'Anna died. I couldn't save her. I don't know now what price to pay.'

⇜ RANAULF ⇝

RANAULF'S BOOTS ECHOED ON the wood of the bridge, then crunched on the frozen mud of the path. The village was quiet, most people indoors, no doubt sleeping off their Yule celebrations. As he passed the tavern he heard a man telling a story, and laughing at his own joke. Roger. He recognised the voice, strong and deep, from the day he had come to the village to ask about Isabella. Roger had told him nothing about that; he stayed out of the business of women, holy women especially, he'd said, but he'd had a lot to say about Gwylim collecting the handmills and speaking roughly to his Winifred.

For so long, Ranaulf had walked through the village, seen men and women in the fields — ploughing, sowing, weeding and harvesting, season after season — and had thought no more of it. He looked across the fields now, left fallow and ploughed over, covered with white prickles of frost, and remembered his first walk to the village. The woman weeding, the little boy throwing stones, his own anger or, rather, his fear of this holy woman. Five days, it had been, since Anna's funeral. Sarah had told Louise she would not see him, and he'd thought it best to leave her in the maid's care, but word was that the anchoress was behaving strangely.

His days had not been easy, but the nights especially had been bad. He rarely dreamed, but ever since he had delivered those few pages to Sarah, his sleep had been full of faces, women's faces in darkness, then emerging into the light, wavering and shifting so that he could see only parts: a pale cheek, a mouth tinged with blue, dark curls that turned to red, a curving neck, a piercing eye.

The sound of footsteps and a hand slipped into his. Eleanor didn't speak, just leaned her face against his hand and tried to keep up. He slowed, looked down at her grimy hair, felt the wetness of her tears seeping through his fingers and onto his palm. At the anchorhold they stopped and he put his free hand on her head. She wiped her eyes and nose on his robe, sniffed loudly and walked away. Louise opened her door, nodded briefly, then closed it again.

He dragged at the parlour door, grateful for the rain that made it swell; Sarah would hear him coming in. It was all so familiar: the stool, the axe cuts in the ceiling beams, the stern window with its black curtain, the white cross stark on the dark cloth — but he kept thinking of his first visit. His cough, his stiff words, her voice so strange.

The usual rustling behind the curtain.

'Sister Sarah. God bless you.'

A pause. 'Father Ranaulf.'

He had nothing to say. This enclosure, forbidding sight and touch, was foolish and wrong. It was killing her slowly, he knew. He lifted his hand, then let it drop again. 'The monks of the priory pray for Anna's soul, and for you. And Louise. The prior has—'

It was a grunt, or perhaps a laugh, he couldn't tell. 'The prior has asked me to say how—'

Yes, a laugh. Scornful. Ranaulf looked down at his hands, scraped some dirt from under his thumbnail. 'Sister, I—'

'Don't speak to me of pity or comfort. I've no use for that.' Her voice was deeper than usual. 'Or prayer.'

'At a time like this, prayer is all we have, Sister.'

'Prayer? I prayed: for days, for weeks; I filled this cell with prayer. I prayed to St Margaret, I read her story to Anna, I gave her book to Louise to keep near Anna. I believed the promises, that she would help if we called on her, that God would listen to St Margaret's prayers. All those promises in the book that you gave me, Father. All in your hand, letter after letter. I did everything I could and my prayers were as nothing.'

Ranaulf felt the sudden licking of flame in his chest. This woman dared to doubt the wisdom of God, she who comprehended so little.

'Sister, be very careful. Do you question God?'

'I do have questions! Why did Anna die? I read the words, the promise that St Margaret made. I even carved her words into an apple so that Anna could eat it. Why did St Margaret, why did Christ look the other way? And Mother Mary too?'

'Your grief leads you to sin, Sister.' For a moment, Ranaulf felt himself on firm ground. 'You presume to know the ways of God. You have tried to control God with your prayers and your rituals. Words on an apple, Sister? I was very clear that you were not to use a charm and you disobeyed me. Faith beseeches, it does not presume to have certainty — that is its nature, to trust without certainty. But you have turned your faith, your prayers, into demands.' He looked down at his hands again. The ink he had spilled on his thumb and palm earlier in the morning had trickled into the lines of his skin like thin black streams, forking then running dry. His sense of assurance was waning. The words were correct, he could quote the scholar, the work, the progression of the argument. But was that what she needed to hear? He thought of Peter and what he might say; nothing came but the old monk's gentle laugh and the blue of his eyes.

He tried again. 'Sarah, I understand how much you wanted—'

'Understand, Father?'

Her voice was quiet and Ranaulf thought of a sword unsheathed, the sound of metal on metal like the hiss of an animal. He began again. 'Your desire to save Anna was born of virtues, the love and compassion that our Mother Mary shows for us, but the ways of God are a mystery.'

'First you speak of faith, and now you speak of mystery.' Her tone was icy.

In his mind, Ranaulf could see the curl of her lip, the open scorn in her eyes. He gazed at the tracery of black on his palm. One miniature rivulet had run down toward his wrist, curved around the base of his thumb, and trickled to nothingness. He took a deep breath and let it out slowly. There was no more he could say, but he would not leave her alone with such bitterness. And so he remained on his stool, feeling the emptiness of the room around him, the failure of his learning and the words he had stacked up in his mind, page upon page, shelf upon shelf. He could not speak, but he could stay; he would do that. He began to silently pray, but did not know how to go on, what to ask for. He gave up, his breath slowed.

The silence began as a small and frightened thing, perched on the ledge of the window, but as Ranaulf sat in stillness, it grew, very slowly, and filled up the parlour, wrapped itself around his neck and warmed his back, curled under his knees and around his feet, floated along the walls, tucked into the corners, nestled in the crevices of stone. A rustling from behind the curtain. He wondered if he could hear Sarah's breath. The silence slipped through the gaps under the curtain and into the cell beyond. A velvet thing, it seemed. It swelled and settled, gathering every space into itself. He did not stir; he lost all sense of time. All he knew was the woman but an arm's length away in the dark, breathing. That was enough.

When the candle in the parlour guttered, he stirred, looked up into the darkness. 'God be with you, Sarah.'

'And with you, Father.' Her voice was lighter, more familiar.

Outside, the village seemed a bright and noisy place, and he began to walk quickly away, then stopped and turned. Eleanor was sitting with her back against the church wall, watching him. He hesitated, looked toward the bridge, then back to the girl, moved toward her, bent and took her hand. He could hear a bird singing, its soft single notes, uncertain, as if it were practising.

❦ SARAH ❧

WHEN FATHER RANAULF LEFT I sat on the floor beneath the parlour window, my back against the stone, spent. I had stood to refuse his comfort, finding a bitter pleasure in throwing his words of sympathy back through the curtain; it was my anger that had kept me breathing since the night Anna died. But he was right: I had been determined, beyond all else, to save Anna, even beyond loving her. I was so busy paying the price, as my Rule commanded, that I had forgotten Christ's suffering. I knew he still gazed down at me from the cross above my altar, but in the panic of my prayers, I hadn't seen it. My anger had crumbled and my strength had left me, until it was only the floor and stones that held me up. I was afraid of what remained.

The silence, offered to me by a man of words, had at first been more threatening than anything he had said, but the stillness reminded me to wait and listen. I began to let go.

His quiet presence had been a gift.

It was cold but I stayed on the floor, shivering, watching the feeble winter light fade from my horn window. I smiled; a year ago I would not have been able to recognise that slight hint of daylight. Nine steps away, in front of me, the door was a dark block. The cold seeped into my marrow.

The stillness was overtaken. Wind gathered and gusted, whispering past my cell, sliding through the tiny gaps in the thatch. I had not closed the shutters to my parlour and the curtain wavered above me. Branches of the oak tree beat at my walls. I'm hollow, I thought. I might blow away.

Sarah, get up. Light the fire. A voice somewhere. I looked around. *Now, Sarah.*

Isabella. I thought she had left me. My joints were stiff when I tried to stand. Moving, setting the wood, fanning the flames, all warmed my limbs a little. I dragged a blanket from my bed and sat by the fire. My curtain billowed, a scent of earth floated in, her hair blew around me like autumn. I picked up a leaf from the floor.

'Isabella, I have your story. Father Ranaulf wrote it down and I keep it here, inside my Rule. The bishop was angry because you promised to stay and you broke your vows.'

Days don't measure love.

I thought she had spoken, but the words made no sense.

'But Isabella, how could you leave, go out that door?'

Sarah, you tell stories to the stones. Tell them about St Margaret.

St Margaret; her story seemed so long ago, I could hardly remember, but I began. 'There was a woman in a dark cell who wanted to fly away, and a man who hurt her. He was important and powerful, and said she would have jewels. But he shouted at her and hit her, pulled at her clothes because he thought she should always do what he wanted. When she didn't he punished her. I remember the smell of straw, a door with nails. A wall, too, just like this one.' I hesitated, looked around. 'I'm confused. Is that St Margaret's story?'

Yes it is. And your story. And mine.

The wind pressed hard, hissing through every crack.

'But my Rule says I should ...' I knew the words that said it was my fault, but they didn't seem as clear when I tried to tell them to this woman who had left. Worn out, I lay down, the straw prickling my cheek. It smelled like the outside world. I was somewhere else, a stable warm with horses, and me on the ground, my head ringing, blood in my mouth. I had pulled myself to my feet and run out into the wind, sobbing.

Whatever I thought I believed, I gave up the struggle for reason and cried for the first time since Anna died. I had tears enough to fill St Christopher's deep river, sobs filled with all that my anger and fear had held on to. Drifts of warmth, the scent of moss, lingered around my face.

Scat moved without a sound, as if she had no weight to shift the straw. She rubbed her face gently against my shoulder, then down my arm, her fur smooth against the skin of my hand. I murmured her name. I had always thought she stayed because I'd tried so hard to make her leave; stayed just to prove that she could. She was not interested in me, I thought, just in her own comfort and warmth, coming whenever she wanted shelter, going to others for scraps, if she could get them. But feeling her warm hum against me, I remembered how often she would sleep against my knees as I prayed, or jump onto my lap when I read, or curl up on one corner of my bed. I put out my hand and she pushed her face against it, her eyes shut into two lines, a pucker around her nose.

~ RANAULF ~

'SISTER, I HAVE NEWS. The dean has sent a message from the bishop. We at the priory are responsible for you, as you know, even though Sir Thomas is your patron, so it was important that we be told. The bishop has considered the situation, Anna and the baby, and with all that has happened he has decided that your enclosure here may continue unchanged.' Ranaulf sat back and exhaled with relief. 'So the account of the incident, of Isabella leaving, I can take it back now and burn it.'

'Unchanged?'

'Sister?'

'The bishop said things may remain unchanged?'

Sarah's voice had a dangerous pitch; Ranaulf shifted his feet. There was something he hadn't understood.

'Anna is dead, out of the way, so we forget she was ever here, ever with child. The grass will grow over her grave. Some woman will look after the baby and the anchoress can continue as she was. Unchanged.' The scorn in her words felt like a living thing. '*Everything* has changed. Did you tell that to the bishop? You wrote down the story of what he did. I have it here.'

Sarah's voice had a silent, sharp edge; Ranaulf could feel each hair on his head rising, a tightening across his forehead.

'The night of my enclosure he reminded me what a gift Sir Geoffrey gave me each day, to be here, secure in my virginity. Gift!'

The last word flew through the curtain and Ranaulf sat up.

'Sister, enough now. Your grief leads you to say things. Be aware of your words. The bishop is your father in God, and Sir Thomas is your patron. They ensure your living here.' Ranaulf heard a rustling and knew that Sarah had stood up. He leaned back a little farther on the stool.

Her voice was very quiet. 'Father Ranaulf, do you ever wonder who fathered Anna's baby? Do you lie awake at night thinking of a young girl, her legs apart, and a man with his arms around her, the two of them moaning and gasping? You thought, like me, that Anna was disobedient and lustful. That she lay with him in the field on a moonless night, or even here, behind the church.'

Ranaulf could feel the creep of warmth into his cheeks. He did not want her to say the name.

'We were both wrong. You did not stay to think, but I knew and I would not admit it. Sir Thomas is the one. He forced Anna. It must have been on May Day. It was supposed to be me. That's what he wanted. He forced her. It's not Anna or me the bishop should be judging.'

Ranaulf could think of nothing to say.

'You can tell that to the bishop. Tell him it has all changed.'

Back in his scriptorium, Ranaulf sat down to work alone. Cuthbert was most likely in the warming room, chatting while he rubbed some feeling back into his fingers; only the cold would keep him from his work. He picked up the page on his desk. With more work coming in, the prior had agreed to pay for someone to be trained to prick and rule the pages. Gilbert had finished the ruling, neat and almost square, but near the bottom of the page was a smudge of grease; the boy learned the skills quickly, but he was from the village and still to appreciate the need for clean hands.

He set down the page. Sir Thomas. He wished he did not know, and there was little to be done. Still, the image of the man and the girl was in his head now, as clear as one of Cuthbert's paintings, though violent and cruel, not playful.

He wouldn't speak, of course. He knew what they would say, knew the words himself: woman is by nature lustful, seeking out man to tempt him; it must have been the maid's fault — after all, she was a village girl. For heaven's love! How had he found himself here, defending women against all he knew, even against the words he had copied? These were foolish thoughts, a path with no way through. He knew that even if he faced the prior's anger and told Bishop Michael or the dean, or even confronted Sir Thomas himself, it would scarcely matter. He saw Sir Thomas looking down from his horse, certain of his power, demanding he be given the Life of St Margaret to deliver to the anchoress. That smug man, certain he would get what he wanted.

Heat flared in Ranaulf's chest: the willow branch, that day on the river path, the whip across his face. He was so slow to recognise his own anger, which crept like a cat after a bird, pouncing sharp and in silence. Anger was a sin, an unruly passion that blinded the heart. Where had he read that? The anchoress's Rule, yes, had called anger a shape-shifter, making a man into a beast.

He stood and walked the two steps to the nearest window. An ache was spreading from his jaw into his forehead, orange-red, battering at him, looking for a way out. Passion: St Jerome had written that anger is passion and passion is incompatible with God.

Thomas grabs Anna's arm, drags her back to him as she tries to run, his whisper mocking in her ear. She shakes her head, tries to pull away, but he draws her tight against him.

But no, Ranaulf thought, Augustine said that anger at sin was not condemned, it was only anger at a brother that was sinful.

Thomas's mouth is white, his lips clenched, his thumbs digging into the maid's skin. He pushes her to the ground, one hand on her chest, one at her skirts.

Christ had felt anger when he overturned the tables of the sinful money-changers in the temple. So, when anger was logical, born of reason, it was a servant of God. Could this be reason when he felt anger in every part of his body?

Anna cries out, but he hits her across the face, covers her mouth and pushes her head into the ground. She kicks her legs wildly, but she is so small, so pale beneath him.

Chrysostom had even said that it was sin not to be angry when there was cause to be. Ranaulf's head pounded, his breath came fast, his fists were bunched by his sides. When there is cause to be — that would be justice.

Thomas straddles her, holds her down, strokes the side of her face. He is smiling.

Justice, anger, passion.

He had written the story of the bishop and Isabella, but he wondered, now, if he'd been seeking justice or simply self-protection. He couldn't tell the difference.

Thomas forces Anna's legs apart with his knees. On her white arms, the bruises throb purple-red.

Ranaulf put his hands to either side of his head, tried to quieten the pounding. The light was dull; the sun that had hidden behind the clouds all day was creeping away. He had never wanted anything to do with women, he told himself, then paused; he was tired of even those thoughts. God had entrusted him with the care of a woman's soul, and Sir Thomas had caught him in this net. And yet to know and not to speak, or act … Was there something he could do where words would fail? A silent act of justice?

The capital *P* had a stem running all the way down the side of the page, creating a patterned blue margin for the words Ranaulf had written. At the bottom, the stem twisted into a fancy knot, then unwound to become the tail of a blue dragon with a long, thin neck, tiny legs, and flopping ears. Above, in the blue-green circle of the letter, was an ornate tree painted in shades of orange, its branches hugging the inside of the curve. Its tiny leaves formed a symmetrical pattern of loops and swirls that tumbled around the gnarled trunk and … was that a figure or the trunk? Ranaulf looked closer. Yes, the shape of a woman, her hair becoming autumn leaves. He wondered if these were Cuthbert's dreams turned to paint and ink.

A bang and he jumped, his arms and legs tingling with shock. How long had he been sitting there?

'Back from visiting the anchoress, Father? It must be grim over there in Hartham.' Cuthbert was at the door.

'Yes, the maid was well liked. It seems a wet nurse is looking after the baby.'

'What will happen now, do you think?'

'With someone to look after the child, the anchorhold returns to what it was: Sister Sarah and Louise, the maid.'

'Life with only Louise, that's harsh.' Cuthbert smiled. 'But truly, life in that cell is harsh. This room is narrow, but to spend a life in that one …' He grimaced. 'At least the sun shines here sometimes. How could I paint without going outside?' He looked down at his work. 'What do you think?'

'It's beautiful, Brother, beautiful. The delicacy of the patterns, such intricate decoration. And I like the way the stem of the letter makes a border for the words.'

'But what about the tree and the woman? The dragon?' Cuthbert asked.

'The tree is beautiful, certainly, but the dragon …'

'It's only a small dragon, and inoffensive, comical even. The words and painting go together; it's like a pattern, like the two colours of thread in that fancy brocade Prior Walter chose for the altar. The one helps us to see the other. And if a woman smiles when she reads …' His words ran out.

'Brother, you argue well, but a woman doesn't need humour when she prays.'

'Surely if we laugh, God must laugh sometimes too.' Cuthbert leaned forward and smiled.

That was the most the illuminator had ever said to him without making a joke, Ranaulf realised. Perhaps he had a point. That last idea was weak, though, even Cuthbert must know that. Our actions don't always reflect those of God, or he would cheat, maim, even kill. There were holy wars, though, and the king's justice … Nonetheless, Ranaulf was beginning to see the value in these paintings, their sheer beauty, if nothing else.

'Well, I'm glad you've made a start, Brother. There are many pages yet to copy, and they will need decoration. Sir Thomas wants it completed for the new year.'

'Sir Thomas? Is this for him? That man! You must have heard the talk over in Hartham: the maid, the handmills, the threats over land. How can one man force his will on so many others?'

'He has money, Brother. And position. And he wants his Psalter quickly.'

'But that's not possible.'

'I've told him it wouldn't be done. By Lent, perhaps, I said, but most likely Easter. I didn't wait to hear his answer.'

⤙ SARAH ⤚

APART FROM LIZZIE AND Father Ranaulf, Louise had kept visitors away from me, no doubt protecting them as much as me, but I told her I would see Eleanor.

'I just went to visit Stella,' she began.

'Stella? Is she a friend?'

'She's Anna's baby. You know, Stella.'

'I thought her name was Isolda,' I said. 'Lizzie told me Anna had heard a minstrel singing a song at Leeton once, about a woman called Isolda.'

'Well I call her Stella. I was going to call her Star, 'cause with her fingers, when she cries, she puts them out like a star, like this.' She lifted both hands and spread her fingers wide. 'Just like a star. Then Father Finnegan told me that in other places they say that word "stella", instead of star. I like that word. *Stella.*' She said it slowly.

'And how is she? Little Stella?'

'She's very little and she cries lots, just like our Will did, but she laughs sometimes too. And Gillie laughs. You should come and … oh, they won't let you come out, even to see her, will they? But when she's bigger, she can come and visit, with me.

And may be,' she began to whisper, 'may be I can teach her some letters.'

'Yes, may be. Do you remember them?'

She nodded. 'Mmm, mostly. I remember "Anna", 'cause I wrote it on the ground, over and over, when Ma said Anna died. She's got my letters, hasn't she?'

'She has.' Two simple letters, I thought, folded over on themselves.

'And her grave's only a bit away from where I buried the baby bird. I like that.'

The dead bird; that seemed seasons ago.

'I'd like to be a bird. Would you?' Eleanor prattled on.

'When I was a little bit older than you, I saw a jongleur at a market, and he could jump and tumble and fly through the air.' I was startled at myself, at this story I knew. 'I called him Swallow, because I thought that's what he looked like. I wanted to be like him.'

'Swallow, that's a good name. What else could he do?'

'He could dance and juggle and balance swords, and he told stories, but the thing I liked best was when three men stood in a line and two men stood on their shoulders, and then Swallow climbed up onto them, as if he was climbing a ladder. He stood tall, stretched out his arms like this, looked up at the sky and jumped, flew, did a somersault in the air.'

'I'd be scared up that high.'

'He wasn't. He looked like he was flying, like he never had to come back to the ground, and he could never fall. That's what I loved.'

'So did he never fall, then?'

'Well, he did once, he told me, and broke his nose.'

'Like that bird that tried to fly and couldn't.'

I didn't answer, angry at her questions that made it seem so ordinary.

Eleanor ran her finger down a fold in the curtain, then poked at it to make it billow, as she always did, thinking. 'Even though you wanted to be like Swallow, they made you come and stay here, in the dark. That's mean.'

'No, I've told you I wanted to come here. And I can leave, if I want to.'

'Do you like the dark best, then?'

I told Eleanor it was time for her to go, and sat down on the straw beneath my parlour window, a blanket wrapped around me. Had I thought Swallow could never fall? Perhaps when I was ten, but I began to understand, as I crouched in my cell just why that leap had made me gasp. He dared himself in the air, knowing he could fall; that was what I loved. I thought I had come to the anchorhold daring everything — to look at the ground, to leap into the air, to face my death and go on living. But I had come like a bird taking fright and hiding in its nest, to be safe from my own body. I had given up Swallow's chance of dying, and with it the chance to fly.

I looked down at the straw beneath my feet, shuffled it apart until I saw the dirt below. Father Ranaulf's voice hung in my mind: *Don't come to God and ask to be safe.* I slipped off my shoes, curled my toes into the soil.

Perhaps it was the tea that Lizzie still brought for me, perhaps it was my body's grief, or perhaps it was a gift: the blood I hadn't shed for months. I pulled off my shift and walked to my altar. I had wanted to be Euphemia or Agnes, sealed up and needing nothing. But Anna and Isabella, even Eleanor and her endless questions, had shown me that holiness was a risk. Blood and pain and bodies. I looked at the crucifix above my altar as if for the first time, at the almond-shaped wound, the drops of blood. Where else was I so like Christ but in this body?

The night was cold, the wind blew in sharp gusts. A dog howled, long and thin. I was sure she was near, in my parlour, but she said nothing.

'Isabella.' A song, four simple notes. 'Isabella, I've been thinking on what enclosure means, and I understand, now, what you said: that the days don't measure our commitment. When Anna died I couldn't see a reason to stay, but I was too afraid to leave — I thought it would be failure. Now I see I can walk out that door like you did.' I wanted her to speak, to help me understand, but I could hear only my own breath. I ran my hands over the ledge of the parlour window, felt the marks where the stone had been cut. 'But it would be hard to leave; these walls have looked after me, mostly, they're part of me now, they're my skin. I know the cracks between each stone, the way the dirt rises into the corners, the curve worn in the place where I kneel to pray.

'And even my curtain: I know the weave, the loose stitches where the cross is sewn on, the fall of its creases. All this time I've been here I thought I would deny my body, and I tried to follow my Rule, but it makes me think on my body more and more. When I eat, even if it's only Louise's pottage that I thought was always the same dull stuff, now I can taste the peas, or the turnips, or whether she's used some parsley or another herb that Anna told her about. I was to shut out the world in here, but sounds and smells creep in my windows and wrap themselves around me. The smell of hay, mouldering berries, the sound of a spade in mud. They're the things that I love now. They've become part of how I pray, how I care for people. Whatever my Rule says, my body is part of that.'

Perhaps the Rule doesn't know everything of God. I thought Isabella spoke, but it might have been the wind.

We were quiet for a time, only the oak tree soughing outside. I remembered its wide branches, the way it arched high, too high to see the top, the way it seemed to sit among the clouds.

'I think I'll die if I don't feel the sun again.' The words came without thought and I stepped back, as if Isabella had said them.

'*EGO TE ABSOLVO*.' The rhythm of Father Ranaulf's visits had not altered, and as usual he did not say very much, but his presence behind the curtain had somehow changed. I crossed myself, listened to his blessing and took a deep breath. I had prayed and thought on this for days, looked for the right words to say, and now I wondered if I would find them.

'Father Ranaulf, could I speak to you a moment?'

'Sister.'

'Anna's death and … other things have made me think about my life in this cell. It's more than a year since they nailed up that door. I want so much to love Christ and join in his suffering. Over and again I've felt that I've failed and, with Anna's death, that God had turned his face away. I'm weary, Father. I've prayed and thought about whether I can stay.' My voice wavered.

'Sister, if you wish to leave, I can make sure that you do so safely.'

I looked to the curtain, surprised, wishing I could see his face. He had spoken without pause, concern liquid in his voice. It took me some moments to shape my next words.

'Some time ago I looked at the crucifix in my cell and I saw, as if for the first time, Father. The stretch of Christ's arms caught between life and death, heaven and earth.' I hesitated, nervous.

'That's me, stretched between my cell and the village outside, between enclosure and the people I pray for. I thought it failure, but perhaps it was what I came here for, my way of joining Christ in his suffering. It's strange to me, but knowing that I can leave, knowing about Isabella, has helped me to stay.'

'I see that.' His voice was quiet.

His three words loosened my shoulders, let me go on speaking. 'I made a commitment and I need to know more of what it means. It seems as if I'm only now beginning to learn. I'm committed still to stay here, but I feel that my vows ... I feel that I can't live as I have been.' Despite his understanding, I couldn't say the words.

'But Sister, I don't see how you can stay and renounce your vows.'

'I won't renounce them, Father. I seek God more than I ever have, but my soul and my body need the sun.'

'Your Rule calls you to contain your senses, Sister.'

'It does, Father, but my Rule is also clear that an anchoress may vary her outer Rule according to her needs and her confessor's guidance.'

'Yes, it is.'

'I'm sure that I can stay here only if the sun can reach me. My body is already weak. Would you arrange for a wall to be built so that I can go outside?' I heard the words tumble from my mouth. 'I'd remain closed from sight, as I am now, and I'd use my garden for prayer and meditation.'

'Sister, I—'

'And our Mother Mary, is she not a garden enclosed?'

'*Hortus conclusus*. That's true, and—'

'I'd behave with the same—'

'Sister, let me speak. I've been concerned for some time that you will become seriously ill. A place to walk outside, a garden as you call it — as far as I know it would be irregular, an anchoress walking outside, but then, this cell has known other irregularities.' He cleared his throat. 'It's my responsibility to ensure your well-being so that you may continue here, for as long as God wills it. I'll pray on your proposal.' He paused. 'And I will speak to the prior. And Father Simon, of course.'

When he left, I stood, walked to my door and back again as I did when I was restless, but this time all felt different. I looked up at my horn window with its dull orange light. Soon, perhaps, I would see the true sun, not this enclosed one.

Was it my own impatience that made me feel it, or was Father Ranaulf rushing my confession? Surely not, I thought, but he began to talk of my garden almost in the same breath as he told me my penance.

'I've prayed about your suggestion of a wall, Sister. And I've spoken with Father Peter. I had thought a garden would be unusual, but it seems that many anchoresses have a garden of some kind. Some quite large, according to Father Peter. We both agree that a simple wall would be suitable here.'

'Yes, Father.' I tried to keep my voice calm, but I couldn't. 'Thank you, Father. I'm glad you, that both of you, agree.' It was no use; I gave in to my excitement. 'I know the sun never shines on my cell so the wall will need to be built out a way, out beyond the parlour door there. It could have a gate just near the parlour door and I could plant chamomile and thyme and—'

'You've built it already then, Sister.' I thought perhaps I heard a laugh. 'It hasn't been easy, however, to persuade the prior. He argued with me, of course, read out the words of the corrody about maintaining the houses and enclosures of the recluse, and noted that there is no garden wall to be repaired. Of course, I'd expected that response, and Father Peter and I had already prepared an argument.'

'And, Father? What was your argument? Can you tell me?' I rushed on, thinking I should be quiet. He had already spoken more than usual.

'Well, I pointed out that the failure to supply access to sufficient air and exercise for a woman of your standing, the daughter of an important cloth merchant, is in itself a fault to be remedied. To repair is to make good a fault, and the absence of a garden wall is in fact the fault. The means, therefore, of rectifying the fault is to provide the garden for which adequate provision has not been made. Clear and logical. The prior had no answer.'

I had seen his whole face only once, through the fog of my anger, but I could picture his smile.

'And you said you would speak to Father Simon?'

'Yes, I've done that, too. The conversation with the prior was only the first of my debates. I expected Father Simon to resist; you're asking, after all, for an addition to the church building. I wasn't disappointed.' He smiled again, I thought. 'But as you may know, Sister, maintenance of the church building is the responsibility of the people of the village, and Roger, it seems, is the keeper of the church fabric. And he is a man with a good will. He said he knew nothing of you or your needs, but his wife always speaks well of you, as do the other village women. So he'll find some men to lend a hand with the wall.'

I hadn't recognised what a quest I had set for my confessor. He'd had finally to convince Prior Walter to allow the men to use scraps of stone left over from the priory building to construct the wall. The prior, claiming he was concerned about stewardship of God's gifts, even to the rubble left behind from building, had spent some time arguing, Father Ranaulf said, though it was more a matter of form than conviction.

When he left I stayed on my chair by the window and remembered his first, rushed visits and single words. He had never before told me so much of himself and the priory. When he'd argued for me, for a garden for me, it seemed that he'd also been arguing for himself. We had both changed, but we also had our own concerns, each on our own side of the wall.

Father Peter had told me of the mercy of God, of his own weary legs, of the surprises he found on his walks to see me, of the cats that hid in the chapel and the angry prior who shooed them away. Father Ranaulf had spoken only a few words, but I was learning to listen to him in a different way. For him, words, spoken or written, were like the seeds that Maud had described to me: set carefully into the ground and tended, they unfurled, leaf by leaf.

I had longed for more from Father Ranaulf, but I realised that I hadn't always heard all that he had been saying to me in those few words, and especially in the spaces between them. I remembered the day, not long after Anna died, when I had thrown back at him his words of consolation. Instead of more words or teaching, he had offered a silence so gentle that I'd felt he had pulled back the curtain and touched my face with the soft palm of his hand.

LIKE MOST ANCHORHOLDS, MY cell had been built in the shadow of the church so that it would never receive any sun. Brother Cuthbert, the monk who had painted St Margaret and the dragon in my book, came to take measurements to make sure the sun would shine into at least part of my garden. He told Father Ranaulf that the walled space would need to be long, and allow enough room behind my cell so that I could go out my door, and at the front would need to extend some way beyond the parlour to where the church no longer blocked the sun. He marked the plan on a small scrap of parchment, and left it with me until the men should be ready to start building. It was so much more than a plan with measurements: the garden would be a little wider than my cell, and Cuthbert drew the huge oak tree in the cemetery that would hang over the side wall, each of its leaves outlined separately and a bird on one of the branches; on the door for visitors, tucked in the corner formed by the front and side walls and nearest to my parlour, he drew an oversized bolt, and in the opposite corner a bed full of blooming flowers.

I looked at the plan often and hoped every day to hear the sounds of men's voices and the clink of metal on stone — but I had to wait. The snow was heavy, melting into slush that stayed on the soil, making it too soggy for building. I had been in my cell over a year, so a short wait should have been nothing to me, but I asked Louise each morning what the weather was like, whether the ground was drying. I prayed and read and sewed, keeping my mind inside with my body.

As the weather turned, Father Ranaulf told the builders to carry down the stones from the priory, and Gilbert, his young assistant, Brother Alain, and Brother Hugo came with them to help. The wall was being built at last, but work slowed, then stopped, then started again depending on the weather and the men making time for it. They were harrowing and beginning to sow, Maud said, and the seeds wouldn't wait.

Father Ranaulf decided to remove the nails from my door once the foundations of the wall had been laid. Given Isabella's story, he was concerned that the door be opened without secrecy, so everyone would know that all was well. I was so excited at the idea of going outside, I hadn't paused to consider what it would mean: that dark barrier unlocked, the seal of my cell broken. I had once thought that the open space would make me blow away.

He heard my confession first, and I could tell, from the sound of his breath, that he was anxious.

'Sister, when the nails are removed, we need to consider your safety. Here is the key to your door, the one that Father Simon has been keeping. It's yours now.'

I took the key from the ledge of my parlour window. It was a simple device, with a large loop at the top shaped into an arch so that it could be easily hung on a nail. Its weight felt serious and solid and, as I closed my fingers over it, I was surprised by its warmth. Warmth that came from Father Ranaulf's body.

He told me to pray at my altar while he went around to the door. I knelt, my heart pounding. Sounds of scuffling, bumping, and the grate of iron on iron. I could not be obedient; I needed to be nearer, to know more. I walked to the corner and put both my hands on the door as I had when I was enclosed. The wood rattled, shook, and I could hear the grunts of Father Ranaulf's straining. He was determined to do this alone, and had rejected Roger's offer of help.

The door began to shiver beneath my hands, and then a sharp, high sound, the wood holding the nail tight. It was still again. I heard Father Ranaulf's grunt. Again the shivering, the struggle, the wood clutching the nail, then the tearing, but a different sound from when the nails were hammered in — an uprooting, a separating that shuddered up my arm, as if it were happening inside me. Travail. Emma's deep groans. I almost wanted it to stop, go back, hammer in the nails again, keep me safe. Another and another, the grating sound of resistance and release, until Father Ranaulf called to me that he would try to open the door.

I held my breath. A single heartbeat between sealed and unsealed. I stood back; the door jolted and stayed. Again he tried, and again. Finally, anger in his voice, he told me he would fetch Roger. I understood: it had mattered that he open the door himself.

Roger spoke so quietly at first, being careful of the anchoress, I thought, that I could hardly hear him. But after a mighty thumping on the door he explained in his usual loud voice: the dampness on that side of the church, the swollen wood, the door's lack of use.

'Best tell Sister make sure she stands away now, Father,' he said, as if the only one I could hear was Father Ranaulf. 'We'll have to dig some soil out from underneath. That'll dislodge it, you see.'

The dull thump of metal on hard earth, a slight shifting in the soil under the door, tiny spots of light that grew, the edge of a tool, perhaps a pick, reaching in, scratching away until a ragged slice of light lay bright along the dirt beneath the door.

'I'll just get me knife in the sides here, cut away some of this moss and dirt, Father. It be well stuck all round.'

The thin scrape of iron on wood, the door shifting slightly, Roger's satisfied grunts. Then a tongue of iron slid beneath the door; it must have been curved at the end because it moved upwards to sit neatly against the wood.

'Right now, Father, you pull the handle there an' I'll pull down here.'

Sounds of straining, the wood resisting. Suddenly light flew toward me and was gone, except for a bright fringe around the door's edges, as they pushed it almost closed again. I could hear the men's voices clearly now, discussing the need to cut back the wood.

'And while I'm at it, Father, how's 'bout I fix that parlour door as gets stuck, or least that's what our Winnie says of it.'

As I sat at my desk, a thin breeze, the musky smell of moss, wandered up to me, drifted around my head and disappeared. I thought of Isabella. I tried to read, but looked up again and again at the door, where Roger's hair, his forehead, his hands appeared and disappeared as he filed its edges, and another pair of hands, Father Ranaulf's I supposed, held it steady.

Kneeling at my altar some days ago, I had thought on this profound moment of unsealing, and now there were two men grunting as they worked on my stubborn door. I smiled. The wood and the damp, like everything else around me, were chipping away the edges of my piety.

THE WALL GREW SLOWLY, as the men snatched time from the fields to work on it. The day that Louise told me it was as high as her knees, I decided to go outside and look at it once it was dark. I unlocked my door and stood for some time in the gaping space, afraid. How had I walked about in the world for so many years and not been aware that its smell and its shape could knock my feet out from beneath me? I thought of Stella and her crying; perhaps she, too, wanted to return to the dark safety she had known.

I do not have words to tell of my first step outside, but to say that I gasped as if jumping into a river. The chill of the night, I knew well, but this air sank into me like a new life. Only then did I grasp how rank my cell was, and how much I had lived in my own smell, thick as pottage. I breathed in deeply and, for all its life, the air felt like a knife in my throat; I coughed so much that I had to go inside and sit until I was calmer.

Slowly I moved back to the door and stepped outside, holding on to the doorframe like an old woman, taking shallow breaths, letting my skin learn this new kind of fresh coldness.

The sky was black above me, covered thick with stars, and when I turned the corner from the back of my cell into the main part of my garden I saw that it was almost the dark of the moon; only the thinnest crescent remained. I blinked, gasped, began to cough again, but less harshly this time. The stones of the outside wall of my cell were slimy, like a soft, wet creature moving at my touch, and I flinched. All I could see was black, but I remembered the damp greenness from my first day in the anchorhold. Now I had to touch it, if only with my fingertips, to feel my way.

I looked across to the garden wall, only a few stones high still, and I wondered if this was what I wanted. It had taken me so long to learn the stones inside, and I would need to start again, one by one, in this new kind of cell without a roof. A rooster's weary crow, a quick shout, a door banging. I turned, walked inside, bolted my door and knelt at my squint. The stone beneath my arms welcomed me.

The night was a creature new to me, its darkness so different from my cell's, its silence alive and breathing. For all my fear, I loved stepping into the mouth of its fierce blackness. I thought of St Margaret being swallowed into the maw of the dragon, then Anna's high, spiralling wail into the black; the night was where I would find her, caught like Margaret in the dragon's belly. Perhaps this darkness would also tear, give up its dead. Until then, I would walk with it, feel its threat.

In the days that followed I listened to the chipping and talking and laughter outside my cell. Words ran together into a low hum I couldn't understand, but at times they were sharp and loud, complaints about borders and grazing. Roger said he had heard that Sir Thomas would make the villagers graze their sheep on his fallow land. 'And make us pay,' he growled. 'We pay to fertilise his land with our own sheep's shit.' The sounds of shushing, then a muttered, 'Beg pardon, Sister'. Some of the other voices I knew, and a young one with a quick laugh, I discovered with surprise, was Cuthbert's. Once when there was a pause in the chatter he began to sing, until the men shushed him, but I could still hear his humming and some snatches of song; I wondered how he and Father Ranaulf shared the four walls of their scriptorium.

One morning there were sharp words. 'What's this here? No one told me aught of this.'

I recognised Gwylim's voice, but there was no answer, only grunting and the clink of metal on stone.

'Bill, I said to you, what's this here? What's a wall for?'

'For the anchoress, steward. A garden. Any more, you'd need to ask Father Ranaulf at the priory.'

'Don't doubt I will. But you can stop work now. No building without Sir Thomas agrees. You'll be needing to get back to the fields, lads.'

'No, this be church work, Gwylim. You well know it's ours to do and pay for. Speak to what man you choose, it's no matter to me, but we'll build this wall.'

'We'll see, then, won't we? Like I said, no building without Sir Thomas agrees.'

There was no more talk after that. I sat in the silence, chilled at the thought of Sir Thomas telling the men to stop. My garden so close, would he punish me and take it away? He had been concerned for me, in the darkness, so he'd be pleased, wouldn't he?

*

The second time I went outside I walked the length of my cell's outer wall, but stopped when I could see the dark gap where the garden door would be fitted. Even though the wall was not then as high as my waist, it saved me from falling out into the village — that dark gap would not.

The ground near the wall was mud, rough and trodden; in some places it piled up and in others ditches and troughs had filled with water. By the light of my lamp I could see the shape of a boot pressed into the dirt. I looked over at the village; blackness, with here and there a flickering light.

I ran my hand along the stones. Anna would have brought me rosemary and chamomile to plant. But she was in her grave, not far away. Would Thomas come again and peer over my wall? Was his desire gone? Or was it anger? They seemed so akin. Louise had told me he would come to the village with Gwylim sometime soon to check accounts and unresolved arguments about land boundaries. My first thought had been to be sure to stay inside, but slowly, as I touched that familiar tender place, I realised that I felt no fear, only grief. Anna was dead; there was nothing more that he could do to me.

Stepping between the puddles, though still I sank into the mud, I put my hands on the top of the wall. I could climb over it if I wanted. It would be so simple; I wasn't strong anymore, but a foot in this gap, one on the jutting stone above. I thought of Isabella; now I had the choice, and I wanted to stay. I turned, stepped over the mud and onto the grass, spread my arms and took weak steps, but as big as I could manage, as if I were a child. In spite of the wet ground,

I lay down. The cold and damp pulled at my back, dragged me toward them. The scrape of bones, that scratching voice. Agnes; I shook her off and looked up, the clouds like a ceiling above me. I remembered the picture of angels in my Breviary when I was a little girl, so many that their wings covered the sky with feathers.

THE SKY WAS BLACK; the new moon a thin crescent. The wall was not finished, but was high enough for me to be able to sit outside, unobserved, at night. Scat strutted along the top of the stones, found a smooth place and lay down. Her contented purr made me feel brave, so I walked to the gateway, still without its gate. It was a dark hole, opening onto the places I had seen only once: the river, the green, Cram Hill. A familiar breeze, the rich scent of moss. I smiled, and Isabella was gone. I could go out with her if I chose; three steps and I would be on the path where everyone walked. I had learned to go places in my mind: to my left, the church and the bridge; to my right, the mill, the duck pond, the villagers' houses, and finally, up on the hill, the manor house.

Of a sudden Scat hissed. A strange crackle … no, deeper than that, a growl, an animal of some kind. A flash of eyes, a long tongue. I spun around to Scat, but she was still on the wall, ears up, tail weaving, looking into the distance; behind her, a yellow glow in the sky. A bonfire, I thought, though why this night? A shout, tight strings of panic. I climbed onto a pile of unused stone and peered through the branches of the oak, its leaves but round buds. On the rise, orange flames leaped and danced, shooting tiny sparks into the sky, but I couldn't see what was burning. In the eerie light I caught flickering glimpses of people running out their doors, alert to that sound in their wooden houses, always vulnerable to fire. They stopped, looked, then sharp shouts, voices jumping, darting back and forward. The manor. It was the manor, they said.

More shouts: Hugo? Mary? Alyce? Wymon? Sir Thomas was still inside, perhaps Gwylim as well. The black shapes of people, some running toward the manor, some running away from it. Villagers bent over, coughing. A woman's voice screamed, 'Alyce, Alyce, get her out.' The night became a mass of horror: flames writhing into the blackness, sparks like laughing demons, moans, calls, a name, a sob, babies crying, the bone-breaking sound of timber falling, an ugly smell floating toward me. Even inside my wall I felt it, the swirl of disaster and panic.

A high animal scream, a movement from within the flames, a horse flickering red and yellow, and I gasped. For a moment I thought that it was burning. It jumped the fence and ran along the river road toward Cram Hill. And another shape, following. A crash as the manor began to collapse. The fire a thing alive, a creature opening its enormous mouth.

In the morning the air was sharp with the smell of ash, even inside my cell, and there were none of the usual noises outside; all was strangely quiet. I had often thought how different silences can be. An anchoress, I suppose, is a student of silence, its forms and shapes. That day after the fire, the silence was one of shock and bewilderment, full of the questions of what was to come, but there was something else binding us. As I prayed, flickers of orange writhed before me, and though I asked God's comfort for all who suffered, I kept my mind away from names. Or faces. I worried for the villagers, but I was also afraid that if I looked more closely, I might discover that I felt relief, or worse.

Louise had been out of her room much of the morning, but she knocked on my shutters to tell me the news. The manor was stone on the first floor with a wooden second floor, and the flames had taken hold most strongly up there.

'Sir Thomas got out, or downstairs, but he collapsed, his clothes alight. Hugo was sleeping in the stables with a sick horse and helped drag him out. The men carried Gwylim's body down this morning. Alyce, Mary, and Wymon were asleep downstairs in the hall. Poor Alyce, Wymon said she was with them as they ran, but a burning beam fell on her. Nothing they could do.'

'Alyce! She's dead? She was young, wasn't she?'

'A few years older than Eleanor. She worked in the kitchen when Sir Thomas stayed at the manor. Thank God, Lady Cecilia stayed at Friaston and wasn't here. Course, she never came when it was for accounts and business.'

Later in the day Maud came to visit. My Rule would have called it gossip, but Maud thought of it as something else, and I had begun to agree. Sir Thomas had been taken to Friaston, badly injured, and Bill had gone to tell the priory. Three horses had escaped — Hugo had managed to unbolt some of the doors — but one had been caught in the flames; the animals in the barn were trapped and died when the stored hay caught alight; feathers lay charred among the rubble of the dovecote.

After a silence, Maud added, 'And who knows how these things start. Happens so easy: a spark, a candle, may be; something in the kitchen. Our young Fulke, you know him — well, not really so young — he was out setting rabbit traps on the lord's forests last night and he says he saw a woman coming out of the manor, her hair alight, he thought. Until he recognised who it was. An' I teased him, he's such a head for fancy, our Fulke. He should write stories, he should.

'Anyhows, Sister, my Billy found us a handmill that wasn't all smashed in the pile of them at the back of the kitchen. Just needs a bit of work to set it right. That'll suit us until the next steward comes on his high horse.'

When she left, I sat at my desk. I had not wanted Thomas to die, had not even thought of it, but I had to confess that for a moment, as the manor collapsed, I thought God might have been declaring judgement. Instead, poor Alyce had died. And Gwylim.

Burned and ill, Sir Thomas demanded compassion and prayers for his suffering. I would pray for him, because I had vowed to do that, though I would have to trust the words to say what my heart would not.

IN THE DAYS THAT followed the fire, more men came to finish my wall. With no steward, and the lord so ill, the usual obligations to the manor were in confusion, but each family still had their own land to tend, especially with the coming of spring, planting seeds and weeding, so I was surprised. There was an air of waiting to know if Sir Thomas would live, a kind of indrawn breath among us all, and perhaps it was easier to be together, working.

'Maybe they want to be sure you stay now, after so much,' Louise said. 'Make sure you have all you need. Maybe they have some thoughts of Anna.' She paused and I heard her breathe out heavily. 'I wonder what will happen to us, Sister, if Sir Thomas doesn't live? Lady Cecilia is a pious woman, and she would look to your care, but she is a woman, after all. I don't know what laws they have for rich folk inheriting land.'

I hadn't let myself think of what might happen to Louise and me. The corrody was signed, the priory had the land as agreed, so it seemed that all should continue as it was. But what of the village without a lord?

'We will pray each day for Sir Thomas to recover, Louise.'

I could hear the men chipping and cutting stone, talking seriously, sometimes laughing and humming. It was the first time so many had gathered by my parlour without whispering or shushing one another. It seemed that they wanted to include me in their lives. Their talk roamed around everyday matters: the state of the newly planted soil, newborn lambs, feed for grazing.

'I've taken me sheep from the demesne land, put 'em back to graze on the corn stubble. And I've taken a few from Sir Thomas's flock as well — not to keep like, but what's left fallow needs the manure. Fair's fair when he made us pay to graze on his land.' It was Roger. 'Who's to stop us? For now, anyway.'

Grumbling began again, words rising and falling, short bursts of bitter laughter, plans to return the boundary stones that Sir Thomas had moved, grumbling about the smashed handmills, voices I didn't know. Words drifted like a squally day.

'The man deserves to suffer.'

Silence for a time. 'I cursed him too, but we can't wish him to suffer. No. Not right.'

'There's Alyce in the ground just there, and Anna, and Sam. We can't wish more death.'

'Anna. Think of the maid and why she died. And he'd have bled us dry and thrown us off our land, given it to the sheep.'

'Strange to think: for all a man's money, all it takes is a spark.'

'And so we must pray for him. He's a man just like us.'

The next morning Louise told me that Roger and Bill had hung the gate. I had opened my door before, but going out in the day was different. I stood from my squint after Terce, turned the key in its lock, and pushed open the door. Even though the morning was dull, I could see nothing but a strange shifting of light and shadows that hurt my eyes. I put my hand up to shield them. Slowly, as they adjusted, I saw my wall, three or four steps in front of me, stone on stone, rough but laid snugly together. I stepped forward to touch it, and walked to the corner running my fingers across its roughness, as if holding a friend's hand. Despite its height, well above my head, I felt that the village could see me, the recluse breaking her Rule of life, opening herself to the sight of others, so I stayed close by the outer wall, pacing slowly along its length. There were the tree, the stones and the mud that I had seen in darkness, but they had been as ghosts to what I now saw: stronger, brighter, more threatening than anything I had known before. When the tree moved it seemed alive and the mud looked as if it could shape itself into a man like Adam.

Towards the corner of the outer wall and the front wall I stopped; Father Ranaulf had told me that Gilbert and Cuthbert had made a bench for me from the thick branch of the oak tree that grew low and long in the churchyard, and had been cut off to make room for my wall. They'd set the bench just below where the branch had once stretched out, a step or two from the corner. It was shaped and rounded, worked smooth, and at each end there was a round face wreathed in carvings of oak leaves and acorns: one face laughing, one serious. I ran my fingers over the serious one and sat down. I was on churchyard ground, above the graves of those I had never known; inside, Agnes ground her dry teeth.

I looked across to my cell wall, slick with green moss. It joined the parlour wall with a rough seam of stones and extended farther to escape the church's shadow. At the corner there was a gate into my garden with a bolt on the inside. I could pull back the bolt and open it, walk by the river, along the village lanes, or into the forest, may be find Isabella.

Perhaps things would change, but I didn't want to go out there. I had barely seen the village, but after more than a year in my cell, its paths, its woods, and its full river were traced inside me. They flowed through my body and I roamed around them, enclosed and unsealed.

❧ RANAULF ❧

RANAULF STOOD AT THE gate. The wood was worn, but solid — and without a handle on the outside. He thought about the first day he had visited the anchorhold and peered around the side of the parlour to the dank shaded grass and the stones of the cell. The new wall would not change that, but he could see that some sun would fall inside the garden, at least in spring and summer.

He moved to the parlour door, pulled at it as he always did, and almost fell backwards when it opened easily. Roger had fixed it, he remembered, though he felt uneasy, unsettled by all the changes. His reaction made no sense, he knew; he had complained of the door, had argued for Sarah's garden, and all had been made good. Still, this was not the anchorhold — nor the anchoress — he had visited that cold winter's day a little more than a year past. He had never seen inside the cell and he would not see the garden, that second space where she would dwell. Irritated at his own lack of reason, he walked into the parlour and closed the door behind him.

'God bless you, Sister Sarah. Good morning.'

'Father Ranaulf. God be with you.'

Her voice was familiar, soothing. He felt himself relax. 'I see that your gate is finished. Your garden is complete.'

'Yes, Roger and Bill came earlier this morning.'

'I had hoped to look at the garden before it was sealed. To see it done at last.' He paused but there was no response from behind the curtain. 'Forgive me, Sister. It's your garden. I suppose because I arranged for the stone and the men, I hoped I might view it. Of course, we couldn't stand in the garden together, or see each other, but if you opened the gate, perhaps—'

'Father.'

It was the old silence, but now they understood each other.

'You're right. I did no more than was needed. I pray that the garden will bless you, Sarah.' The word came so easily. Sarah.

The ritual of confession and absolution, that well-worn path, helped to settle him and he sat quietly for a time before he spoke again. 'We at St Christopher's are praying for Sir Thomas. The prior has visited Friaston and says he's very ill. The physician does what he can, but we must wait on God. The thought of Sir Thomas and his pain stays with me, whatever else I have thought of him.'

'Louise and I pray for him, and Father Simon says Mass for him. It's all we can do,' Sarah said.

'It is.' Irritation rose in his throat again, pushing him to argue at such simple words, however true they might be. Nothing was simple anymore. He had thought his anger at Thomas had been in defence of the young maid, anger purified because it was on behalf of another. But the flames accused him, the spectre of the burned man followed him as if the fire had sprung from his own desire for revenge.

'God is merciful,' Sarah said. He looked at the curtain, wondering if she was speaking of Thomas, or of him, her confessor. But it did not matter; her words were a consolation.

❦ SARAH ❦

ELEANOR WAS QUIETER THAN usual. I thought perhaps it was the fire, and so many deaths in a short time: Anna, Alyce, and the baby bird she had buried, even Gwylim. She had seen him often and had been scared of him, his big hands and his voice that shouted even when he was talking, she had said. She had little to do with the manor, but she understood enough to know that Sir Thomas controlled the villagers' lives, even if from a distance.

I asked about Anna's baby because I knew it would take her mind off all that had happened.

'She still cries, but she looks at me now, and I can make her laugh. And, Sister, when she laughs she makes her hands like stars too.'

'She must like you, Ellie.'

'Mmm. Has Gillie brought her to see you yet? She said she was going to.'

'Lizzie came to see me and give me some herbs for my tea, and she asked if Gillie could bring Stella the next time she comes. And I said yes.'

'Good. It's mean if you miss out, just 'cause you're here. And can I see your garden, Sister? Has Father Finnegan seen your garden?'

'Not yet, Ellie.'

I was embarrassed still at the luxury of my garden, and apart from Louise, Eleanor would be my first visitor. I had wondered if Father Ranaulf and I might speak together in the garden, but then I remembered the words of the demon in the story of St Margaret. A man and a woman might sit together, thinking they were safe because they were speaking of God, but the Devil would use that to tempt them. By looking at each other and then by touching they would sin. I loved my books, but I had been thinking carefully about their words and about who had written them. Not all words are to be read in the same way.

I pulled back the bolt to open my gate. It was heavy and browned with rust; I wondered whose barn or workshop it came from. Some outbuilding of the manor, perhaps. Eleanor and I were shy, our first sight of each other without a wall between us, and though I wanted to hug her, all I could do was stroke her hair. Her feet were bare and thick with mud past her ankles, and I remembered her offer, the first time she visited, to take me where there was good mud. There were streaks of dirt on her face as if she had tried to wash, and in the daylight her red birthmark had less of the dark shadow the glimmer of my candle gave it. She was carrying a bundle wrapped in sacking.

I pointed to the thyme and chamomile and rosemary I had planted and showed her the faces on the ends of my bench.

'I saw them the day the men carried it here. That boy Gilbert said he made it with Brother Cuthbert. I like the happy one best,' she said.

We sat together and she moved close to me. The warmth of her body, touching my legs and my arms, was both memory and revelation. The light movement of her hand when she brushed her hair from her face, her thin arms, the outline of her shoulder beneath her shift, the swing of her legs that didn't quite reach the ground — they were all recovery.

If my first steps outside had been shock and awakening, sitting with Ellie was a return home. I closed my eyes.

'Sister.' She shook my arm. 'Sister, I want to show you this.'

She lifted the bundle onto her knee. 'I thought you might be angry but I want to show you. I went to the manor house just to look a bit, though Ma said I wasn't to. But I went anyway. And under some other stuff, just in a corner where it was hard to see, under that grey ash stuff, I found this.'

She pulled away the sacking and handed me a small book, so damaged that it would not completely close. The leather had burned away from the wooden covers and the pages were wrinkled and wavy, most of them crumbling at the edges. I let it fall open and turned the pages. The words, written in a block in the centre, were smudged in places with black, but clear enough to read; it was a Psalter. The outer margins were scorched and dark, but even so the paintings made me gasp. Flowers and rabbits and birds and trees and creatures that I had never seen before — half-man, half-bird; dragons and monsters with a head at each end. And on the first page, King David under a tree with his harp, curls in his hair, his face turned upward as if he was listening.

'That monster there's my favourite, that one with a head like a bird and a tail and legs like on a dragon,' Eleanor said. 'And it's done in those good colours.'

'See this, Ellie? Just here, that shape is a *V* for virgin, for the Virgin Mary.'

'That's the wood in the barn, not a letter like in a word, and look, there's Jesus — he looks a bit like Stella — and Mary and Joseph, and that's an ox peeking at the baby. It's a picture, not a letter, Sister.'

'It does look like wood, but the man who painted this — and I'm sure it was Brother Cuthbert — is so clever that he can make a letter part of a picture, and those letters there — that one and that one — see, all together they say *Virgin*.'

'Could we read this, and could you could you teach me more letters, Sister? And can I keep it? I think Ma won't want me to but if you say …'

'Yes, I think that you found it and you should have it. No one will take it now it's so badly burned. But if you think your ma will say no, perhaps you could leave it here, and when you come to visit we can look at it together. And I won't forget it's yours to take whenever you want.'

When Eleanor left, I sat at my desk and turned the Psalter's pages. I thought that one day, and I was learning to judge the right time, I would ask Father Ranaulf for a quill and some ink, perhaps a few small sheets of parchment. We would learn together, Eleanor and I. Our secret. I thought of him, a scribe, seated at his desk, copying letter after letter. He had told me that a book of psalms for Sir Thomas was finished and ready to be delivered, and though he knew it was his responsibility, he wanted to pass the task to Brother Cuthbert. 'I find it hard to look at the man after …' That was all he said.

So the book had been delivered.

On some pages I read the psalms, but I looked more often at the illustrations. I thought of my embroidery and admired Cuthbert's skill, so fine, but with such a world inside his head. I took the pages of Isabella's story out of my Rule and tucked them inside the Psalter's back cover. Some stories must be told.

SIR THOMAS'S CONDITION REMAINED the same, and though uneasy questions hung around the village, each day pressed its needs: the weeds had to be pulled, the animals fed, the lambs tended, some late sowing finished. The village settled back into its familiar routine. A new steward had been appointed and work on the demesne began again. I wondered why the villagers weren't as alarmed at spring as I was. The sun was brighter than I had ever seen it, the grass shone, and the leaves on the oak tree grew thick and fast.

Just as I had learned day by day to live in my cell, I began to learn about my garden. I walked around it touching each stone, counting my steps: eighteen on the longer side and ten across. I knew that most of my garden would always be shaded by the church, and even though the days were warming, it held on to the chill of night. On the outside wall of my cell, the moisture had begun to dry, though the fur of moss grew lush in the gaps between the stones. The grass was growing back by the wall where the men had dug and trampled the earth, tiny single shoots that thickened each day. The feathery chamomile stalks had new buds.

It was such pleasure to feel the sun that I allowed myself only a short time outside each day. At first, I thought it was from fear that I was sinning, that I had broken my vows, but really it was a fear of intensity. The sun is touch; it had always been the caress of a hand, the gentleness I longed for, but since my isolation, it had become much more and for a time I clung to the familiarity of the darkness.

One morning, a breeze made me shiver and I walked to a patch of garden where the sun was shining. The scent of moss and earth drifted past me. I lifted my robe and pulled it over my head. My shift was thin, and the air was cool on my arms and legs, but the sun warmed my skin, licked at me, played around my face, ran its fingers along my arms, across my breasts, and down my legs.

It seemed to me that Christ called to me and touched me. My Rule tells me that I must come to know God by controlling my senses, by keeping the flesh in need and not allowing my eyes or nose or ears to lead me back into the world. I had read and reread the words, wearied myself, tried so hard to be a holy woman, beaten my body and heart against stone. But that morning, it was as if I turned, and love was there, simple and without rules.

I remembered then the story near the end of my Rule; it says that Christ is my lover-knight who longs passionately for me, who went into battle to rescue me and died for the sake of his deep love. It advises me to touch him, my lover, with as much love as I might feel for another person. When I read that, I see Emma kissing Godric and other things I can barely say, of skin and mouths and faces caught somewhere in pain or ecstasy. That day, the sun on my skin, I remembered the night of my hair shirt and prayer and felt the heat in my belly when Thomas first touched me, the flutter of Eleanor's fingers when I drew letters on her palm, Anna's hand wrapping around mine the night we ate the apple together. But mostly I thought of Swallow, how I had gasped to see him tumble, his red and grey stripes spinning against the sky. I stretched out my arms and looked up as he had during that first leap, looking for flight but knowing he could fall. That moment of risk — now it was mine.

AFTERWORD

I first read about anchoresses when I was doing research for my PhD on the story of St Margaret of Antioch. Initially, I was intrigued and a little horrified.

Sealed in forever? Never to see the world again? How strange these intensely religious women must have been, I thought. During the enclosure service, burial rites were even read over the anchoress, and some had a grave dug inside the cell to remind them of their living death. But then I began to think about the women themselves, the ones making this choice. Who was the anchoress? Why did she choose enclosure? Was she afraid, excited, certain, doubtful? What about her family? And what would this small dark place be like as a home? In my mind, I went inside the cell. My central question was always: what was her experience, bodily, emotionally, spiritually, mentally? She was no longer just a weird idea; she was a woman. Sarah. My anchoress.

I visited many English churches with archaeological or documentary evidence of a cell. Most of the cells are gone — only a squint remains, or perhaps a trace of a building on the external wall of the church — but even those bare remnants helped to evoke the women who had once lived there.

There are few detailed descriptions of how anchoresses lived, although information can be inferred from wills, accounts and other documents that make mention of an anchoress. There are also the 'Rules of Life' written to guide the women, the most famous of which is *Ancrene Wisse*, written in Middle English in the thirteenth century (which I quote in the novel). From such documents it is possible to glean details about their daily rituals, the architecture of their cells, the expectations of their behaviour — and even some clues about their transgressions. The Rule's specific prescriptions — for example, that an anchoress should not gossip, keep a cow, teach children or hold documents in safe-keeping for others — suggest that such things happened, and were seen to undermine her commitment to being enclosed from the world. Such glimpses of the ways women broke the rules, more than the ways they obeyed them, allowed Sarah, my own anchoress, to draw a little closer. With a basic framework of facts, supported by lots of material about spirituality, church teaching and attitudes to women, my imagination filled in the spaces.

If you want to read more about daily life for anchoresses, modern English translations of *Ancrene Wisse* are readily available. Hugh White's translation (Penguin, 1995) has a very accessible and informative introduction. A thorough, and more technical, introduction by Robert Hazenfratz is available at http://d.lib. rochester.edu/teams/text/hasenfratz-ancrene-wisse-introduction

Rotha Mary Clay's seminal book *The Hermits and Anchorites of England*, originally published in 1914, is available online at http://www.historyfish.net/anchorites/clay_anchorites.html

Anne K. Warren's *Anchorites and Their Patrons in Medieval England* (University of California Press, 1985) is detailed and thorough and while technical in some places, offers an essential overview.

For life outside the anchorhold, material is plentiful. Roberta Gilchrist's *Medieval Life: Archaeology and the Life Course* (Boydell, 2012) uses archaeological evidence to reconstruct medieval rituals of life, death and the afterlife. For medieval village life, see Barbara A. Hanawalt's *The Ties That Bound: Peasant Families in Medieval England* (Oxford University Press, 1986) and Judith M. Bennett's *A Medieval Life: Cecilia Penifader of Brigstock, c. 1295–1344* (McGraw-Hill, 1999), which uses documents to reconstruct the life of one peasant woman. For the agricultural and ritual cycle of the village year, see Frances and Joseph Gies, *Life in a Medieval Village* (Harper Perennial, 1990). Mark Bailey's *The English Manor c. 1200–c. 1500* provides a selection of manorial records.

For a clear and accessible description of a scribe's work, see Christopher de Hamel's *Scribes and Illuminators* (British Museum Press, 1992). M.T. Clanchy's *From Memory to Written Record: England 1066–1307* gives a detailed discussion of the practice and implications of the written word. Jocelyn of Brakelond's *Chronicle of the Abbey of Bury St Edmunds* is a translation of a chronicle penned between 1173 and 1202; it provides wonderful insight into the daily life and political manoeuvring of a large and influential abbey.

ACKNOWLEDGEMENTS

Writing is mostly solitary, but many people have helped and supported me in many ways. I'd like to thank Flinders University for a Field Trip Scholarship to the UK to explore anchorholds, and the friendly, precise work of Flinders University Library staff, especially its Document Delivery Department. Gladstone's Library (aka St Deiniol's Library) in Wales offered warm hospitality and scholarship support that gave me quiet time to write; thanks especially to Peter Francis. I am grateful to ArtsNSW, Varuna the National Writers' House and the Byron Bay Writers' Festival for the enormous encouragement of an Unpublished Manuscript Award, along with two weeks of peace and beauty at Varuna in the Blue Mountains.

My heartfelt thanks to my two marvellous agents, Gaby Naher and Rachel Calder, who saw the possibilities of my manuscript, helped me punch it into shape, and provided a wonderful blend of care and expertise. I am very grateful to the editorial teams at HarperCollins (Australia), Faber & Faber (UK), and Farrar, Straus & Giroux (USA), who have welcomed me warmly and been professional and thorough in bringing into being a beautiful book. My thanks especially to Amanda O'Connell, Denise

O'Dea, Jane Finemore, Michael White, Shona Martyn, James Kellow, Alex Russell, Kate McQuaid, Lizzie Bishop, Marsha Sasmor, Lenni Wolff and Rodrigo Corrall. My love and thanks to my editors: Catherine Milne, Hannah Griffiths and Sarah Crichton, whose enthusiasm for the novel brought me to tears, and has kept me believing.

My writing friends — too many to name all of them — have urged me on with good advice, coffee and wine. My thanks to Nigel Featherstone, Nikolai Blaskow, Amanda Lynch, Richard Calver and Marcus Amman. My love and gratitude to Maeve Castles, Michelle Fahy, Jess Cadwallader, Biff Ward, Di Lucas, Jenn Shapcott, Jenni Savigny and Gay Lynch, who read drafts of the novel, gave precious feedback and helped me see its possibilities, and to my mother-in-law, Beryl, who has been so excited for me (and poured the champagne).

Love and huge thanks to Judy King, who told me years ago that this would happen, listened to my doubts and struggles, translated and gave advice on the intricacies of the Early Middle English language of *Ancrene Wisse* and helped me with the Latin. Undying love and gratitude to my children, Jess, Myf, Dan and Demelza, for traipsing around English churches helping me look for squints or signs of a cell and becoming probably the most educated children on matters of the anchorhold, whether they wanted to or not. Being mother to them has given me most of what I know about embodiment. Above all, always, my love and thanks to Alan, for reading, talking through ideas, seeing me through the many patches of doubt, celebrating with me, and for believing all this was possible.